Amongst and Above All

HISTORY CANNOT CHANGE A MAN.
MAN CAN CHANGE HISTORY.

Willie Hirsh

HILDEBRAND BOOKS

an imprint of W. Brand Publishing

NASHVILLE, TENNESSEE

Hildebrand Books an imprint of W. Brand Publishing
j.brand@wbrandpub.com
www.wbrandpub.com
Printed and bound in the United States of America.

Cover design by designchik.net

Amongst and Above All /Willie Hirsh —1st ed.

Available in Paperback, Kindle, and eBook formats.
Paperback ISBN 978-1-950385-19-5
eBook ISBN: 978-1-950385-20-1
Library of Congress Control Number: 2019954527

Much of the background information for this story was readily available online. Many thanks to Wikipedia, Quora, just to name a few.

I want to thank my Publisher, JuLee Brand, collaborating with me once more on this project.

Chapter 1

T wo shots pierced the silence of the crisp winter air and echoed across the United States Capitol building.

A few seconds earlier the Supreme Court Justice asked the President-elect to move a bit closer, and then started the ceremony by asking him to raise his right hand and place his left hand on the Bible. His voice was heard over the loud speakers repeating the Presidential oath. The Supreme Court Justice then declared, "Congratulations, Mr. President!"

Rufus Barker was sworn in as the President of the United States, taking command of the Oval Office and becoming the commander-in-chief of the United States military. Then, came the shots, fired so closely together they almost sounded like one bullet. The First Lady of the United States fell first. The second shot the Supreme Court Justice's neck and tore his carotid artery apart, which sent him down next to the President's wife. He died a few seconds later.

Chaos erupted as the FLOTUS's chest unveiled a growing bloodstain, darkening her purple overcoat as she lay underneath the President. He saw the bullet entry mark that killed his wife before she hit the ground, but his mind was frozen and he couldn't grasp the implications.

"That's a great way to start a presidency!" Secret Service Agent Evan Harris uttered loudly as he immediately jumped to cover the President—the body he was ordered to risk his own life to protect. *It's not the CIA's happy day,* he thought as he looked for the President's physician.

"Doctor!" Harris screamed.

Dr. Rintler, the President's personal physician, yelled from the temporary grandstand a few benches up from the podium.

"Let me through!" Rintler yelled coarsley.

Rintler was short, and hunched slightly. He made his way to the podium and crossed by dozens of Secret Service agents engulfing the area.

The bullet that killed the First Lady missed the POTUS by a few inches as he stood at the podium. The Supreme Court Justice saved the President by asking him to move closer. *Was it coincidence? Or was it part of a larger plot?*

Those questions raced through the minds of the protectors.

Tom Phillips, the Vice President-elect, and his wife, Gina, were saved because they stood behind the Supreme Court Justice.

People on Capitol Hill screamed and ran, with many glancing around trying to figure out where the shots had come from.

The Secret Service agents protecting the President took immediate control. Phillips had not taken the oath for his position yet. Agents shielded him and his family in case the attack on the President was still active.

Dr. Rintler checked the First Lady's pulse and shook his head.

Rufus Barker was the most powerful man on the planet, and this was the most unparalleled situation recorded in modern history. No presidency ever started this way. Now helpless, dazed and confused, he whispered to his physician, "Can you save her?"

"I'm afraid she's gone," he murmured, his voice shaking. "I'm sorry, Mr. President." He could not hide the fact that he was still in shock from the terror attack.

The physician shook his head firmly and crawled his way to the Supreme Court Justice's dead body.

The podium area was congested with twisted people on the ground, groaning, coughing, and screaming in panic looking for help as the situation was still paralyzed.

The CIA and FBI operatives scanned the area carefully for the source of the attack, or for signs that it might continue. They exchanged calls in their central communication center to move the President to a secure place.

Hundreds of bodyguards protecting the international dignitaries in their charges, were ready to take a bullet, or shoot to kill. No questions would be asked, even though this task was supposed to be assigned to local law enforcement.

Everyone took responsibility for their own lives. Emergency protocol cut off all satellite communications to prevent the attacker—or attackers—from using any form of communication. Blocked roads appeared around Capitol Hill almost instantly, and police cut off any potential escape routes.

International media broadcasting the ceremony live speculated if the President was alive or not. Their guest contributors wore designer suits and fashionable ties and masked themselves with serious, somber faces as they adjusted themselves to the grave atmosphere. They immediately speculated who and what was behind the attack. They all looked to blame someone. They connected imaginary dots and drew dark pictures of a worldwide Jihad on the United States. Some blamed the American policies around the world, as they always did.

"It's ISIS," declared one commentator.

"It's Al Qaida," confirmed another and someone else wagged a finger at the camera. "With ties to the 'Muslim brotherhood,'" he added.

The daring assassination attempt triggered the biggest global investigation probe in the history of the United States since 9/11. Speculations and theories started to pop up live on national TV. Every theory imaginable was thrown in the mix to see what stuck to the wall, and created anxiety among the listeners who gobbled up every piece of information.

Blood stained the Capitol Hill limestone floor as evidence of a personal and national tragedy. Rufus Barker's ceremonial tuxedo was stained with the blood of his wife and possibly others. The scene looked like something from a Hollywood studio, except this was real and it was a nightmare.

January 20th would be remembered. The sun could not offer warmth, even though it was shining and glaring in the center of the blue skies above. The frozen ground held cold with no mercy. A couple of runaway distant clouds floated aimlessly and dissipated along the horizon, keeping the Almighty as witness to the cruelty that man that can inflict on each other and, in this instance, disturbing the foundations of the biggest democracy on earth. On the other hand, the brief pastoral atmosphere of the Capitol was misleading. Something in the air seemed to send the message that no one, no place was safe anymore, despite the vast amount of security and advanced technological intelligence programs in place it proved that despite all of this, it was easy to throw the nation into a whirlpool of horror.

Ambulance sirens wailed in the distance, cutting through the crowded streets to reach the victims. Special task force vehicles closed in as well in a coordinated chaos that the Capitol had not seen since the crash of American Airline flight 77 on the Pentagon, that was piloted by an extreme Islamic Jihadist.

Police officers pushed bystanders out of the way of emergency vehicles. Every second felt like an eternity for Evan Harris as Dr. Rintler tended to nearby victims.

"Damn," cried Evan. *I could have done a better job protecting Mrs. Barker.*

"It's not your fault!" said the physician. "It's a broken system."

The President lay still by his wife, overheard this and replied angrily, "Get help, Evan. Get your agency to move their butts!"

"A little longer, Mr. President. We are trying to make sure the area is secured!"

Evan pushed the President down further. He drew his handgun with the right hand and with the other he picked up the Bible from the floor near the President. He held the Bible's twisted pages tight to his chest, insinuating he got a message from God, *I am with you.*

Messages started to flow in with clearance from the FBI director in Evan's earpiece.

"All clear to move the President! Clear the path to the building," Evan ordered the agents next to him. The agents cleared up a safety path from the west lawn of the U.S. Capitol into the safer senate building.

"I am not moving!" The President raised his voice. "What about my wife?" he asked with tears in his eyes.

"Paramedics are making their way now, but, unfortunately, I regret to say that your wife didn't make it." Evan put aside his emotions and tried to keep the President out of danger. "You are the President now, our new leader, and must be evacuated to a safe refuge area immediately, sir!"

Jet engines roared above the Hill.

"It's a precaution, sir, securing the air space just like we did on 9/11," added Evan in a calming voice as he helped him to stand up. The President looked down, seeing for the first time his wife and the Supreme Court Justice dead on the ground as agencies cleared the area for the paramedics and rescue professionals.

The nearby Andrews AFB dispatched and scrambled an emergency formation of four F-16 jet fighters equipped with AIM-9, Sidewinder, infrared homing, Air-to-Air missiles, and AGM-65E, semi-active laser homing air to ground missiles to intercept and engage any military threat from the ground or from the air.

All civilian aircraft were routed 100 miles away, creating a "no Fly Zone" around the Capitol, with fighters threatening to shoot down anyone who would cross the airspace under the emergency closure.

"I'll get up myself!" cried the President as he tried to push Evan away.

"OK, Mr. President!" Evan had no choice but just to encourage him to do this as fast as possible.

Rufus Barker was not used to his new title yet. His attention was on his wife, who lay dead in the bloodied coat they chose together for the event.

Rufus's entire Presidential campaign stormed his mind like lightning just for a fraction of a second. *Was this all worth it?*

He asked himself if anything on the campaign might have triggered the plan to assassinate him. He won the election a couple of months before on a platform that basically accused his opponent of building a mighty military machine to fight a ghostly enemy while he gutted the social programs in the country. He accused his opponent of selling out the American people's privacy on social media, accusations that were exposed by a former CIA analyst. He had also accused him of damaging the agency's reputation and caused demoralization among those in uniform.

Now Rufus Barker questioned his own platform. He pushed away the suspicion that the assassination was connected to an accusation during the campaign that the elections were rigged by using data information to target 'perusable' people in certain districts that could swing the entire election in his favor.

Rufus denied the allegations of foreign involvement, or that these countries hacked social media retrieved behavioral data from each American citizen, and added fake accounts with disguised negative ads to sway people's opinions.

"My opponents went crazy," he announced time after time.

He hoped that the dust would settle as soon as he knew one thing for sure: the assassination attempt changed him, and it would give him the biggest test of his life. The President knew that the entire world would probably speculate the country's next step. How soon might the attackers retaliate, against whom, and how?

"Mr. President, we need to move." Evan still clutched the Bible and raised his head to look at his surroundings. He ignored the noise and commotion, and checked for any new threats.

He glanced at the Ulysses S. Grant memorial from the corner of his eye. *Peace Monument*, he scoffed at the irony and then looked out at Garfield Circle, which was heavily guarded by other covert security forces. He thought, *just wait you fucking bustards, just wait! You started a game and hope you know how it will end!*

Rufus stood and took a long glimpse at his dead wife, but Evan didn't allow him to mourn her death for too long. There could be another attack at any moment. Terrorist groups always had a back-up plan if the first failed, and perhaps it was now when the President was standing. Evan ushered the President and the vice president to the clear path.

As the President was moved away, Rufus promised himself he'd change the world. He decided to keep his scheduled trip next month to Saudi Arabia to address the Muslim world, perhaps with a slight delay to re-examine his strategy. A new way of thinking was necessary to deliver a different kind of a message, a message that would carry a meaning based on new intelligence and developments, one which would determine his future steps.

The local police were teamed with FBI agents and commanded by their chief to storm a 20-block area and hold random suspects, especially those bearing Middle Eastern features. They were to ignore the fact that profiling was not a popular act with the Supreme Court and happened to be one of the issues that President Rufus campaigned to fight against.

"No racial profiling in TSA," he claimed in many a campaign stump speech. Now, however, Rufus would not give a flying crap if an entire Capitol building full of foreigners were rounded up, arrested, and put in Guantanamo Bay for interrogation.

The honored guests on the grandstand were forced to stay frozen in place. They crouched down in their seats or between the aisles as they waited for instructions. Divers scanned the near-freezing water of the Lincoln Memorial Reflecting Pool for a possible hiding threat.

About three minutes passed, until it was relatively safe and every step for safety was taken to the highest extreme. Evan moved the heavily-guarded President into the Senate building. The President's wife and the Supreme Court Justice's bodies were examined by the paramedics and were taken for autopsies to the nearest medical facility, Bridge Point Hospital.

The Secret Service refused to let the President accompany his wife's body to the hospital for fear that there was an alternate option to strike the President if the first attempt to kill him failed.

Constitutionally, the President's running mate was not in power to take over the presidency officially in case of an emergency, since the vice president-elect was not sworn in yet. His wife, son, and his best friend Frank Dabush, stood next to him and were pushed into the lower level of Emancipation Hall after the President, as armed agents led the way first. The eight members of the Supreme Court who survived the attack were hurried into the building as well.

Once inside, Frank grabbed Evan's hand and pointed to the vice president-elect and urged, "Have one of the Justices quickly swear in the vice president!"

Evan pulled the Bible from his inner pocket coat, and asked for a quick ceremony for the vice president-elect. Rufus witnessed the surreal occasion while the wheels in his brain turned. He resented the confusion and signaled to take charge. He felt as he was soaring like an eagle and witnessing the scene from above, stretching his wings over the surreal ceremony. The act to swear in his running mate felt like déjà vu, and reminded him of the impromptu ceremony to swear in Lyndon Johnson aboard the Air Force One during the flight back from Texas after the JFK was assassinated.

His widow, Jacqueline Kennedy, stood in witness in her pink bouclé suit still stained with the blood and brains of her murdered husband. Rufus felt like he was watching a movie running double time.

Evan handed the Bible to the Supreme Court Justice and quickly swore in the vice president, adding an emotional dramatic statement of his own. "Democracy is fully restored now, and the power is transferred back to the people, our greatest democracy was put to the test by evil forces. The Supreme Court is united and we shall prevail, may the Lord bless our President and bless the vice president, help them to find the way for long-lasting peace and justice. I wish to our wounded a full recovery and condolences to the victim families of our great nation. Congratulations and good luck, Mr. Vice President!"

No one was given the time to exchange handshakes as they were moved deeper into the building for safety.

This officially started the manhunt and war on terror. Counter-terrorism intelligence agencies around the world would stir the pot of future events. They'd work tirelessly to figure out who tried to kill the President and why.

Chapter 2

Eighteen months ago.
The Golan Heights, Northern Israel

The Qunaytriya border pass in the Golan Heights, under Israeli control since 1967, separated the two enemy states of Israel and Syria. This war-torn stretch of land was in regional chaos for the last few years, and was under joint control of the Red Cross and its Israeli equivalent, MDA-"Magen-David-Adom," ambulance and paramedic services.

It was a bitter cold winter night with a nonstop drizzling rain. The weather didn't interrupt the rescue mission operation by the Israeli Military who sought to save injured Syrian citizens and transport them to Israeli hospitals.

Looking down from the Golan Heights to the valley below, the serene, flickering lights of the Israeli kibbutz and towns were the last stronghold of the enemy expansion agenda, but gave Syrian refugees new hope for survival.

Guns and rocket-propelled grenades were heard exploding near the border, shredding town after town in the war-ravaged region just south of Syria and adjacent to the mutual borderlines of Israel, Jordan, and Syria.

Skilled, experienced Israelis in military uniforms helped to sort the twenty-something refugees in the border pass seeking medical help. Israeli policy was always to help and save lives regardless if those lives were friend or foe. Physicians grouped those who needed immediate attention, prioritizing based on the seriousness of their injuries. And, as always, children came first.

"This, you will not see in the news," murmured the young military nurse to Dan Eyal, a Mossad agent who stood next to her.

"We are just doing our jobs, Dvora. I don't care about BBC, CNN, and others. These are people, families. Forget that they are coming from the most ferocious enemy we ever fought!" replied Dan compassionately to the young first lieutenant who joined them in selecting the most injured for the fastest treatment.

Dvora, a slender, athletic 20-year-old paramedic, and her first lieutenant, Ilana, served the mandatory military service in the Medical Corps and were in charge of filtering the refugees based on their medical conditions. Both were clad in heavy military winter coats, olive green uniforms, and muddy military boots, and orchestrated the processing with skill and confidence.

Dan Eyal, a former decorated Army officer who joined the Mossad intelligence agency and successfully performed a few confidential missions behind enemy lines, watched the Medical Corps service men and women performing their duties with devotion. Dan stood aside from the middle of the night action, without any single complaint, other than cursing the weather.

Dan's average height and weight made him fit for a 43-year-old man. He wore a similar winter coat without the military insignia patches. He combed the area and felt proud of his country that helped poor people with unfortunate fates.

"What are you doing here?" asked Ilana. She gave him a curious look. "Are you a physician?"

Eyal stared at her and simply said, "Just like you. I'm selecting who gets treatment. By the way, nice to see you again." He chuckled.

She scoffed and shot back, "If you were only not married!" She then moved away and left Eyal with Dvora so they could greet the refugees at the selection point.

A Sikorsky CH-53 helicopter waited nearby to transfer them to the appropriate hospitals for treatment, the same as the helicopter had done for thousands of their brothers and sisters treated before.

A child covered with a blood-stained blanket crossed the line with a young female who wore layers of torn clothing to warm her up. The child cried as the physician, a captain, immediately examined the near-fatal wounds. The child's face was unrecognizable. The doctor looked up at the young women and shook his head. She glanced at the physician with teary eyes, unable to speak, her hopes of good news faltering.

"Live? He?" she asked with a trembling voice in broken English and touched the physician's arm lightly.

"He needs a miracle. . .he needs surgery right away to stop the bleeding," he said, as he continued to check the tiny lethargic body.

Dan overheard to the conversation, and showed the physician his Mossad agent badge before turning to the woman. "We can't promise, though we will try our best. We have the best medical team," he said, his assured voice calm and soft, as if were trying to convince the distraught woman as well as himself that they could perform a miracle.

"Will he survive?" whispered Eyal to the physician in Hebrew.

The doctor nodded his head, then he turned to Dvora.

"Transfer him immediately to Rambam; it's an Israeli hospital in Haifa, 20 minutes away," he said.

Without delay, Dvora carried the child to the helicopter. She walked straight under the draft created by the whipping rotor blades, and unintentionally ignored the mother and the man next to her, who both risked their lives to cross the Israeli border to save their child.

Dan followed the nurse without paying attention to any protocols.

The child's parents rushed after Dvora, but another female soldier in uniform blocked their way. "Hey, hey, hey. . .wait, we need all your information first!!"

"I'll take care of that," called Eyal.

"It's my baby there!" the mother cried.

"It will only take a second," the soldier said, holding a tablet that logged information into a computer data base as the nurse loaded the child into the aircraft.

Eyal assisted the parents with submitting their personal information and then guided the mother towards the chopper.

The mother freaked out when she saw the rotor spinning, clearly worried it would take off without her. Dan accompanied her and held her arm gently. "They will never go without me, right?" she said as she gasped for air, worried that she would be left behind.

"You are flying to Israel with your son; and we will save him. I'll personally take care of you, I guarantee" promised Dan.

"My son," she screamed with panic, stretching her hands forward.

"He is not leaving without you, and he is in good hands now," Dan said as he tried to calm her down. "Once we get your info, we will all join your child."

"It's time to close the pass! Evacuate!" a voice called through a megaphone.

Dan helped the traumatized parents into the helicopter, and made sure that the couple could see his face. He was their savior and planned to see them again when the ordeal was over.

The cabin light in the helicopter was dimmed and the only illumination came from surgical lights. Two surgeons and three nurses tended to the child to ensure that the life support equipment was fully engaged. The medical procedure to stop the bleeding started as the child's parents held hands and wept softly.

Dan sat next to them and put his arm around the father to comfort him. He was sure that the war trauma was so dramatic that all they could do was to trust that they were in good hands.

"How long have you been married?" Dan asked, in an attempt to distract the distraught couple.

"A little over a year," she answered, as tears streamed down her face. "This is my husband, Farouk, who also is wounded on his back." The pilot received the signal to take off.

"How is he?" she asked the nurse when she saw her son motionless on the surgery bed. Dan knew the experience must have surreal for the boy's parents. The nurse nodded her head, signaling that things were alright. The mother raised her hands to praise the Almighty.

"My enemies are saving my son and pulled us out from hell," she murmured. In the meantime, her husband passed out, his head landing on Eyal's shoulder.

The nurse helped Farouk lie down and raised his head with a pillow as she checked his pulse and blood pressure.

She pulled Farouk's shirt away to expose the deep shrapnel wound that was bleeding heavily. "He lost a lot of blood!" she exclaimed. She bandaged it, and calmly looked at Jamila.

"He should be OK until we get to the hospital," she said, her voice calm and soft. She then continued assisting the surgical team without saying anything more.

The mother watched the child's heart monitor beep, examining its rhythm, and praying to the only God she knew. The beep was a music to her ears and she prayed it would not stop.

"OK," the surgeon said, signaling that they stopped the bleeding.

"What's the child name?" the surgeon asked.

"My son's name is Jamil. I am Jamila and Farouk, my husband. May Allah bless you and your hands, doctor!"

Jamila clearly realized that, in her country, death ruled; but in Israel they cherished life, even the lives of their enemies. In her homeland, they would probably be all dead by now. The heavy fighting amongst the many combatant fractions shredded her town and left many for dead with no help from the international community, no intervention from the United Nations. What little aid was sent to help the refugees was stolen by the rebels themselves. It was total chaos. She could not imagine her other family members and friends surviving the war. She was lucky to listen to her husband's advice to flee to Israel and take their chances for a better life.

Chapter 3

For 12 years, Katarina Belinkova worked in the American Embassy in Moscow. The Embassy was located close to the horseshoe turn of the Moscow River in the Arbat district and a few minutes' walk to the Krasnopresnenskaya bus station. Many of the western countries' embassies were located nearby–Britian, Canada, and Poland installations.

Katarina was a 33-year-old Russian bombshell. She had the body of a supermodel; long, wavy, blond hair; green, almond-shaped eyes; and pouty, beestung lips. She wore designer clothing, probably happily supplied by her colleagues in the embassy. Katarina was a quiet person, and not the flirty type.

Her femininity had a strong presence that no one could ignore, and it was hard not to make eye contact with her. Few could resist taking a glimpse of this angel on earth. She was considered a good worker who minded her own business. She came from a small family town near Moscow, and was the only child of elderly parents who were chicken farmers. She was invited to every embassy party around the district but declined to attend, respectfully, with polite rainchecks she never cashed. Katarina had a security clearance to access emails, schedules, and information about almost everything at the embassy.

Every Tuesday, she walked to the bus station after work, making sure she was not followed. She boarded bus line 216 that looped through the Tverskoy District and got off half an hour later at her housing complex.

She was a single woman, and even though men lavished her with attention and gifts, she ignored them; instead eagerly awaiting her arrival home to greet the love of her life, her black Russian Terrier puppy.

This particular Tuesday sported unusually warm comfortable weather for October. As usual, she walked to the bus waiting behind a short line. She walked confidently and made sure, out of habit, that she was not followed. She'd cross the street from time to time, and check out the displays in the storefront windows. Katarina carried a black purse containing makeup, a wallet, a few rubles, other miscellaneous trinkets, and an envelope with a pack of printed pages was tucked in her side pocket.

The bus came on schedule, spewing out black smoke behind it. She boarded and walked all the way to the back but found the bus fully occupied. A chubby, balding man in his 60s, politely asked her if she wanted to sit and immediately stood up without her response.

Katarina sat on the bag the man left on the seat, which was identical to her bag, including all the personal belongings. She gave him her bag instead, which included the envelope with all the printed papers she smuggled out from the Embassy.

Spasibo. "Thank you." The man kept an icy expression on his face and no further words were exchanged. He inserted Katarina's purse in a larger black bag. The man, an FSB (Federal Security Bureau) agent, got off at the next station. Dima

Petrankov looked more like an accountant with a lifetime desk position rather than an intelligence analyst agent for one of the most ruthless agencies in the world.

Dima, with his heavy pear body shape and constantly drooping eyeglasses, appeared harmless. He could not keep his shirt tucked in, and always battled with an exposed shirt-tail at his back. At times, toilet paper trailed from his shoe. He limped slightly, favoring his left leg due to an injury from a car accident which he claimed was an assassination attempt on his life.

Dima's misleading look disguised the fact that he was the No. 1 transmission analyzer in his intelligence agency. His ability to draw important information from a simple routine email, even encrypted transmission and texts, was phenomenal. He was a mathematics graduate of the Moscow University during the USSR regime, followed by a stint at the KGB, and later moved from agency to agency until he was assigned to his current mission for the last 12 years.

Dima exploited his friendship with Katarina, whom he met on the bus. Katarina looked at him as the father she missed since he passed away a few years ago.

At the same time, per his recommendation, Katarina got her job in the American embassy. Dima never asked for anything until now, but times had changed. The purebred, loyal Russian comrade to his Tsar now gave way to one who worked for the highest bidder.

The American Embassy security and the CIA knew that local embassy workers met periodically with Russian agents, and one of them was Yuliya, Katarina's comrade. Most of the information was not significantly important, since they had no access to the computer server and the encrypted secret information. Katarina had higher security classification than her local workers and access to a higher level of non-classified information. Her elevated position in the embassy garnered attention from the Russian intelligence world.

Chapter 4

One week after the assassination attempt

Hassan Abu Shikri sat alone in the living room, nervous and without a way out, for the last week in his apartment hideout. In an effort to redirect his thoughts and calm down, he watched TV and played video games. He was told that the apartment was rented by the Iranian Revolutionary Guards in Georgetown.

A week ago, he was on the roof of the Wilson Center leaving the scene at about 10 a.m., two hours before the assassination attempt. He met another person using identification codes, since they never met before as per the plan. Still, he felt he was suckered into it.

He examined the man up and down, trying unsuccessfully to put a name or a title to his face. The man didn't waste any time and asked Hassan to lead him to the roof the day of the attack. Hassan used his building digital access card to enter the electric gate. They slipped by the security desk and waved hello to the guard who knew Hassan. The distance to the elevators was short, and the doors opened immediately. The lobby, usually packed with people during normal business hours, was relatively empty due to the inauguration.

Hassan led the man to the top floor without exchanging a word. The man had an enormous mustache and a few days' beard peeking out from under his scarf. The rest of his face was shielded by a large pair of sunglasses.

From the top elevator floor, they walked up one flight of stairs and stepped out to the roof. Hassan shut off the alarm with his remote-control device, given to him by the building management as part of his job. The man pulled a white plastic poncho that covered his tall body, and then stepped onto the roof after Hassan.

The roof, as with all the buildings in the area, was exposed to aerial surveillance by drones that detected any disturbances or suspicious activities. The white poncho blended in with the white roof membrane perfectly. No surveillance would know he was there, the planners thought.

Hassan was never an insider on the plot. He was kept out of the loop and was used as an aide due to his position in the building. He didn't know what the purpose of the assignment was until he figured out that it would be tied to the inauguration when the weapon was brought in, part-by-part. The people who engaged him were well disguised and always covered their identities.

The man on the roof acted very cool. All of his movements were very mechanical, as if shooting people was nothing new to him. After Hassan showed him the rifle storage location, the man assembled the pieces like the trained expert he was. He cocked the gun twice to ensure its effectiveness and then inserted the bullets into the cartridge so it was ready to use.

Five minutes later, Hassan went back down, leaving the man on the roof. He crossed the lobby and exited the building, but couldn't shake the feeling that someone was watching him. The concierge greeted him with a smile, but Hassan rushed by without acknowledging him.

Then, the actions taken by his recruiters hit him hard. He felt an urge to tell someone, *anyone*, that a terrible thing was about to happen, but he couldn't. He was trapped between the hammer and the nail. He left the block, and cautiously avoided the street cameras. About 15 minutes later, he ordered an Uber, despite his directives never to do so. The Uber got him straight to his apartment. Hassan realized his mistake in ordering the car, which could be used as evidence against him if he was caught. The feeling that someone was following him lingered. *They want to make sure I obeyed my orders,* he thought to himself.

Hassan immigrated to the United States with a diversity visa lottery program and planned to have a successful future. He was hired as a janitor to work in the building as he went to college full-time. His major was in chemistry.

On a clear late evening, two weeks before the assassination attempt, a masked man approached Hassan as he left work and suggested they go for a walk. They boarded a van with two other masked men inside and zoomed off.

"Where are we heading?" asked Hassan, concerned.

"District Heights," answered the driver.

"Just driving around suburbia," added the other, in a failed attempt to calm down the young student.

"Why?" Hassan insisted.

"It's a fun ride, you will see!" the driver exclaimed. "Just twenty minutes of fresh air!" The men exploded with a loud laughter.

They drove around in circles, looking for something around the malls, which were scheduled to be closed soon.

Then, in a cluster of a few fast food eateries, they found what they were looking for: a lone young woman walking to her car from a long day of work at a minimum wage job.

"There she is!" exclaimed the driver.

"OK, get her on the right side and open the door!"

"Can't open the door while driving!" the driver responded to the man who seem to be the leader.

The screeching tires left their marks on the asphalt as the van skidded to a stop next to her. Hassan was stunned as the two men quickly snatched her off her feet and forced her inside the van. They covered her mouth and preventing her from screaming for help.

These men are definitely professionals, Hassan thought in horror.

He was not sure where all this would lead, or what part he might play in it, but the scenario reminded him that the 9/11 terrorists had fun in the days leading up to the attacks. *Is this what they are planning for me?* The thought crossed his mind and he shivered.

The woman was strapped down on the back seat and seat-belted in place for good measure.

"The van is registered in your name, Hassan!" said the leader as he laughed. "We got you the job and gave you a credit card in your name. It's all planned out, my fellow countryman!"

"You trapped and manipulated me, you motherfuckers!" Hassan screamed as he watched the girl crying softly. One of the men taped her mouth shut.

"We chose you, Hassan!" replied the leader.

They preferred to speak in English and Hassan tried to understand the reason. They didn't sound Iranian, so he ruled out the Revolutionary Guards. They sounded like Russians, and surely weren't his countryman as they claimed.

They drove for another 30 minutes toward Virginia and the girl's muffled cries grew to irritate the leader. He decided to join her on the back seat and punched her in the face to shut her up.

Hassan witnessed all of this and was not sure he would live to tell the story. *But they still need me for tomorrow; that's what they said,* he thought.

Finally, they stopped the car in a small park and turned off the lights. The dark silence in the park was surreal.

"You go first!" ordered the leader, peeling the woman's clothes off, layer by layer. They kept her seatbelt on to help restrain her. She was petite but strong. Not strong enough to fight off bigger men, however.

"No! No!" Hassan replied, horrified. He refused to take part in the rape.

The man pulled his handgun and cocked it, putting the muzzle against Hassan's forehead. "It's not a request, Hassan. It's an order."

The other man in the back stripped the struggling woman. She fought Hassan as he reluctantly insinuated raping her, though he did not penetrate her. He wasn't hard. He was terrified. Though, the men holding them both prisoner didn't seem to care.

The leader videotaped the act, clearly showing Hassan's and the woman's faces.

They tied Hassan to the car seat and then took turns brutally raping the woman one by one, for three hours, and documenting the act.

"A car is behind us!!" said the driver, looking at the back mirror.

"Police?" asked the leader, concerned.

"They just stopped at the other side of the street and turned off the lights!"

"Perhaps some love birds, but don't take any chances, let's get out of here!" he commanded.

The exhausted woman heard the conversation and started to scream; however, her voice was not heard.

"Should we check the people in the car?" asked the driver. "Do you think they can see our license plate?"

"No, too far and too dark!"

"Let's get out of here!" Without turning the van lights on, they drove slowly out of the park.

Hassan felt trapped. The documented rape couldn't be erased and could be used as extortion if he decided not to cooperate with them at the last minute. He doubted the police would believe he didn't actually rape the woman. The woman might be able to save him with her testimony, if she lived to testify.

Hassan could be blamed and spend his entire life behind bars in a military prison or worse, in Guantanamo Bay.

Hassan's worst fears came true when later that night. The men videotaped themselves shooting the woman once in the head in a secluded part of Huntley Meadows Park. They left her body there. They made sure to get video of Hassan standing near her dead body.

Driving back, the leader calmly explained to Hassan that the video would be kept for exchange of his cooperation in the plot. They viewed the video that showed that two man forcing the woman to the van's floor, the third man with a gun pointed at Hassan. More than anything, it would be a dishonor to his family, his friends and himself if they ever saw that video on TV.

Hassan understood that he was automatically guilty in the eyes of the prosecutors if they chose to use the video as evidence to turn him in. The rental van was registered in his name and would be the last nail in his coffin. They had him.

Thoughts of suicide versus collaboration stormed his head. However, they made sure to steal this from him as well. They took turns all night to protect him until the next morning. Hassan tried to think of a way to prevail, but his heart raced, and he felt short of breath and experienced chest pains.

They told him what they expected. The job was offered to him. The credit card and his rental apartment, were all planned by the agents, who followed his every footstep the last four months.

The agents rotated every day, checking his daily routine, checking his friends, sexual behavior, and eating habits.

Hassan made for an easy target. He had no political views, and basically minded his own business. He did not participate in Pro-Islamic or anti-Iranian government rallies. He was really wanting to assimilate in this country and society and staying away from the boiling pot of political agendas.

The Iranian agents profiled him as a 'naïve' Millennial who constantly played computer games since he was able to afford them. He was not classified as stupid, but perhaps as a little intimidated being in America. It was his dream come true, it was a country he always wanted to live in.

Hassan was ordered to stay in the hideout apartment after the assassination until they could move him out of the country. At this point, he didn't know where all this would end and if he should trust anything that they were saying. Perhaps he was already a dead man.

He was not sure what the assassin would do with the rifle after his mission was completed. *Would he leave it on the roof or store it back in the chimney?* he wondered.

"It must be all there," he said aloud.

The apartment stored all his necessities for a few weeks. He made it there with no problem, getting the keys from the top electrical box on the side of the wall as he was instructed. The apartment was dark. The mini blinds were closed and made the room feel very stuffy and claustrophobic.

A strange feeling engulfed him, and he shivered occasionally. He was not used to this. He figured that they didn't kill him right away because they wanted the authorities to think he was a lone wolf and no one else was behind the plot. He was sure that the Wilson Center would be investigated once the probe moved forward, and that his name would be probably tied to the assassination. This would give the real assassins time to disappear. So, perhaps no one was coming to help him as he thought. Perhaps even someone would disclose his place in order to capture him.

Hassan was not a soldier type or cool spy with a poker face. He had to make an analytical decision and worked toward it. *They will not let me live,* he decided. Basically, they needed to shut him up for good and release the video at the same time. This would create a dead-end for the investigators.

Even if he reported the plot to the police, he was not sure they would protect him, so perhaps speaking to the Imam he met when first came to the United States would help.

Chapter 5

Ten days after the assassination attempt on the President, the defense community started to gather pieces of intelligence information from open sources like 'Osint' and centralized them in a computer model they called 'dust chips' in the FBI and CIA command centers. Other hacking sources by 'Non-Conventional Cyber-attack' forcefully collected information from around the world, paying attention to the source of instability in regions, to plan the next steps. Many questions were on the table. Was the assassin a lone wolf? A Jihadi group? A nation with a political agenda?

The CIA, aided by the NSA, the largest security entity in the world, could hack any smart phone, and intercept any calls or text messages around the globe as they searched for key words to solve the puzzle. Drones with listening devices roamed the skies over strategic regions, transferring the information in real time using the most advanced quantum and computation communication systems that were virtually unhackable. The race was on to capture the assassins before they could flee the country. Those extreme steps were taken under the emergency protection Patriot Act, even though it was a controversy with the Supreme Court and Rufus during his campaign.

Rufus Barker, following the forced resignation of Gene Bennett, the previous CIA director, due to his failure to provide true intelligence from abroad on the attack during the ceremony, appointed Marcus Barbour as the new director of the Central Intelligence Agency. The Senate approved him quickly and a week later, Vice President Tom Phillips, invited his close friends and staff to the CIA director's swearing-in ceremony at the Naval Observatory, which was refurbished as his residence in a 1974 Congressional decision. Frank Dabush was there, the only NRA member representing the American Gun lobby club, excited and proud as a peacock.

Frank was well known in the political arena in D.C. He always invited politicians from across the political rainbow to enjoy an evening with their spouses or girlfriends at one of his extravagant parties in a five-star hotel. His favorite party was renting an entire boat and sailing the Potomac River, roaming up and downstream for hours, ending at sunrise, which gave guests plenty of booze and a good time that cost him a fortune.

They all liked Frank and were looking forward to being on his guest list without political boundaries. Some were questioning if Frank had the appetite to run for an office one day. He always chuckled and said, "Who knows?"

Frank was first to congratulate the new CIA director after the vice president. He smiled. "Good luck, Mr. Director, you have a lot of work ahead of you."

Tom, who himself was adjusting to being "citizen number two," didn't wait for his CIA director to answer and chuckled nervously.

"Don't push it, Frank. Let him enjoy the moment. We have the best man on the job." They laughed politely and raised a glass of Veuve Clicquot champagne to celebrate the occasion, of course paid for by Frank and expensed to the NRA.

"What's with your wrist? I see you wearing this leather band all the time," Patrick shot at Frank.

"This leather piece keeps my hand in place!" He chuckled and rubbed the band.

Tom, a career politician, always found himself in the right place at the right time, even if it took switching from one side of the aisle to the other if necessary. An early private Presidential exploratory commission found him as an insignificant figure and recommended he lose his Presidential dreams. But he wouldn't let go of them that easily. He thought he would replace Rufus Barker as President in eight years.

He got to be Rufus' running mate with Frank's help. Frank donated a hefty amount of money to Rufus' campaign in exchange for considering Tom for his running mate. Tom was supported by his good friend Frank, who brought with him the endorsement of the NRA and its inflated bank account.

Tom's résumé included his time as a senator under the Democratic platform where he ran for the Oval Office a couple of times. He'd known Rufus for many years, and they shared the same political views, which is why they made a great team. His quiet demeanor, reasonable responses, and analytical brain were a good mix in a good advisor. As the President used to say occasionally, "It's the right fit. . .fits like a glove."

Tom was of average height but athletic, and believed in a healthy lifestyle. He was a committed vegetarian and organic food lover, but he made sure not to mention his diet on national TV. His reddish face and short, thick, white hair made him look older than he was. His clean eating didn't prevent him from being diagnosed with leukemia, which he kept a secret.

On the other hand, his friend Frank Dabush, a former arms dealer, made his career and fortune buying and selling

surplus armament around the globe. He sold to drug deal-
ers in South America—and anyone from any country for any
purpose—who would pay. The Israeli Air Force was one of
his top customers, selling its old fleet of aging jet fighters to
third world countries in South America and the Balkan states.
Frank made a fortune brokering the refurbishment of those
old fighters by the IAI, the Israel Aerospace Industries. A
vivid spy book reader, he admired John Le Carre's books and
sometimes indulged in an Agatha Christie mystery. The most
inspired book he read was about Eli Cohen, a Mossad agent
caught in Syria, charged for espionage and hanged in the city
center of Damascus.

"Money doesn't smell," he used to say, "as long as it's legal."

Defense contractors were doing business with Frank as
well, upgrading and refurbishing old generation equipment,
and these deals bought him many powerful friends in the
political world of Washington, a win-win situation that everyone noticed.

Tom Phillips liked having him around, and they discussed
anything and everything. It was natural to appoint his friend
as the Vice President Chief of Staff. Frank accepted the job
with no regrets. After all, Tom owed his political career to
him, and was always there to help financially, either with
fund-raising or personally.

The prestigious job required a top-secret security clearance by the NSC. Frank, the son of Hungarian immigrants,
was approved by Congress. They saw him as another Henry
Kissinger, who was also an immigrant's son. Frank thought
running the Eisenhower Executive office building—the
vice president's headquarters—showed him that money
could buy a high political office. All he needed was enough
money and the right connections, and if possible, he could

go even higher, maybe becoming a cabinet member or a senator.

Marcus, the CIA director, decided his first and foremost priority was to follow President Barker's request to investigate the assassination attempt that resulted in the death of his wife and the Supreme Court Justice. Normally, the CIA didn't investigate crimes on American soil, but the President asked him to work with the FBI to find the men who killed his wife. In addition, the President instructed the vice president to assemble an inquiry committee, led by a special investigator, Gordon Donovan, a former senator from Wyoming. Donovan was to investigate the events leading to the assassination and submit a report within one year. Frank was the link between Donovan and his boss, the vice president.

FLOTUS was laid to rest on her family's estate in Arizona. Due to the continuing state of emergency, the President was not allowed to stay and mourn with the family, and was rushed back to Washington after the funeral.

Chapter 6

The same day.
CIA Headquarters, Langley, Virginia.

Two hours after the CIA director was sworn-in, he immediately left the party, got into his limousine and entered the agency building 25 minutes later. He walked the corridors of CIA headquarters with a deliberate, noisy footstep to mark his presence. He sat in his office overlooking the dense forest that surrounded the complex and sank into deep thought as he considered his next steps. "He's got too much on his plate," everyone murmured in the ceremony. *Would the world be the same?* he asked himself.

God help us, he whispered, and opened the executive desk drawers one by one, inspecting them for bugs. An agent always will be an agent. He forced a smile and decided not to make the whispering a habit, because someone might be listening.

After a few minutes, he decided to continue his power walk through the corridors, crossing offices and waving to his staff as a mark of his new command. A new era of espionage for the agency had begun. He passed by his personal administrative assistant's desk and barked sharply without even looking at her, "Call all the desk heads to a meeting, 10 minutes sharp."

"Yes, sir," she replied sarcastically and gave him a dirty look behind his back, while secretly lifting her middle finger. She knew it would be her last day on the job if Marcus had seen to that. He turned and yelled back, "Everyone, including Threat Analysts, Counterintelligence, Counter-terrorism, and Analytic Methodologists." He made sure his voice echoed loud and clear.

President Barker appointed Evan Harris as his personal agent to attend all the FBI and CIA briefings, and to represent him as liaison with the departments. Carrying the highest security clearance and access to all information, he could cut down wasted time among the agencies by reporting progress directly to the President.

Direct daily reporting from the trenches ensured that there were no smear tactics, evidence cover ups, or attempts to hide system breakdowns. Reporting would help to uncover who was responsible for a failure, a breach of security, and any signs or triggers that were ignored or overlooked.

The head of the counter-terrorism and Iranian desk, Patrick Stevenson, conducted the meeting in the conference room as the director observed the tense faces. Marcus felt that Patrick should run the meeting and introduce all the people in the room. They were trying to pile up all the information that the FBI collected and displayed them on the large screen.

Patrick, a former rear admiral, served in Afghanistan and Iraq as a fighter pilot, and was responsible for compiling a list of identified targets that later were destroyed by launching cruise missiles upon approval from the political leadership. As a jack-of-all-trades, he also ran the Iranian desk and was high in the hierarchy to one day replace Marcus Barbour as the chief of the CIA.

He joined the CIA after he retired from the Navy, at the request of the former director who knew of his ability to resolve issues under pressure in the field. After he was grounded, most of his military career demonstrated that Patrick showed sharpness at analyzing information—or disinformation—as it surfaced on his network. Finding targets at an enemy's weak points was his specialty. Patrick was 5'11", had cold, Icelandic blue eyes, and a square face with a semi-bald skull. He looked a little older than his mid-50s.

Evan Harris, on the other hand, was in his early 30s, and had an athletic build with a thin, but muscular and strong body. He was just a little more than half of Patrick's age. A former Navy seal team ST/6, he was part of the Warfare Development Group, Special Forces.

Evan had many missions deep behind enemy territory lines searching for insurgents in the mountains of Afghanistan. He was a natural spy and joined the CIA first as a covert operative agent. It was an easy pick for the President to select Evan, a courageous soldier awarded with a Purple Heart medal and the Distinguished Service Cross, among two of the highest medals in the military service. Evan become the second set of eyes and ears everywhere he went. The President gave him freedom to attend any meeting, and to collect and review any data despite the discontent from the FBI and the CIA, agencies that preferred to work alone.

With experience thinking out of the box, he had been a killing machine when needed, or an intelligence officer when circumstances required his attention. Evan was an analytical man, who was described by his colleagues as a cat with nine lives. He shot the leader of group called "Agents of Allah" in Iraq, and therefore he was also a target by Jihadists.

No one paid attention to him in the room, as he was considered as an outsider spying on them for the President. Evan put his ego aside and couldn't care less.

Patrick read the FBI synopsis of the last few days of the investigation aloud and pointed to photos on the screen behind him. Then he raised his eyes toward the head of the departments and cleared his throat.

"Anything?" Patrick growled.

"No one has claimed responsibly yet. Our agents around the world are checking the gutters of every Arab capitol for clues," responded a specialist.

"Thank you, Harvie. We need to walk the extra mile here. . . meantime, what we know is that the bullets came from Madison Drive, close to the Smithsonian National Museum," he said.

"Yes, which is 4,700 feet away. The Wilson Center behind the William Jefferson Clinton building, which is in the same direction and two miles away," replied Harvie, a short, stout computer science analyst.

Patrick continued. "The laser trajectory kit used, despite the slight deflection of the bullets, is on par with your assessment." Patrick stretched his back, which made him look a little taller than he was. Sometimes, he was sarcastic and made people laugh at the most tense times, however, it was not the right time to joke now.

"It's a very tense time! Everyone is nervous," Marcus said. What he heard didn't make him very happy. Deep wrinkles plowed his forehead as he tried to come up with ideas for a new direction. His narrow eyes and long skeletal face ensured that no one would want to meet him alone in a dark alley.

He tightened his lips. "What else can the forensic analysis report show us? Anything?"

Patrick looked at Harvie. "Yes, the two bullets were recovered from the crime scene wall. The FBI reconstructed the crime and preserved all the evidence they could, including possible DNA. They collected the victims' clothing to test for

GSR (gunshot residue) and sent them to the CBI (Colorado Bureau of Investigation) crime lab in Denver. They were too powerful and after the first bullet hit the First Lady and Jerome, the Supreme Court Justice, they continued their way with a slight deflection, the second bullet almost missed and therefore its direction of origin using a laser trajectory kit, is an accurate assumption."

"Show me the direction of the bullets and the alleged building where we assume the bullets were shot," Marcus demanded.

Patrick inhaled deeply and continued showing the building roof's aerial photo presentation. Suddenly, Marcus yelled, "Stop, stop, stop. . .go back one frame, go back!" He focused in on the pictures, excited. "What's that?" he asked as he pointed to the roof of a building photo.

"That's a drone camera shot from above during the inauguration. Why?" Harvie said as he adjusted his glasses.

"Zoom closer, can you?"

Patrick zoomed in on the photo. The powerful camera produced a photo clarity that was able to zoom in and show a needle laying on the roof membrane. Something on the photo triggered Marcus's attention.

"What building is that?" he asked.

Patrick delayed his answer and selected his words carefully. "The FBI reported that every roof, every room in all the buildings surrounding Capitol Hill were checked for clues, including visitor's lists in museums, hotels, airlines, etc. The roads in and out of the Capitol were blocked, which yielded zero results." Patrick sounded skeptical even to himself and looked straight at Marcus.

The director rolled his eyes and turned to his staff, which was composed of the best minds the agency could hire and asked bluntly, "Was this video shot before or after the bullets fired? I see the date on the video to be January 20th, 11:11 AM, about 51 minutes before the shots were taken."

The analysts, each one with his own area of expertise, concentrated to come up with answers. The team simply did not adjust to the new director's enigmatic method of thinking; instead, as advised, they focused on questions such as: What was the motive and purpose? What was the risk versus achievement? Who was the real target? What would the assassin profile be?

It seemed like a dead-end but Patrick continued to press the issue.

"Look closer," exclaimed the director. "What do you see on the roof of the Wilson Center building?"

All the eyes focused on the photo of the white roof top looking for clues.

"Nothing! Anyone see anything?" Patrick asked the room looking for encouragement and support.

They shook their heads silently with agreement that there was nothing suspicious in this photo. Others raised their eyebrows and rolled their eyes slightly. Even Evan's sharp eagle eyes could not come up with anything reasonable.

Patrick, a detail-oriented man, put his ego aside and replied, "Not sure if you are advising me that someone attempted an assassination from the Smithsonian building, as it is very difficult to escape from. It's an open area and the assassin would expose himself to cameras and the enforcement forces carpeted this area!"

"Agreed, however from the Wilson center, despite the distance what do you see? No obstacles, a straight line to the podium!" Marcus said, cracking his fingers nervously one by one.

"Assuming the bullet direction analysis is accurate," added Patrick, challenging his boss.

"But of course, we can miss that, giving the CBI the benefit of the doubt, and there is something else you don't see in this photo." The director tightened his lips.

"Do you have a photo of the bullets after they were fired to compare?" asked Marcus, without letting go of his prey.

Without points to connect, the exercise was a waste. But his IT team immediately found what Marcus requested, separating the roof photo frame and put both, before-and-after, next to each other for comparison. One photo before the shots were fired and one photo after. Since both photos were taken not on the time of the day or weather, they looked somewhat different, especially with the sun's direction.

Murmuring analysts chatted amongst themselves, softly analyzing the difference between the photos.

"See on the roof before the shots, close to the building parapet heading south!" Marcus exclaimed, as he raised his hands. "Zoom-in to this point!" he instructed.

The photo was zoomed in and the group could see vividly the roof membrane as it was from a few inches distance.

"Looks like a patch," claimed one in the room loud enough to wake up the dead.

"Oh, yeah!" exclaimed another.

Chattering came again.

"It's not a patch!" Patrick shot back. "It's a cover made from the same roof membrane material, it looks like a small white fabric tent."

"To cover what?" Harvie asked anxiously.

"The assassin's weapons," cried Marcus loudly. "That's what I'm guessing! See the sun create a shadow of the tent? It doesn't show the other photo!"

"But we checked this every inch of this building!" cried another staff member.

"Zoom in on the 'after' photo. . .there will be no shadow, no patch!" Marcus raised his voice even higher. "It means that right after the weapons were used, they were stored somewhere in the building, 10 days later!"

He separated the last words slowly one after the other to make his point.

Chapter 7

"We have the bullets," stated Patrick to Marcus, ten days after the assassination attempt.

The discovery was announced during the morning briefing before heading back to his office. "More precisely, a SRS99-AM sniper rifle equipped with an electronic scope for precision targeting with 7.62mm bullets manufactured by Israel Military Industries (IMI)." Evan Harris joined via a teleconference from his office in the White House.

"How the fuck did an Israeli sniper rifle materialize on the roof?" asked Evan, his eyes wide.

Marcus, a meat-and-potatoes kind of guy, kept his office simple. No artwork or expensive furniture or a credenza full of family photos. On the shelves lining the back wall stood a large cast iron model of the long-ago decommissioned frigate he served on in the Navy. His mind raced as he cracked his knuckles and checked Patrick sitting in front of him. "Did you find anything else on the roof?" Marcus changed the subject.

Patrick sipped from his coffee and put the mug back on the desk.

"Yes, immediately after the roof photos were analyzed, we sent the force to lock down the building-" Patrick was cut off and clicked his tongue in surprise.

"And?" Marcus stared anxiously at him.

"They combed every inch of the building and found the rifle dismantled in the top of the boiler room chimney," Patrick replied as he scrutinized Marcus' motionless face.

"It's an inside job, Patrick!" Evan suggested as he grabbed a couple of pastries.

"We should coordinate with the FBI. They checked all the building personnel," Marcus cut Patrick off as he responded to Evan. "Keep this out of the media's reach until further notice. What did you find from the personnel search?"

"The information was kept confidential and not disclosed to the media. We got the list of the building workers before and after January 20th and we're analyzing them." Patrick jumped in fast before he would be cut off again.

Patrick, ready for the new long day in the office, was motivated by the findings to push his team for more information using informants and collaborators working with the CIA field agents abroad, and collaborators with the NSA and FBI domestically.

"The police were looking for the public's help to find an unmarked van that was sighted nearby and reported by a private citizen. It was the same area where the naked body of a girl was dumped on the ground. She'd been raped and murdered. The police are trying to identify the van, which was not reported as missing yet." Evan coordinated the info to his CIA comrades.

"As long as the police are not trying to link the van to the assassination, we can investigate our case without interference from the police or the public," said Marcus.

"It's a domestic crime, under investigation of the FBI!" Patrick informed his boss, who perhaps was looking to tie any event in town to the assassination.

"Perhaps there is a link, and the FBI will keep me in the loop," Evan informed them both.

"You are lucky man!" Marcus sounded a little sarcastic. "I wish we could get some coordination here!" Evan ignored the remark, because he knew that the President knew what he was doing by asking him to connect the two agencies.

The public was encouraged to bring up any piece of information to solve the puzzle. Some identical vans were confiscated by the police and examined by forensic experts who found no evidence that connected them with the assassination. However, Patrick's team did find that Hassan was missing from his job in the building where the deadly shots came from.

"Investigators checked in rental car companies and located a van that fits the description," reported Patrick to Evan Harris who was surprised that this info came to Patrick first. *Looks like not all the information he should know comes to him,* he thought.

"Any connection?" asked Evan.

"It's still early. The van has been confiscated by the FBI examiners." Patrick hoped to not piss off Evan on that info that came to him first. In an effort to soften the blow, he added, "It just happened, you may have gotten the text."

Marcus changed the subject to prevent competition among the men. "We analyzed the security videos and saw Hassan, a building employee, entering the building. With him was an unidentified man, and they went to the roof. He had a bag, perhaps containing the white poncho he left behind." Marcus explained.

"Poncho?" asked Evan. "The FBI is looking for Hassan; he has been missing from his job since the day of the attack." Evan thought he scored a point knowing this info first.

"We are learning about Hassan," Patrick stated. "We are asking our allied intelligence agencies to pitch in."

"We know he rented a van similar to the one reported in the park," added Marcus.

"So, you have the van, now we are looking for Hassan. Is he a suspect?" asked Evan.

"Yes, Hassan might be a key person to the riddle; he worked with a team, although left the building before the shooting. He didn't actually do the shooting," answered Patrick.

It was a few days after the murder when the van was found, and the forensic evidence was badly contaminated. Hair samples of many previous renters were found. Then, after combing the van with a tweezers, investigators found what they were looking for. . . a small piece of fabric caught in the seat belt lock with traces of human semen.

The rental company disclosed all information of the van rental history and there were a few renters before and after the January inauguration date and with a possible time of the murder. They concentrated on the last renter.

"It's strange that the van was returned back to the rental depot in the middle of the night the day after the assassination," informed Patrick.

"Camera images?" asked Evan.

"Very bad images, can't identify the driver, he hailed a cab down the street." Marcus said.

"You think it was Hassan?" he continued.

"Not sure, the FBI might have Hassan's personal statistics to compare, and he was limping slightly," said Patrick. Evan was impressed at how some information passed between the two agencies.

"Hassan Abu Shikri was the signatory on the van lease." said Marcus.

"No, it's too easy!" claimed Evan when Hassan's name and evidence surfaced in the video conference meeting. Evan connected the dots and didn't jump on the first clue because it might take him farther from the truth.

Patrick, Marcus, and Evan agreed. A professional killer will not leave so much evidence on the ground to indict him. Hassan's cell phone account disclosed the Uber ride the day of the attack and the address where he was headed. Since then the cell phone was not in use and could not be traced.

"I can't believe a professional killer would leave such a trail. Perhaps Hassan is a small fish in this case, but I am sure if we find him, he can tell us about his partners," said Patrick and they both agreed.

"I am sure there is more to it, and there are more people involved in this case," Evan stated confidently.

"The van informer, a private citizen, reported that the driver came out of his car, perhaps to pee, but he could not be identified. He didn't pay attention to it too much until it was advertised by the police." Patrick was reading from the report on his desk that was issued to him while on the conference call. "Perhaps with an identification lineup, his memory will come back, but that's the FBI responsibility." added Patrick. His boss nodded in agreement.

"The fact that Hassan did not report to his job at the same building, and a sniper was the assassin, is enough information to start with. The President needs to be confident that this will be resolved as soon as possible," Marcus said decisively.

"The FBI is deeply involved in the girl's murder case and tied this investigation with the assassination," Patrick read from the repost. "The FBI worked with the police detective task force, assuming that Hassan did not act alone, looking for a lead to find the rest of the terror cell, to find who is behind the attack. . . what entity. . .however the FBI is cooperating with all agencies."

"Is the President looking to retaliate? Entity?" Marcus asked Evan, who scoffed.

"No!" chuckled Evan. "For God's sake, Marcus, he is not starting a war, he's just anxious to know the details. His wife was murdered!" Evan exclaimed.

"Once we have Hassan, we can find the sniper. 'Small fish attract big fish!' " stated Marcus as he tightened his lips assuredly. Marcus was not a fan of the Israeli Mossad intelligence agency, and refrained from asking them to collaborate or assist in profiling and tracking people, even though they could do it well.

Patrick, who previously collaborated with the Mossad, thought they might hold clues on activities of terror cells around the world. Many times, Israel warned foreign governments of a planned terror attacks in their countries, including adversaries, and saved thousands of lives. However, when it came to any connection to the Middle East, they were the No. 1 source to seek for help. It was time to ask his boss to put ego aside and quietly ask for assistance.

It was very well known that 'old dense' politics created a disconnect among federal and foreign agencies. Patrick wanted to restore the connections and move forward. He worked with the Mossad on other international missions, especially with his top agent, Dan Eyal. He knew how they operated and understood their mentality. The Mossad kept an inventory of potential terrorists, monitored their routes, actions, training camps, and tapped their communication lines via social media by imbedding a Trojan horse. Doing so was key to identifying new plots.

Marcus read Patrick's mind. "You don't need permission to call the Mossad," he said hoarsely. Patrick was relieved. He'd received the green light.

"OK, Patrick, restore the back-door line to glean what the Israelis might know about the assassination," added Marcus. He was referring to a direct, encrypted line between the Mossad and the CIA.

"Don't forget who called us minutes after the 9/11 attack on the World Trade Center, and directed us to focus on Osama Bin Laden." Patrick tried to win a case that was already won. Patrick wanted to penetrate Marcus' head with a drill and squeeze his skull to understand how his brilliant mind operated.

Marcus scoffed and went to the window to look out at the world below. He imagined how beautiful life could have been without the animosity between humans.

"Patrick, I know you're their biggest fan, but I was burned up in Iraq with a WMD that was never found, and I don't want to point fingers now. . . every federal agency hammered us for our poor performance!" Marcus said.

"You blamed the Mossad?" asked Patrick, surprised.

"Oh, yeah, they orchestrated the voodoo dance around the WMDs and encouraged us to attack Saddam Hussein!" Marcus snapped at Patrick, as he raised his hands in frustration. Patrick didn't expect the harsh response.

"The President was hard on attacking Iraq by any means, and he didn't need the Mossad's permission!"

"The agencies confirmed that weeks after that there is no WMS, the Mossad didn't know?" scoffed Marcus.

Patrick did not forget that; he always knew that if you didn't ask them, they wouldn't tell you. All Patrick wanted, for now, was to crisscross what they both knew, which perhaps would help the investigation. At least on that, they both agreed. Patrick had a good relationship with agents working in the Capitol embassies, especially the Israelis.

He periodically met with them especially the heads of the North Korean and the Iranian desks.

"You remember the Marine platoon trained to remove road mines in Israel?" Patrick asked.

Marcus nodded and Patrick continued, "They also learned how to fight in an urban combat, from house to house, in a simulated village for a month. . .they completed their tour in Afghanistan with no casualties. I was there once, in the infantry base of Tze'elim training camp in Israel by invitation of my friend, Dan Eyal!"

"So?"

"So, they saved American lives!" exclaimed Patrick in defiance.

"Let's focus on the assassination; the President is looking for answers!" Evan said.

Marcus knew the story. The Israelis delivered experiences to the American soldiers, which saved many lives in the war of terror in Iraq and Afghanistan. As a matter of fact, they all came back alive after their Afghanistan tour. No one would appreciate this, until he himself witnessed the Israelis methods at work.

Chapter 8

Mossad's profile of Hassan Abu Shikri drew an abstract picture of a normal family. His father was Iranian and his mother a Syrian, and they lived a secular life on the outskirts of Teheran. Hassan also liked the traditional lifestyle, which he followed as a gesture to his family history he left behind. He easily blended in with any culture due to his light-colored skin.

Hassan was on the Mossad's watch list because of his European "terror path" from the United States to Tehran. He stopped in Syria and also visited terror camp sites.

Dan was assigned to the Israeli embassy in Washington to link the agencies. He met with Patrick in a small coffee shop in Alexandria, Virginia. After a short, warm greeting where each made sure he was not followed, the men exchanged memories from past missions before they got serious about current events.

Patrick was 15 years older than Dan, but didn't look it. Time had been kind. Dan, was in his 40s and still in fighting form, tight and muscled.

"Any contact by the ICO?" asked Patrick.

"The ICO has 10,000 points of data information about Hassan, profiling his past and behavior path, his likes and comments on Facebook, Twitter, and Instagram to draw a picture of who he is and what he believes in. Would he join a terror group? Don't forget that ICO is a private Israeli cyber and spy organization and it is offering its information to the Mossad for profit; they did mention messages to someone who called himself '*Zikit*' in some of the email transactions from a third party, but not directly from Hassan."

"You make me laugh, Dan. Your agency will not pay for information. Who is *Zikit*, how did ICO get the data?"

"*Zikit* means 'chameleon' in Hebrew."

"Is he an Israeli? Can ICO track him down?"

"ICO uses social media platforms to spy and collect information. The information is used to predict a certain behavior that in some cases, politicians around the world use to persuade voters to vote for them, or target them with a deluge of commercials . . . or in our case, to predict groups who are venerable to be persuaded to join terror groups. Our headache," explained Dan.

"Can ICO predict or change people's behavior?" Patrick asked.

"In theory, yes, and it was proved. Now experts claim that 70,000 people in one swing district alone actually voted Rufus Barker in power last November."

"Pennsylvania? The swing state?"

"Exactly"

"Can ICO hack-"

"Yes!" Dan cut him off. "Hack active phones and spy on personal activities, conversations, and even videos. However, Hassan and The Chameleon were not hacked yet; we are trying hard though."

"I am sure the NSA is trying the same, not sure what information they have to share?"

"I want you to meet a colleague of mine," Patrick said as Evan walked in the coffee shop, straight toward Patrick with a smile.

"I've heard about you," Evan said, staring at Dan with a profound glance.

"I hope good things," Dan joked.

"Where are we?" asked Evan.

"We're trying to locate Hassan before he disappears into thin air," replied Patrick. He ordered three coffees and a few pastries for which the shop was famous.

Dan looked out to the street. Patrick sat with his back to the street and Evan was on the side when Dan whispered, "Don't look out, someone is taking photos of us."

Automatically, they both looked, ignoring Dan's warning.

A black Ford Explorer was parked across the street with a camera zooming in on the trio. The photographer was sitting in the back seat with his window down while the driver was behind the closed darkly tinted window.

Evan rushed out to identify the SUV, but it zoomed up the road like a missile and disappeared in the morning's rush hour traffic. He returned to a throng of slack-jawed customers.

"Let's get out of here," Dan said as he set a $50 bill on the table.

They left the coffee shop and stood on the chilly sidewalk where they hailed a cab.

"Is someone following you, Evan?" asked Patrick.

"Why would anyone follow me?" he asked, puzzled, as a cab arrived.

"It's getting interesting, Patrick. Looks like someone wants to know my moves. Who the fuck are they?"

"Did you identify the car?" Dan asked.

"No, it's a black Ford Explorer and there are thousands in the city," he scoffed.

"Might be Islamic Revolutionary Guard agents," said Dan.

"Are you sure?" asked Evan.

"That's what we all think right now since Hassan is Iranian; there must be a connection."

"Not necessarily, but it's an option. Where are you going?" Patrick asked.

"I'm heading to the White House." Evan was troubled. He wondered who might be trailing him.

"I am flying back to Tel-Aviv. I have some ideas how to help you and need to clear it with my boss," replied Dan.

They separated and each headed to his destination but promised to keep in touch.

Patrick took his notebook and, excited, went straight to his boss with the data he got from Dan so far.

"The Mossad's pointing fingers at the Revolutionary Guards," Patrick said.

"Why? Because Hassan is Iranian?" asked Marcus.

"Does the name 'Chameleon' sound familiar to you? Or 'Zikit'?" he asked.

"Huh?" Marcus raised his eyebrows. "Is that what came up in your meeting? The jungle is full of chameleons, why?" Marcus leaned back on his chair and scoffed as he eyed Patrick.

"Unit 8200, is a department in IDF intelligence based near Tel-Aviv, and works closely with the Mossad. It's equivalent to our NSA intelligence base in Cypress," Patrick explained.

"It's OK to keep the communication freely across the pond Patrick, but what is this Chameleon?"

Patrick was frustrated when he saw Marcus rolling his eyes at the mention of unit 8200 and said, "This Chameleon entity communicated with other people across the globe and it seems as if Hassan might know them."

Marcus sat motionless, his expression frozen. He took a minute to digest the information.

"So, what are you saying? We are not looking for a Jihadi terror group?" Marcus cleared his throat.

"No, that's not what I am saying, what they are saying is that Hassan is an outsider, like 'Event Horizon,' the boundary but not the core, when the real people or a group called themselves 'The Chameleons' and the lead man is known as 'The Chameleon.'"

"How did they come up with that?"

"The Israelis were monitoring The Chameleon for different purposes."

"Can we get more information about The Chameleon? This will open some new avenues for us," suggested Marcus. "The Mossad didn't come up with connections to 'Soldiers of Allah'?"

"Not that they mentioned. Who are they?" Patrick asked.

"Not to be confused with 'Agents of Allah.' Evan killed its leader. We just received a video as you arrived, and the FBI said that the Soldiers of Allah claimed responsibility."

"Wow," Patrick exclaimed. "A Jihadi group claimed responsibility, right? Did the FBI check its authenticity?"

"You answered your own question; I will share this with the FBI and NSA to crisscross information and start searching our town. We all need to validate the video, where it was taken, surrounding images and sounds, furnishings, details, etc. Just another place to look for answers," said Marcus.

"There's no way Hassan could escape the roadblocks in town if he didn't have the assistance of a terror cell right here in our back yard. . .He must be still here!" Patrick declared.

"I am afraid we are all looking in the wrong direction; someone wants us to use our resources investigating other areas in vain." Marcus was concerned.

"Could be. . .Hassan could not pull this off by himself. Now we have The Chameleon on one side and the Soldiers of Allah on the other side. Are they all the same or separate entities? Mind boggling," said Patrick, sounding skeptical.

"I suspect that he was used by a professional agency, perhaps an adversary, perhaps a country backing this operation, who knows. . .I've never heard of 'Soldier of Allah' before," Marcus replied.

"OK, then, Marcus, I'll look into it!" Patrick left his boss's office and he knew exactly what his next step would be: he'd launch a huge probe to question mosque after mosque and question everyone about Soldiers of Allah and Hassan Abu Shikri. He hoped that the Mossad would activate his ICO proxy and perhaps expose the entire group, especially the man who was on the roof and pulled the trigger.

Soldiers of Allah, he whispered gently and shook his head as he walked back to his office.

The vice president, who was in charge of the investigation for the President, requested information about the progress through his Chief of Staff, Frank Dabush.

Patrick discussed his conversation with his boss without disclosing the group who claimed responsibility, which was considered top secret, classified information until it could be confirmed. Frank promised to intervene with the local search to make it easy on Patrick to investigate the case and offered Evan as an alternative. "The President will give Evan up for that case," Frank promised. "He is the best at this shit right now, and you know it!"

Patrick discussed with Frank only the info he needed to know as a politician, and nothing more. Frank was easy to deal with and known as a nice man, however, when it came to politics, he kept his cards close to his chest and didn't like to share his thoughts with everyone in the White House, especially the vice president's staff.

Frank's meteoric rise to his position as a NRA lobbyist and to an arms dealer stained with some bad blood deals could and probably would be hurting his own country. But now, it went unmentioned.

"It's all legal," Frank used to say, and he was right as long he bribed the politicians they respected. When Frank was asked once at a cocktail party a question on how he would explain capitalism in four words he said, "Grab whatever you can!"

Chances were that federal agents who were not familiar with the Middle East demography could not distinguish between the differences of one Middle Easterner to another unless given a few signs of what exactly they were looking for. Middle Easterners came in many forms, from those with blue eyes and light skin to those with black eyes and dark skin. Therefore, the authorities kept the roadblocks after the inauguration for an undisclosed schedule. Routinely, roadblocks were there for couple of days until the town was cleaned up.

The Capitol looked more and more like Kandahar, Afghanistan, with the military chasing Taliban terrorists rather than looking like the symbol of the most powerful nation on earth. The National Guard sealed the city, checked all vehicles and examined all residents and visitors, and monitored airports and waterways, 24/7.

The town was relatively quiet during normal evenings in D.C. A handful of pedestrians could be seen on the sidewalks, and at midnight, the city fell into a deep sleep. Taxis and a few cars traversed the streets after most of the downtown restaurants served their last customers before closing. Silence covered the city like a military curfew.

Frank suggested a conference call to send Evan to investigate a couple of Iranian Shia mosques in town and religious centers in the area where Hassan lived. Evan thought it was nice for Frank to suggest reassigning him to covert operations, and he planned to visit the mosques immediately. He was flattered to know that he was personally selected by the President to be his personal bodyguard, but that was not what he yearned for as a full-time job.

"Looking into the Revolutionary Guards made sense given the info disclosed earlier by the Mossad."

Evan briefed the President and the defense secretary in the Oval Office. He didn't mention that he was followed by a foreign agency, at least not without having solid proof that was the case.

"Do you see any connections between the drone incidents—ordered by the former President—to the attack?" asked the defense secretary, who was anxious to blame the former administration for the event.

"If it was a retaliation, why did they shoot my wife and the Supreme Court Justice?" the President asked.

"They probably missed," replied Evan. "But we really don't know yet."

"They probably aimed at former President Cole and missed," insisted the defense secretary.

"President Cole was a couple of yards from us. There's no chance a professional sniper would miss a target by that much," replied Evan.

Evan was cut off by the defense secretary. "Perhaps not a professional sniper, but trained by professionals."

"It's a plausible theory. . .the trigger suspect left the building after 10 minutes, and was limping on his left foot," Evan said.

"The same guy one who entered the building with the suspect, what's his name. . .Hassan?" the President asked.

"Yes, the same guy," Evan confirmed.

"Do we know anything about him?" the defense secretary asked.

"No, not really, we are trying to match him with thousands of suspect images using the NSA imaging program. He was pretty much covered up to avoid identification." Evan added his theory, "The drone incident in Iran was a possible form of retaliation, sir."

"So, they just missed. . ." the President started. He could not see the connection between the two, since the drone incident occurred during the previous administration. If that was the case, why did they shoot his wife and the Supreme Court Justice?

"Perhaps they were looking to assassinate the former President who gave the order, and they just missed," the President concluded. Evan nodded his head and concurred.

"The irony was that the drone was hijacked by the Revolutionary Guards, right?" asked the defense secretary.

"We can't blame anyone, guys. This fiasco can't be pushed and to blame others; we need the motive fast so we may know who to turn to dust soon, that's all!" The President seemed to lose his cool, and raised his voice to emphasize the need for a direction.

"That's what politicians do!" Evan scoffed. "But, yes, this drone came with a self-destruction system that could have destroyed the drone if activated. When the pilot declared that he lost control of his drone, his superior gave the order to destroy it. The system malfunctioned and instead, both sides lost control of the aircraft that flew aimlessly for hundreds of miles away from its original course target in Iraq. The wind ended its trip in the outskirts of Teheran; it exhausted its fuel supply, and killed civilians, including many school children." Evan remarkably detailed the event that drew worldwide attention to the United States and its war on terror in the region.

"That's history, Evan. I know the details," said the President.

The President and Evan agreed on the assessment that the assassination attempt should not be blamed on the former President and vowed to not leak this assumption to the press to avoid another round of a feeding frenzy by the media.

"I wonder," asked the President, as he rested his legs on his desk, "why they didn't shoot it down when it entered their airspace?"

"True!" Evan said and Alvin jumped in, "They wanted to hijack it, sir."

"This question was asked many times. It was our most advance stealth drone. Radars couldn't detect it, so in the end it exploded on a school with its entire armament," said Evan.

"By the way, Marcus informed me that you are assisting those investigating mosques around the town, just keep me informed, I'll call you when needed." The President sounded frustrated with the progress and hoped the media would cooperate.

"Yeah, perhaps I'll find some starting threads of information. I will personally investigate one of the mosques Patrick asked me to visit," Evan added, knowing this task would bring him straight into the lion's den.

"I wonder, why you?" asked the President.

"It was actually Frank Dabush's idea. He thinks on the same level."

"Oh, Frank, the character who is involved with everything and anything," chuckled the President, showing his revulsion.

"It should be a personal visit, to calm the community down rather send detectives and make a big fuss," Evan said, reading the President's mind. The defense secretary concurred.

"Got it!" he answered laconically.

Barker informed the Pentagon to immediately ground the entire drone fleet operations in solidarity of support to the Iranian victims until the situation was cleared up.

The media somehow hit TV screens as usual with their own connections. The President made it clear that he would not allow such incidents to happen again under his watch. They've made the connections and called it even, for now.

The media immediately praised him for the move, not knowing that in his heart, he wanted to annihilate Iran and vaporize it. But in his position, he could not speak his thoughts as many Presidents before him had done.

"Evan!" called the President.

"Yes, Mr. President?"

"You understand I trust you to resolve this case, right?"

"Yes, Mr. President. I do," Evan replied stoically.

Chapter 9

Alexandria, Virginia
Three weeks after the assassination attempt

E van buttoned up his winter coat, shivering from the cold air. He parked his car in the NRL Federal Credit Union building across the street of the Shia Iranian Islamic Center on Cherokee Avenue.

He parked at the end of the lot and displayed his official badge on the windshield and thought, *You can't trust anyone these days.*

Carefully, he crossed the street toward the community center, ensuring that he was not followed. He entered the two-story red brick building through a single vestibule door entrance. He looked outside from the lobby to check the parking lot and saw a few cars parking at the center close to the building, and a few parking on the street. It was important to remember the picture so that when left the building, he'd see any changes that could signal a threat. His agent-like senses had, over the years, blended with his personality. "Always check your escape route," he was told again and again by his superiors.

The Shia religious building was used by Iranians as a community center to mingle, meet friends, exchange job information, and enjoy cultural activities for the entire family. It was generally a peaceful place. He heard children playing in the day care center and they sounded like any other children would sound: happy, with free spirits and no worries. When he approached the unoccupied reception desk, he noticed the camera on the corner of the ceiling above and smiled, showing his official badge.

While waiting, he checked his surroundings one more time. The door leading into the center was controlled by an electric lock. The camera could swivel electronically as needed. He heard the buzzer sound and looked up into the camera. A minute later, a young bearded cleric with a white thobe, a long robe worn by Muslim men, opened the door and asked in heavy accent, "Can I help you?"

"Yes, I want to meet the Mullah, please!"

"Do you have an appointment?" he asked politely with a smile.

Evan pulled up his badge and showed it to the man who acknowledged it with a nod. He let Evan into the building and asked him to sit in a waiting room.

Evan was very happy to get inside the warm building. Shortly after, another man wearing a bishet (a dressier cloak) over his thobe and who resembled the ayatollah entered the room. He held a cane and greeted Evan with *khosh amadid*, ("welcome" in Farsi), then added, "I presume you are Evan Harris?" Evan shook his hand and nodded his head slightly. "Yes, I am here to meet Mullah Afshin Shiraz, I assume it's you?"

"Yes, that is me, Imam Afshin Shiraz!" he corrected his title, smiling at Evan's mistake.

Evan smiled back and kept this as polite as possible in order not to offend the community leader. The Imam radiated a kind of a good, peaceful man of God, someone who resonated with a calming ambiance about him. The men walked into the elder's ample office. Evan noticed all the window shutters were pulled down. The man read his mind when he said, "It's a tough time for the community," he shook his head and added sadly, "We are keeping a low-profile."

"Are you seeing any changes in the community since the attack?" asked Evan with a low voice. He wanted to keep the conversation as normal as possible and not seem like an interrogation.

"Yes, strangers are sending hate messages and have defaced the building with graffiti," he answered with real sadness.

"My apologies for my ignoranc-" Evan began before the Imam raised his hands and softly said, "It's OK, we didn't complain, we have had many hate calls asking us to leave. We just need the police to protect us."

"I understand, I'll bring this forward," Evan promised.

"I didn't expect you to know the differences between Imam and Mullah," the Imam said gently.

Evan chuckled and look at the Imam's twinkling black eyes.

The door to the Imam's office opened and an older man entered. He smiled at Evan as if he'd known him for years.

The two whispered in Farsi and then Imam Afshin Shiraz introduced him to Evan.

"This is Imam Ali; he wants to show you the prayers room in preparation of an obligatory prayer, soon."

A pair of enormous carved wooden doors with religious symbols that Evan didn't understand led into the prayer hall that was covered with prayer rugs. As anticipated, the large room was warm and cozy, and a few people were preparing for a prayer. He was sure it filled to capacity with Jumu'ah prayers on Fridays early afternoon.

"Would you please take off your shoes?" Imam Ali asked politely. "We are about to start a sermon; would you care to stay?" Imam Ali asked softly.

"I would, but I have a lot of work in front of me," Evan answered. For a moment, he thought about how to get to the point without being too aggressive.

"How can we help you?" asked Afshin with a calm smile.

"Do you want me to come at a more convenient time?" asked Evan. He pulled a few photos from his pocket and silently laid them on the table.

The Imams gazed at the photos, awaiting an explanation. Evan was not sure if he was acting or not, so he continued to spread out the photos. They all looked alike–the same man, same image, the same identity.

"This is Hassan Abu Shikri," Evan said. "Is he one of your members?"

"Why, what are you accusing him of?" Afshin asked, his eyes wide with curiosity.

"I hope he is not in trouble?" said Imam Ali with surprise in his voice.

"Hassan is an Iranian student and connected to the murder of the First Lady and the Supreme Court Justice during the Inauguration ceremony, and we need to find him, fast!" Evan's tone of voice was replaced with an official one, which got straight to the point.

"Do you know Hassan?" Evan asked.

"Oh, sure, I have seen him before, but understand that we have a few thousand followers and don't know what they do or where they are."

"That was my next question. When was the last time you saw him?"

"A month? Two?" The Imam clicked a few keys on his computer keyboard and nodded his head. "Not on my list, but I know the face!" he finally exclaimed.

"Has he any friends? Roommates maybe? Do you know where he hangs out?" Evan asked in rapid fire.

"He is not a member; people may come and pray without being a registered member, like a guest you know. . .we maintain their privacy."

"Have you noticed or witnessed any unusual activities among your young congregation? A discussion you might have overheard? Are there any missing members? Anything you can share with us even if you think it's not an important detail or significant information?"

"People already asked us those questions," the Imam said, his eyes growing large and curious. "What else can we add?"

The Imam didn't wait for an answer and added dramatically, "Our congregation is a peaceful one. We do not mind politics; but honestly, I do not recall any unusual signs worth investigating, although I will be glad to share any with you if they relate to the event, if I have any. Our hearts are with the American people; we do not preach for violence and want to live in peace without worries with our neighbors." Afshin took the emotional path. Evan wondered who they were and if they were really loyal. He glanced around the office, which had bare, white walls, with no adornments other than a photo of the Ayatollah. Some religious accessories rested on a table and Evan couldn't make out what rituals they were used for. "If it's tied to the assassination attempt three weeks ago, we will help!" Afshin exclaimed, catching Evan by surprise.

"We believe Hassan was hosted by a friend while he waited for his dorm at the university. So, some people hosted and know him, I was hoping that you would know, if perhaps he slept here or in another center."

"He was not sleeping here; I can assure you that," Ali confirmed.

Evan pulled out a business card, put it on the table, pointed to it, and said, "Let me know if you see him, or you hear anything. . .he might be in a grave danger from other terror groups. . . any information you bring forward can help. Keep this interview confidential please. OK?" Evan put on his coat and got ready to leave the building. He had mixed feelings. He felt surreal, like he was floating between imagination and reality, like he was the main character in a movie. Something told him that the holy men knew more than they admitted.

"It's difficult; I'll do my best to inform you of any inconsistency with the congregation," the Imam said and raised his hands up in the air as if to say 'it's up to the almighty above. The only one who has control over the situation, Allah.'

"A friend brings a friend," stated Evan. "Everyone knows something. I would appreciate if you call me. You have my card." Evan turned around to leave after they all politely bid goodbye.

The cold air struck his face like a thousand needles. He hated winter and remembered the vacation time he spent with his friends in Florida just before the inauguration. He would take the heat and humidity anytime over the cold winter in the northeast. He let out a juicy curse.

Light snow flurries greeted him, lingering in the air with a variable wind direction as he walked to his car. His SUV was parked toward the end of the parking lot next to a line of mature, tall trees, standing bare in the snow behind a few peaceful townhouses where smoking chimneys marked the active fireplaces. It could have been a romantic scene. He pushed his car's remote control to start the engine from about 50 feet away to warm the cabin in advance. In an instant, a huge explosion rattled the neighborhood buildings with unimaginable force. Shock waves could have brought down the Empire State Building with the amount of explosive that blew his car to pieces. Shattered, twisted metal fragments flew up in the air. The explosion ignited the gas tank and created a secondary explosion a couple of seconds later and the vehicle was a shredded piece of metal skeleton. The flames sent a large black mushroom cloud of smoke into the sky, melting instantly the falling snowflakes in its path.

Evan's slim frame was catapulted forcefully onto the ground a few feet from where he stood, slamming him on the thin layer of snow accumulated on the frozen asphalt.

He moaned loudly as he gasped for air before he lost consciousness.

Chapter 10

Hassan became instantly tense when the intercom buzzed in his secret apartment hideaway.

A few days had passed since the event and he hadn't heard anything, so the obnoxious buzzing brought him back into reality. He had a few days to worry and plan his next steps forward, and every day that passed by was harder on him. He was told that he would be in the apartment for just a few days, and that his "bosses" would help him, but he didn't know how.

He had no choice but to stay in the apartment. The TV was the only reminder to him that time was passing. His food and provisions were dwindling, yet, he feared to leave without knowing where to go. He found a loaded handgun in a drawer under some clothes and wondered if it was unintentionally left behind.

The media was not aware of his existence. *No police requests were made with his portrait, and that was the good thing,* he thought. . .total silence, not even a mention of the rape on TV, the murder of the poor girl from District Heights, no mention of any names or suspects, and so, far no one was in custody for the murder or the attempted assassination. *It was weird,* he thought, *that the media collaborated with the defense agencies.*

Hassan was frustrated and wondered, sometimes aloud, if the men who blackmailed him would put into action their threat to release the video recording of the rape and murder and turn him in. He never thought he would end up this way in the new land. The device used to record and transmit the videos might also be leaked to others. Hassan believed it was just a threat and that was his hope, even though he doubted he'd ever go free.

He speculated on the court's punishment, if he was convicted in the rape and killing of the poor woman. He wondered if he could prove he didn't actually rape her, and that he certainly didn't kill her. Perhaps he would turn himself in and explain how he was used and taken advantage of, but how would he explain that after all this activity, he knew no one? He didn't know the faces or names of his blackmailers. The rental car was in his name. *No one would believe me,* he thought.

The intercom buzzed again, and interrupted his thoughts and brought him back to reality. He had no way out now. He could not see who was buzzing the bell downstairs, since the person stood with his back to the intercom camera. After additional rings, he felt he had no choice but to press the intercom button and ask, "Who's there?"

"Hassan, open door, it's me... me, Walid," the man spoke in broken English and with a strange accent.

Hassan wondered, *Who the fuck is Walid? Was he one of the guys who was supposed to help me? Where are the provisions they promised to bring?*

The man waited an additional few seconds before buzzing again impatiently three times in a row.

"Hassan?" the man yelled. "You are in a great danger, Hassan. I must evacuate you to a safe place... I am here with food! Some fresh food. Halal from the corner!"

He heard giggling in the background and he felt cold sweat run down his back. *Something is wrong here. It was wrong all along, but this time is the end. It's the end of the line!*

But. . .what if he was wrong and the man was here to help? He sighed to try and calm his heart. He could actually see it beating in his chest, but breathed deeply again and pressed the intercom button to open the entry door.

Then, suddenly, he regretted not escaping the night before when he saw the rent envelope addressed to him that the landlord shoved under the door. *What was I thinking?* The apartment was rented under his name. No one cared if he needed anything. He pushed the thought away as he wildly grasped at his escape plans in the minute or so before Walid and company reached his door. He needed to decide his next step and stick with it no matter what.

Hassan knew he didn't have the brain to analyze conspiracy theories. The apartment was comfortable, and it was a place he would love to live in if it was not for the circumstances he was in. Last night, he saw the news, which covered the SUV explosion in Alexandria next to the mosque he visited a few times with his friend. He wondered if there was a connection.

Perhaps, these guys are disguised federal agents? he wondered, then rushed to the window and pulled the curtain slightly a side. No, it was not surrounded by FBI cars or guns pointing at the apartment windows.

Hassan's hands shook as he took the gun from the drawer in the bedroom, made sure it was loaded, cocked it, turned off the lights, rushed back to turn the door lock off, sat on the sofa across the front door with a big pillow on his knees and waited. *Try to stay cool,* he commanded himself while focusing on the entrance.

The doorbell did not ring again, but someone turned the latch open without waiting for an invitation. The door opened one notch and the light from the corridor spilled into the apartment foyer and living room, painting a beam of light on the floor. A shadow blocked the light and hesitated to get into the foyer, keeping the door only slightly open.

Hassan recognized the man who drove the van. He wore the same jeans and checkered shirt that Hassan could not forget, and it was glued to his skin. He didn't cover his face with the scarf as he did during the videotaped rape and murder of the girl, and he limped into the room. He smiled like the Joker from the DC Comics. He stood close to the threshold, trying to spot Hassan.

Another person appeared just behind the Joker. He pushed the door open as he shoved the Joker into the room and pulled a gun from behind his belt. It was equipped with a silencer and once he spotted his target, aimed the infrared beam at Hassan's forehead. The second man kept his face concealed with a scarf. The Joker spotted Hassan as he got used to the darkness, and understood they were in control of the situation, the second man pulled off his scarf, smiling contentedly. Hassan sat helplessly on the sofa, awaiting his execution. He held his gun in ready mode under the pillow. His hand shook uncontrollably. The guests did not know that Hassan had a different plan in mind other than to wait for a bullet to split his skull in two.

"Hello, stupid," the Joker said sarcastically and let the third man in. The men now all stood in a row in front of Hassan and the door closed behind them.

The infrared beam moved around as the second man shifted position, while he explained to Hassan what his role in all this was. The men were a perfect target as they all stood in front of Hassan, with confidence abounding, and satisfied that another leg of their mission was nearly complete, with hefty paychecks on the way.

Without removing the pillow on his knees, he carefully adjusted the gun under it, and Hassan pulled the trigger three times, shooting the three men dead before they had a chance to react. Hassan was stunned that he actually did it. The closed room made the loud shots sound louder and that distressed Hassan, but he realized that he didn't have much time to recover, if he wanted to live to tell the truth. He needed to escape at once.

Allah ho Akbar, he muttered as blood from the victims poured on the floor and sank into the carpet. The victims' guns were spread close to their bodies as they didn't have a chance to fire.

I fucking knew it, he shakily murmured. He didn't ignore the fact that he was close to death as well. He was tense to the point where he couldn't think. He breathed deeply a couple of times, as he learned to do when he was under pressure. He needed to leave immediately.

He picked up the gun and tucked it behind his back. He then invested a few valuable seconds to frisk the pockets of the dead men and found a big wad of $100 bills—possibly as much as $10,000—which he shoved in his pants pocket. He took their wallets and any identification and shoved them in a plastic bag inside his backpack, and then he picked up his coat and left.

He wanted to take photos, but they didn't have cell phones and his cell phone battery was dead. The men forgot to confiscate his cell phone, and the apartment didn't have a phone line, computer, or a Wi-Fi connection device. It was totally isolated from the outside world, and perhaps it was better this way.

One thing was for sure: he'd stay away from the mosques and Shia religious centers for now. They were all probably being monitored and under surveillance. He figured that now, not only were the Americans looking for him but also the Iranians or perhaps the entire international intelligence community. He probably was the most hunted man on the planet. *What next?* he wondered. Hassan was not sure in which part of town or neighborhood the apartment was located, but he needed to move on.

Wailing sirens marked the fast-approaching police cars entering the neighborhood. *They were fast*, he thought. Now, he appreciated his decision to grow a beard and cut his long hair which made him look much different than the student he was. He grabbed the last pretzels left from the five gallon jar and left the building by the back door. He noticed the camera and lowered his face. He walked a few blocks with no apparent direction, just as far away from the scene as possible, and hailed a cab.

Chapter 11

Dan Eyal was in the West Bank, disguised as an Arab merchant in the Jericho Casbah. He walked down the street, but not alone, as others from his unit mingled in the market that teemed with life.

They'd intercepted communications between the town of Jericho and Moscow regarding a video related to a terror group called the Soldiers of Allah. It was the name that Hassan Abu Shikri came up with, but the content was encrypted and hard to break.

The man they were looking for was a well-known figure in the local political scene and ICO was able to locate him through his cell phone. He sat in a Narghile shop playing backgammon and exchanging gossip with some locals.

Two shielded Army trucks, equipped with machine guns, blocked the street from both sides, and faced backward for a fast escape. No one suspected what would happen next as three Mossad agents known as *Misterhe'bim*, (from the Arabic word meaning disguised as Arabs or literally, a mystery) approached the smoky shop from both sides, entering one by one in short intervals. A Molotov cocktail bomb exploded next to one of the Army vehicles and the soldiers opened fire on the attacker. Tension rose instantly.

Dan signaled to the suspect while he drew two handguns and instructed bystanders to calm down.

The other two agents quickly outflanked the man in his 50s, dressed in a European designer suit, raising him above the local population's appearance.

The man froze in place and didn't resist. "What is wrong? Why, why?" he asked in Arabic.

The bomb accelerated the mission and they pushed the man out of the store. Dan called one of the vehicles to approach them and get out of the Casbah before the rest of the Jihadists could join in.

As they left, a second Molotov bomb exploded next to the man who threw it, killing him instantly. Dan had already shot him in the leg a second earlier, which prevented him from throwing the bomb.

"Get in, fast, fast!" shouted Dan and encouraged the targeted man to get in.

The people in the store started to get restless and chanted against the arrest by raising their fists in the air and cursing the Israelis. Both trucks disappeared as fast as they came, and shot off in different directions, to confuse those who might be after them to save the man arrested.

Dan was relieved when it was all over and thanked his troops.

"Aslam Abu Mansour, the producer of the video, has been captured," Dan reported to his boss.

Chapter 12

G ad Jacoby, chief of the Mossad agency of special assignments, knew more then he wanted to tell, and always kept his best card close to the vest for potential future negotiations. He might need a favor in return for information, and they knew it. There were many open questions that the Mossad were trying to answer with their spy games in the post-cold war era. Once again, the United States and Russia were involved in a mini cold war, and this time, China was a player as well, pursuing its own agenda and ready to play an equal role.

"We have in our custody, Aslam Abu Mansour. It seems that he has connections with The Chameleons, the group that might have been hired to assassinate your President."

Dan was sitting in his boss's office when Patrick picked up the phone and, after a short, polite greeting, Patrick said, "Great job, guys. Perhaps Abu Mansour will help. Any personal info about Hassan that might help us locate him?"

Dan answered right away, "Hassan was born to a mixed parentage–a Sunni minority Kurd mother and a Syrian Shiite Muslim father."

"Go on," encouraged Patrick.

"He came from a small town of the northwest region of the Sunni Kurds, a depressed minority in Iran, close to the Iraqi border, and didn't care about the Ayatollah's religious revolution too much." Dan cleared his throat and continued, "As the son of a Sunni mother, he never had any chance to have a successful career in academia, where most of the seats were saved for the Revolutionary Guard families first, even though his father was a Shiite Muslim. Hassan didn't wait for others to dictate his future and left his war-torn country." Dan held his breath and waited for a response.

"Was he radicalized?" Patrick grew impatient.

"He might have visited terror websites out of curiosity, but Hassan does not fit the stereotype of a terror organization member."

"Oh!" Patrick acted surprised. "Why do you think that?"

"There was no affiliation to a terror group, or any Islamic group, including the Soldiers of Allah. This group just surfaced after the attack and it's a fake organization."

"Why would anyone do that?" Patrick asked, confused. "They claimed responsibility; we are now investigating the video!"

"OK, I understand, but there is no trace of any financial wiring, bank accounts, fund raising, money laundering, or online recruiting, like any of the other terror groups. You are wasting your time investigating the video, Patrick." Gad tried hard to convince his colleague from across the pond.

"Of course, Patrick," said Dan. "We found out that Aslam was hired to make this video. He is a small porno producer in the West Bank and will produce anything for money. He hires actors to shoot videos, including weddings, in his studio," Dan insisted.

"Why go to Aslam? What's the purpose of the video?"

"To sabotage traces of the people who ordered it. . .to blame others!" claimed Dan and Gad agreed with him.

"He knows who ordered the video?"

"Of course, but he kept his mouth shut. It will take time; we are still squeezing him little by little in our cellars, his client could be a member of The Chameleons." Dan inhaled deeply.

"Perhaps what you are saying is the truth, and I respect your on-ground infiltrating spies. What do we know about The Chameleons?" Patrick asked.

"It's a brutal gang composed of the filth of the former Soviet Union gutters. After the fall of the Soviet Union, all hell broke loose. Everyone wanted to put their hands on the weapons scattered all over the former Soviet bloc, especially the nuclear arsenal left in the Ukraine," Dan explained.

"They traded plutonium with North Korea, Iran, and other third-world countries to produce dirty bombs to protect against the Western countries that pressured their regime," added Gad.

"I am sure many died because they didn't know how to handle radioactive material," scoffed Dan and Patrick and Gad laughed.

"Now regarding Hassan," Gad sighed, bringing back the main suspect on this case. Patrick cut him off.

"What you are telling me is that Hassan has no connection to the Soldiers of Allah terror group or to The Chameleon?"

"True, that's what we think!" exclaimed Gad.

"But is your organization considering that Hassan was linked, importantly connected, or just sucked into the group that was responsible for the assassination? He might know someone?" asked Patrick loudly in defiance.

"A group, in a group, in a group, just losing track," explained Gad.

"I'm just asking!" Patrick insisted stubbornly.

"There was no apparent motive we can come up with; we need to know how and where the attack was originated." Patrick took a deep breath and exhaled softly.

"It's normal to move in circles. Whoever planned the attack is a master of 'catch me if you can,' " Gad assumed.

"He wears many hats," guessed Patrick.

"Yup, he takes you around the world, but it could be someone right in your backyard."

Patrick absorbed every word the men said. It was a different way of thinking. *I should speak to Marcus to run a separate investigation within the FBI investigation,* he thought.

"Wait, Patrick, what about the rape in Virginia? Hassan was involved with a couple of other guys," Gad asked.

" 'Other guys' sounds suspicious," said Dan.

"Perhaps they were members of The Chameleons," suggested Gad.

"What possible motive do The Chameleons have in all this?" asked Patrick.

"A proxy, nothing to do with your domestic politics, assassins-for-hire for example, money. . .I have my ears everywhere, Patrick," said Dan.

"Well, we uncovered photos that incriminated Hassan in the rape. The rape victim was later murdered." He sighed loudly as he scrutinized Gad's reaction.

"We got a copy of the video, but don't ask us how!" Gad and Dan chuckled.

"Your offensive cyber experts discovered it, I assume?" Patrick was sarcastic and knew when not to ask too many questions. He let Gad continue.

"The only reason we initiated a file on Hassan is that he was a person of interest, and used the same path that terror groups used to penetrate Europe as a refugee. He was on a watch list. That's all!" Gad cleared his throat. "He has no record of being trained in terror camps or visiting Jihadists; we assume that Hassan's employment in the building was part of the assassination plan. The planners have planted Hassan, pure and simple!" Gad stopped to take a sip from his coffee.

"Shifting the blame on to others?" Patrick was amazed on the clarity of the analysis.

"Yes!" exclaimed Gad.

Patrick sighed softly and sank into deep thought. The Mossad just opened a new way to investigate and perhaps it was better not to involve anyone other than his boss, not even the FBI.

"Could your cyber intelligence ICO hack his phone for information?"

"We tried that, no phone, no CC, no trace; someone prepared him for all this, but he might be using one with a different name, or a different number," Gad suggested.

"Always nice to pick up your brain, Gad, thanks a lot."

"Someone in the Mosques must know Hassan," suggested Dan.

"You should also look for other sources for answers; there are many layers and scattered puzzle pieces. I'll do what I can to supply you with information from my team on the ground!" exclaimed Gad.

Patrick knew that Gad was referring to his secret unit imbedded within the Arab societies around the Middle East that was also responsible for stealing the entire Iranian archived nuclear program and delivering it to Israel as one of its missions. They also brought Aslam Abu Mansour from the heart of the Jericho swamp for interrogation at the Mossad agency.

Gad promised to keep in touch with the CIA and have Dan Eyal on standby to assist. Basically, Patrick never liked the clever student who always shot up his hand every time the teacher asked a question.

He wanted to hear more from everyone else, but what could he do when he called the Mossad and they reshuffled the cards in his head? His head was exploding, and he asked his assistant for a Tylenol and a glass of water before realizing that she hadn't started her shift yet; it was 7:00 a.m. in Langley.

At least he could report some progress to his boss and the President, who wanted to put this away before his promised upcoming tour to Saudi Arabia, which was the next main source of headaches for the CIA. Patrick let out a huge sigh. "Fuck," he murmured under his breath.

A knock on the door caused him to move his head quickly to see Evan Harris enter the room.

"Hello, Evan, who let you in so early?" he asked with a smile.

"I have my ways, Patrick," Evan replied confidentially.

"Yeah, how is your recovery going?"

"Pretty good, no issues, I feel like a new man!" Evan said.

"We were very concerned a-"

Evan cut him off and asked, "How's the investigation of my car explosion going?"

"Evan, I wonder if this had anything to do with the people who followed you to that Alexandria coffee shop, remember?" Patrick asked.

"Yeah, someone was out to kill me, no doubt, and I can't come up with a trace or a motive," Evan sighed.

"Motive?" Patrick was surprised. "You are the President's bodyguard. You're living one breath away from the most powerful man on Earth, and investigating a mosque that's possibly related to the murder of the President's wife." Patrick got excited and emotional.

Evan nodded.

"Anyway, thanks for the assistance," Evan said as he thought about the Mossad agents. "Patrick, listen, this must be a domestic terror group, someone who has access to our military storage. The explosive was Army-grade composition C-4, similar to RDX, which we use in our military," Evan declared.

"It was stolen probably from t-" Patrick started.

"It was a professional job. I was lucky to remote-start the car, otherwise we would not be speaking today."

It was the first face-to-face conversation in awhile and Evan expressed his anger over the sloppy investigation on his murder attempt. No one was arrested, nor did anyone have a clue where to start investigating.

"Too much is going on; all the resources are directed to the President not to a- " Patrick began.

"There is a fucking link here, Patrick, don't you see? Why someone would want to take me out? Think!" It was Evan's turn to get excited and loud.

"Shhh, lower your voice," Patrick scolded. "Might be. . .but please let me finish!" Patrick raised his voice.

"OK, what next? Why am I here?" Evan asked.

"I want you to volunteer for a mission," Patrick said.

"How did I get so lucky? What's the mission?" Evan asked, his curiosity piqued.

"First, Marcus and I agreed with Frank Dabush that you should be away from here for a while to shake your followers, and, second, you will be going to Moscow!"

"Frank? The same Ol' Frank cares about *me*? Wow!" Evan laughed and Patrick was silent. "Frank always finds me new assignments." He laughed, then stood up and approached Patrick's office window to watch the sunrise. "OK, Patrick, why Moscow?"

"The chief, Marcus, was working on a separate case that originated in Moscow that no one knows about. They suspected a mole in our embassy. There are activities leading us to believe that the Russians are involved in spying after the Presidential race and the elections. They were trying to redirect public opinion with fake profiles on social media to elect President Rufus who actually won."

"Really, another Russian involvement in national elections?" Evan smiled.

"If the Russians want someone to be elected, it's not necessarily a good thing if he was elected," grunted Patrick.

"I do get it, Patrick, but why am I going to Moscow?"

"Katarina, one of our embassy workers, is in touch with a Russian agent who asked for all the President's movements, schedules, campaign events, and overseas trips."

"That stinks!" replied Evan anxious.

The door opened and Patrick's executive assistant stood in the doorway.

"Good morning, gentlemen, aren't you early birds today! Can I get you coffee or something?" She smiled kindly.

"Sure. Black, no milk or sugar." Evan jumped on the opportunity "I hope the coffee here is good!"

"The same for me," Patrick said. His assistant nodded, left the room, and closed the door behind her.

"Where were we?" asked Patrick.

"Oh, yeah, I asked if Katarina is connected to the assassination case?" asked Evan and wrinkled his forehead.

"Our embassy security manager, Bob, works for me and will fill you in on all the details once you arrive; your assignment is to track her down with the man she sees and find out if the Russians are involved with the assassination, directly or indirectly!"

"Sounds like a fun job!" exclaimed Evan, but on the inside, he was happy to be assigned to an overseas mission again.

"After you are done, kill them both!" Patrick said calmly.

Evan scoffed nervously. "*Boom, boom,* just like that?"

"Yes, the order came from Frank Dabush himself!" Patrick said.

"There's got to be more to it," said Evan. "Either you aren't telling me, or you just don't know!" Evan insisted. He knew that orders could sometimes come down the pipeline from the top government officials, through their assistants, and ignore protocol or a legal release from the Supreme Court.

"If the shit hits the fan, who can I blame? The vice president or his Chief of Staff?" Evan was not amused by the command.

"Marcus backed it up, and as usual, the state will deny any involvement in the case. You'll be fending for yourself. Not the first time you did that, Evan!"

"I'd be more comfortable if Marcus gave the order."

The door opened and the administrative assistant entered with coffee and few pastries. Evan grew silent. "She read my mind," said Patrick.

Evan was in deep thought. He grabbed the coffee mug and took a couple of sips. This was not sounding like a simple mission. Odds were that it could escalate, as it always did when the Russians were involved.

Patrick pressed the intercom and called his assistant. "Is Marcus in yet?" he asked.

"I'll find out," the assistant replied.

A minute later, the phone rang, and Patrick picked it up.

"Yes, he is here as scheduled. Can you join us?"

Patrick hung up the phone and said calmly, "The chief will be here in a minute; can I offer you anything else? Bourbon? Vodka?"

"Are you crazy, Patrick? It's not even 8:00 a.m.! No thanks, it's too early for a drink, the coffee will do," Evan said.

Patrick ignored Evan and pulled out a bourbon bottle from a cabinet and poured some of it in his coffee.

"Sure, this'll keep me up!" Patrick murmured, amused with himself.

After a short break, Marcus arrived.

"Evan, my man, how the hell are you?" Marcus was geared up, walking in dressed in a $2,000 designer suit and a tie to accent his white shirt.

He sounds so happy for this time of the day, Evan thought.

"Is no one sleeping in the CIA these days?" All chuckled with Evan. "Doing fine, what about you?" Evan smiled.

"Busy, busy busyyyyeee, very busy," said Marcus. Patrick let the conversation flow between the two as he sipped on his souped-up coffee.

"Evan wants to hear it from you!" Patrick exclaimed.

Marcus pulled up a chair and sat next to Evan. Patrick went to his bar and poured two glasses of bourbon; one for Marcus, and one for himself.

"You guys are really getting drunk so early?" Evan joked.

"That's the fun part of our business!" laughed Marcus. "But seriously, it's a confidential mission overseas by the order of the vice president. He can authorize an order to eliminate a foreign agent of a foreign country without the Supreme Court intervention, in emergency cases," Marcus explained. He gulped the bourbon down in one shot as if it was a glass of water. His face showed no signs that he was at all affected by the drink.

"The vice president probably concurred, but who actually decided to send me to Moscow? Also, I tried to figure out why the President is willing to give me up as his bodyguard for his upcoming trip?" Evan was curious.

"Why? Do you miss this Middle East shithole?" scolded Marcus. "Besides, he knows and he blessed the idea, but wants to stay out of the decision to avoid an international diplomatic conflict in this case explodes. He doesn't like spies!" Marcus poured himself a second bourbon.

Patrick and Marcus laughed, but Evan remained serious, his head spinning.

"We had a session between sessions and Frank Dabush threw the idea in the air to loan you out for the mission. After a short consultation, we thought it was perfect, since we want you out of the country for a while," said Marcus.

"I told him that!" exclaimed Patrick.

"Here we go, Evan!" came the raspy voice of the CIA director. He raised his glass and Patrick followed suit.

"You want me to assassinate a woman?" Evan scoffed nervously.

"That's our business, Evan. We could send others, you know, but we think you are the perfect agent for this assignment. This is our new espionage headache that must be resolved; if, in the end, you think she deserves to live, we'll leave that up to you!"

Evan was relieved. He didn't like the death sentence of a women by anyone, and that gave him the room to decide otherwise. Marcus caught him with the right cord.

"It's a simple mission," said Patrick, defiantly.

Marcus changed the subject.

"The mission was kept to a handful of people; just us, the VP, his COS Frank, and the President!"

"You assume that Katarina is a double agent?" Evan asked.

"The answer is that Frank Dabush has connections with some underground people in Russia and the Eastern bloc. Don't forget, he is Hungarian, immigrated when he was two years old, and speaks six languages, so his people leaked Katarina's activities to the VP's office." Marcus took a deep breath and Patrick added, "We have your back, Evan!"

"Can we use her to our advantage if seen otherwise?" wondered Evan.

"Evan, that's up to you to decide. Frank Dabush can only advise but not direct. First, find her, ask the right questions, and be careful, she might be dangerous!" Patrick advised. *Apparently bourbon can calm people down,* Evan thought.

Patrick pulled Katarina's photos from the folder on his desk and Marcus whistled softly.

"She is a bombshell," he said, amused. "It's easy to focus your attention on her; she might have used her figure for dangerous spy games."

Marcus played the game; he knew that he was sending Evan into the lion's den, the Russian FSB who might be involved in the American affairs would protect its interests and not allow an asset to escape.

"Your passport and diplomatic visa are ready, and the reason for your visit is for an exchange with another diplomat who 'suddenly' got sick and needs urgent medical treatment in the United States," Patrick explained, pushing the rest of the file toward Evan for his review.

"Nice excuse; it's like, *really,* the FSB will *really* swallow this bait?!" scoffed Evan as he flipped through the folder.

"Don't worry, you will blend in. You look European." Patrick laughed.

"He just needs to dye his hair a little blonder," murmured Marcus, as he and Patrick laughed and poured themselves the rest of the bourbon.

Evan hoped to validate the information he got. He didn't trust everything that was thrown at him. He would have to use his own judgment in the field as he always used to do, especially to find any connections to the murder on Capitol Hill.

CHAPTER 13

L ate the same day, Dan reported to his boss and came up with the idea to assign Farouk and Jamila to the CIA to assimilate and help to retrieve information from the local Iranian-Islamic communities about the assassination attempt.

The weather in Tel Aviv was warm and muggy, and the streets were full of people and tourists swarming the town to take advantage of its bars and beaches.

At the top of the Mossad building, M picked up the call transferred to him by his assistant. At the same time, he motioned his agent, Dan Eyal, into his office.

"Not a bad idea," M agreed. "Did Patrick agree to this idea?"

"Oh, yes, he had to run this with his boss, it's a legal issue," said Dan.

"The world would be a better place without lawyers," Gad shot back and laughed. "Patrick asked me to extradite Aslam Abu Mansour."

"Wow!" Dan was surprised "And?"

"I explained that it's a very complicated legal issue; everyone knows we arrested him in broad daylight and leaders from both sides of the aisle will be asking questions soon." M was skeptical.

M was a nickname, short for *Memune* meaning 'the appointed' or 'in charge.' M led Dan to patch himself in with the special Mossad department called *Yomint*, which specialized in recruiting agents from around the world. It received new recruits from towns conquered by Jihad groups, saved by the Israelis trying to cross the border for medical help.

Thousands of people escaped certain death to seek asylum. People who sought revenge were not qualified, people with values, like Jamila and her husband Farouk, were perfect candidates.

Dan was a familiar face to Jamila and Farouk, and Gad thought it was a good idea for him to speak to them first.

The Yomint department thought that Dan did not have the persuasive skills to convince candidates to join the agency, but that didn't keep Dan from trying to help.

Jamila and her husband recognized Dan, who had helped them enter the country, and greeted him with warmth.

"This is my friend, Alon Mishal," he introduced the Yomint officer to them.

"Jamila, your son has recovered from his injuries," said Alon Mishal in fluent Arabic with a perfect Sunnite dialect. He smiled and squeezed his electric cigar between his lips.

"He needs additional rehabilitation for a few weeks to adjust to his new life here in Israel without fears of bombing and starvation," Jamila replied. She offered the men coffee and sweets.

Alon, a veteran recruiter, led the Mossad's efforts to add new agents to their spy forces, and Dan knew he couldn't compete with Alon, so he allowed him to continue.

Alon was a hefty, balding man with a chiseled face and high cheekbones. He had a rough, tough exterior but inside had a heart of gold.

"Well, you can stay in the kibbutz for as long as it takes, your adoptive family will take care of all your needs," he said, doing his best to sound positive.

"We can't go back," said Farouk and pointed North toward his Syrian village. Alon cut him off.

"We know the situation; it's not safe for you to return. The rebels lost ground and the Syrian military made sure that no one would be able to come back, nor do they want you to come back!" exclaimed Alon.

Dan, Farouk, and Jamila nodded their heads in sorrow. "Your village is totally destroyed to the ground, no infrastructures, no food, the Red Cross aid and international food supplies for the refugees were stolen by the soldiers on both sides," Alon added.

"I know. I assumed our families were all killed!" growled Farouk angrily.

"Thousands who stayed because they had no other choice died," added Jamila tearfully.

"They didn't stay, no one stayed. . .their evacuation routes were blocked so the atrocities would be hidden from the international media," said Alon, adding, "They were murdered with nerve gas."

"If a Muslim kills a Muslim, he is not a Muslim," said Jamila, believing that the Koran verses were misinterpreted. "When it comes to war among our Muslim brothers, they all think their interpretation of the Koran is the real Koran!" She scoffed angrily.

"Bending religion to fit radical extremist's own agendas, giving them a license to kill other Muslim brothers; something went wrong in the years since the glorious prophet of Islam created the third most popular religion on Earth with two billion followers," said Farouk.

They both sound like visionary people, Dan thought.

Alon listened, and waited for the right time to move on to his agenda. Gaining their trust was a very important step before investigating their personalities and aptitudes to determine if they were skilled enough to work for the Mossad. It was an interview rather than a social meeting and Dan's presence was important, since the couple already trusted him.

"The Muslim world decays societies and leaves ruins all over the Middle East. Millions immigrated to Europe and the United States seeking refuge," Alon explained, paving the way to his real agenda step by step. "Muslim neighborhoods in Europe and the United States are flourishing, but we need eyes to make sure that what happened in Syria does not happen in Europe or America."

Dan could not resist the opportunity and asked, "Do you want to stay in Israel or immigrate to a Muslim community in Europe or the states?"

Jamila looked at him.

"How interesting is it that Islam's most notorious enemy, you, of all enemies, the Jews, would be the ones who welcomed us with open arms and saved us from annihilation. You gave us a new sense of hope and future to live our lives in peace," stated Jamila, getting emotional as her hand praised the Lord above.

Dan didn't get his answer and Alon glanced at him as if to say, "Calm down."

Alon already thought to himself that they might be the perfect candidates to become spies on terror cell groups embedded in host countries.

"You know the cost to assist refugees and the cost of medical treatment of thousands of Syrian refuges in local hospitals?" Alon didn't wait for an answer and completed his thought, "It costs us millions of dollars, and we get no help from the international community, no donations or Red Cross assistance; it's us alone on this. No one asked us to do that."

Jamila and Farouk paid attention, with looks of appreciation in their faces.

Alon stared at Dan to see his reaction and then shifted the subject to recruiting.

"Your country is blessed!" Farouk exclaimed, and raised his eyebrows. "Your people are the chosen people by God, and he blessed your country." He got emotional.

"I want to ask both of you a favor," Alon said and the couple looked at him.

"What favor?" asked Jamila, skeptically.

"Would you want to see your son one day as an engineer or a doctor? You see, your son is happy and getting healthier every day. His adoptive family will take care of him while we will train you for a trip!"

"Trip? What trip? Where?" asked Farouk, surprised.

It was time to put the cards on the table.

"We want to achieve a better world for everyone, especially for your son and other families who suffered just like you. Don't you want to be part of that mission?" Alon continued enthusiastically, hoping they'd gravitate to his side with no pressure.

"Sure, we want to help." Farouk was careful in choosing his words and used a softer tone of voice. He looked at his wife, who said nothing.

Alon tried the emotional path first. "Perhaps their ideology changed over the years of war and destruction, who knows?"

"We will train you for that mission, all expenses paid, and you will live in Tel Aviv. Once the training is over, we will send you to help other immigrants in a country of your choice."

Their faces radiated with determination. "Sure, we want to know what it is all about," said Farouk as he examined his wife's face for her reaction.

"Is this payback?" Jamila was amused at her husband's ignorance.

"It's return on investment. I won't ask you to do something you don't want to do," Alon replied calmly.

Jamila and Farouk hesitated, and were not sure if they could live up to their saviors' expectations. They were happy that their son's recovery was progressing well, and that he was happy making new friends and leaving his old life behind.

They knew they must pay back the country that helped them, but the offer seemed too sweet, too perfect.

"I assume that not everyone was approached to be recruited by the Mossad?" Jamila asked with a frown. Her reaction surprised the two agents.

"Many preferred to return to their homes after the medical treatments to tell their stories later, but they might have died in a new military attack. If they were lucky, they were saved by the UN refugee agency UNHCR to find a new home somewhere abroad living on social support. Does this sound like a better option?" Alon said.

"How long is the 'better world' training course?" asked Jamila and her face showed that she already knew what it was all about.

"A couple of weeks and then we send you to an internship in a country under a supervised mentor th-"

"Wait, what about my son, he comes with us abroad, right?" cried Jamila.

"Of course!" replied Alon, even though he knew it was a coldhearted lie.

"But until then, you could visit your child time to time between training sessions, excursions overseas and routine duties!"

"You are adding new components to the duties!" cried Jamila.

She was certain her guest that claimed he came from the government to check on their well-being was a Mossad agent. Their reputation crossed borders and, in a way, Jamila was flattered to be chosen to make the world a better place if, in the end, her family would rest in a safe, quiet place and be taken care of.

She looked at his business card on the coffee table and laughed and then she looked straight at Alon and Dan.

"Is my son your hostage?" Jamila asked fearfully.

"Of course not, he will be proud of you when he grows up!" Alon exhaled.

A few hours later, Dan boarded the non-stop midnight flight from Tel-Aviv to Newark, New Jersey.

CHAPTER 14

J ust before Evan left for Moscow, he asked to meet Dan and Patrick, this time in Patrick's office in Langley.

"No coffee shop meetings anymore," Evan murmured to himself.

Dan hurried through the airport after landing in Washington and entered a black SUV waiting for him at Reagan National Airport, a short distance from the Pentagon.

The office had more character than Marcus' office. Photos from his military service as a Navy pilot decorated the walls. Just like Marcus, he had a few metal cast Skyhawk airplane models, miniatures of the real plane he used to fly operating on Navy aircraft carriers.

"Just wanted to catch up with the latest before my flight." Evan sounded apologetic as he took a seat on the black leather couch.

For the next half an hour, they chatted about new developments, and analyzed hints from all over the globe.

"I smell trouble," Evan said.

"We excluded the Soldiers of Allah from our suspicion list because we found where it began and we have the producer in our custody. He refused to talk or mention his client," Dan reported.

"But he admitted forming the group, right?" Patrick wanted to be sure.

"Yes," Dan answered laconically.

"But he refused to talk, or he didn't know his clients?" Evan drilled Dan.

"Could be both; our agency will fill us in on any progress. I understand you wanted to extradite Aslam to the United States?" asked Dan.

"You know how to smuggle people. You did it before." Patrick chuckled to himself as he reminded Dan of the Nazi kidnapped in Argentina and was brought to trial in Israel and also the "Atom Spy" who was kidnapped in Rome and was sentenced in Israel for spying.

"Well, the CIA has unmarked 'white jets' to fly prisoners from country to country. You can send one to Tel-Aviv," laughed Dan.

"Fair enough!" Evan replied and laughed. "I'll take American Airlines later!"

"I am sure your agency scrutinized every detail of the assassination plot and you have a long list of suspects," said Dan.

"Not really. The list is short, and we are trying to shorten it further by eliminating the fake news," said Patrick.

"You have three bodies in hand killed by Hassan, but no clues?" Dan said. "Other than Aslam Abu Mansour, my agency has nothing to offer other than to imbed Jamila and Farouk in local communities, real fucking refugees."

"What about The Chameleon?" asked Evan. He wanted to know everything he could to help his mission succeed.

"Your agency intercepted those transactions from Aslam Abu Mansour to his client in Moscow. They are connected to Hassan. I remember you said that."

"Perhaps it's for you to find out," Patrick said as he glanced at Evan.

There was silence, and Patrick could hear the top Israeli spy breathing heavily. He knew his comrade was about to embark on a trip to Moscow. The small sitting area was cozy and the conversation was friendly, however, there was a lot of tension.

"I know," replied Evan gravely. "We are anxious to know if you have anything to share about The Chameleons' operational tactics," he tried not to sound too desperate.

Dan knew that M shared information on a 'need-to-know basis' only if it could benefit the Mossad. Many times, information was kept confidential since the Mossad agents were in the line of fire, and exposing their activities could sabotage their missions. This scenario happened in the past when former U.S. Presidents exposed vital intelligence information with the media, and missions behind enemy lines had to be terminated.

"I know you guys are covering Europe and the Middle East and have better ways to get your information on the ground," Patrick said, trying another tactic to extract information. Dan lingered before answering, not wanting Patrick to suffer too much as he waited for a response.

"Well, Patrick, my dear friend, I have told your agency a few times that electronic surveillance, 'the eyes in the sky' as you call it, is not a match for field agents. You can listen to all the phone transactions you want, and the terrorists will use boots on the ground, or motorcycle messengers with messages in sealed envelopes. You must have more boots on the ground." Dan selected the precise words so as not to offend his friend.

"Well, I *am* boots on the ground!" exclaimed Evan, who was taken back a little.

Patrick convinced himself to contact foreign intelligence agencies like the Israeli Mossad agency or the British MI6, or even the *Mukhaabaraat* (Jordanian intelligence services) to assist in obtaining data. It was a normal request among allied agencies.

"The NSA 'Dagger Complex' intelligence based in Germany is all over it and we are analyzing calls, texts, emails, and videos that might give us the starting point," replied Patrick. "But we are lost, and your agency helped us a lot in the past."

Patrick knew the Mossad's reputation and its experiences, something most intelligence agencies could only dream about, however he wanted more. He wanted to get straight into their servers and take what he needed.

"Look, Patrick, we do have information from our agents, who are monitoring hundreds of Jihadists, what we call 'the Jihad path' from Europe through Turkey to Afghanistan and Iraq to their training camp grounds. We track some down and kill them with no questions asked. If we meet them in the middle of the road, then we get rid of them execution style, although some escaped and would always reappear somewhere else on the planet. However, we don't miss the second time. Hassan Abu Shikri is not a stranger to us, but for now he is not a terrorist, just a curious young guy. We know his family, and as for The Chameleons, we are still investigating its origin." Dan defended his point.

Dan was not a novice in this business, Patrick thought. He exhaled deeply and let out a soft whistle. He knew Dan as a high-ranking reservist in the IDF who served in the intelligence service, an arm of the Commando battalion, for his entire time in military service. Tracking and killing terrorists were two of his primary skills. Collecting information from the Arab crowd was a risky business, in fact, he was informed about Dan's last mission in Jericho that brought Aslam Abu Mansour to the table, ruling out the Solders of Allah.

Patrick admired Dan's analytical mind and tried one last time to draw out more information about Hassan by asking point blank, "Is Hassan definitely involved?"

Dan was decisive and let out a soft sigh before repeating something they all already knew. "We see no evidence that he was brainwashed or radicalized. If you claim that he is still in the Washington D.C. vicinity, then check the area mosques."

"Sending over your new agents' refugees to us might help," Patrick acknowledged.

"Look, it takes more than one man to perform this kind of terror attack. It takes planning, money, logistics, network, and motive," Dan reminded Patrick as he waited for a reaction.

"Sure!" exclaimed Patrick. "Planning-Iran. Money-Iran. Logistics and Network-the Revolutionary Guards. Do you need a reason to destroy 'Big Satan'?" Patrick was wired up. "Hate! Spread fear, sabotage the American democratic pillars, spread the Shiites' religious views around the world and. . ."

Evan nodded his head. "The President and I were thinking that the stray drone attack launched eight months ago by our military that missed the target has something to do with it."

"The Iranians are tough and they will retaliate; after all, they need to show that they are standing neck to neck with the United States for their own internal political control. They are expected to push the envelope, and hit us without escalating to a full blown regional war." Dan took a deep breath.

"The attack was approved by former President Cole. Hitting a school and killing 52 children could trigger revenge," Evan said. "And then retaliation might be the motive! The motive is important; it might lead us to the source and perhaps you know more than we do!"

"Relax, you'll find the way! Perhaps all they want is for the man who gave the order to openly apologize and compensate the victims' families," Evan added, referring to the apology and compensation his government paid the Turkish victims of the Israeli raid on boats that infiltrated Israel's territorial waters and breaking the embargo on Gaza.

"President Cole is gone. It will be President Rufus to decide on compensation. Perhaps they aimed at Cole and missed?" Patrick asked.

"Well, Rufus will not take any responsibility for the previous administration. He would easily believe that the real assassination target was the former President, who stood right there between him and the Supreme Court Justice at the inaugural podium." Evan was confident in his statement.

They put their minds together and acted as a think tank. Patrick's mind was running data at lightning speed and suddenly he felt claustrophobic in his office. He poured a glass of bourbon and offered some to his guests, both politely declined.

He swallowed the drink in one gulp.

"Alcohol withdrawal." He chuckled and felt better.

Dan knew that drinking a glass of bourbon in one gulp would send him to the emergency room with cardiac arrest.

"So, you both think we have a motive?" Patrick asked.

"This could be what the assassins want us to think the motive is," Dan suggested.

"Perhaps," Evan said.

"From our records so far guys, it might be that the assassins are trying to frame Hassan, but it can't work!" exclaimed Patrick.

"The fact remains; we bombed a school and not the military headquarters of a terror group. Personally, the President and I are not proud of it. That can trigger revenge, you know." Evan got back to the same retaliatory motive. "And . . . yes, I agree that Hassan is a small link but it's important to put our hands on him fast!"

"Do you mind if I smoke?" asked Patrick as he pulled a cigarette from a Marlboro box in his drawer. When none of the other men complained, he lit the cigarette and inhaled the bluish smoke deep into his lungs. He poured another glass of bourbon.

Dan wondered who paid for the top-shelf liquor in his office. "I need to ask for another bottle, because Marcus drank most of it!"

Evan and Dan chuckled. They took this fact for granted.

"I can't imagine how your liver looks after an MRI exam!" joked Evan.

"Guys, shit happens in a war!" Patrick exclaimed, remembering the details leading to the failed attack and ignoring the liver joke he'd heard so many times–too many times.

The runaway drone incident was highly publicized and brought with it global outrage. The media condemned the attack and shredded the previous administration to pieces. The POTUS apologized and it looked like the incident was over and forgiven.

The media didn't stop showing the Ayatollah of Iran, the supreme leader commander, participating in a few children's funerals, and promising to retaliate against "Big Satan," and punish "Small Satan," Israel.

"There was no evidence that the Revolutionary Guards were involved!" Dan argued. "The Iranians are in our back yard; we know what is happening there!" he continued.

"So, do we!" exclaimed Patrick. "Our Fifth Fleet is spying on them 24/7."

"Hassan was Iranian," Evan pointed out.

"True, but that's just a coincidence!" said Dan.

"Hassan is a good cover for the planners," Patrick said. "Not ruling out that this is a Jihad case like 9/11."

"We are all killers for different reasons–some are and some are not justified," Evan replied.

Patrick was not amused when Evan mentioned that part of his mission. He knew that Dan would immediately pick up on his task abroad so he changed the subject, "For me any terror attack is a Jihadi case!"

Dan explained his ideology, "Not all terror attacks are Muslim, that's old school ideology, Patrick. Separate the two, otherwise you will fight the wrong fight in the wrong place. It also depends on who you ask."

Patrick was not sure if Dan was reprimanding him and then he stared at Evan. "We are in full contact with our NSA branch in Germany. We asked to intercept any information about The Chameleons and especially to see if there are any connections to the Iranian secret service or the Revolutionary Guard. . .any ties to the assassination team."

"*Zikit*,'" called Evan and chuckled at the Hebrew translation of the name Chameleon, "Does that mean The Chameleon might speak Hebrew?"

"Good question, Evan! I didn't even think of that," Patrick shrugged.

"Perhaps a few words, perhaps he knows us too, perhaps, perhaps, it's all perhaps, and it's open to interpretation," Dan said.

"I want to prepare for my mission the best I can, this is why I asked you to join in today, I know you have a long trip ahead of yo—" Evan said softly.

"My intelligence unit 8200 will keep watching you guys as always."

"I know your reputation, Dan. I am sure you haven't told me everything you know, because you don't want to sabotage your sources by mistake. I hope we can have dinner in Georgetown when all this is over," Patrick said reassuredly.

"*Inshallah*," Evan replied in Arabic, meaning "with God's will" and added, "I'll bring my entire team; they will appreciate the gesture!"

Patrick scoffed. "I will wait for Evan to join us when he is back! Meanwhile, I have to prepare the POTUS for his upcoming trip to Riyadh. What I wanted to confirm, Evan, is that our NTC (National Tracing Center) which uses a scientific technique to trace guns, makes sure that your gun's serial number is properly erased. No evidence should lead back to you, you know?!"

Evan let out a huge sigh. "Fuck!" he exclaimed loudly. "The rifle used in the assassination attempt was sent to the Federal Bureau of Alcohol, Tobacco, Firearms, and Explosives' laboratory center in Beltsville. Using acid etching techniques doesn't always work. That's what the technician told me. We need to trace this weapon's origin and track its route another way."

Dan was paying close attention and replied, "I understand."

Evan looked at his watch. "Time to go; my driver is waiting. I'll see you when I see you. Keep me informed at all times."

They exchanged handshakes and wished Evan success in his mission.

After Evan left the office, Patrick continued the conversation.

"So, a new method was developed called EBSD, Electron Backscatter Diffraction, which was used in the Boulder, Colorado facility. The researchers are still developing the method by using electron microscopes to examine the atoms of the metal that was damaged beneath each number or letter; it was not ready and it might take time to find the owners of the gun."

Dan understood little about the methods to trace a gun once it left the Israeli manufacturing plant. He knew more about the gun itself and wondered if there was a connection between *Zikit*, the head of The Chameleons, and the gun used to assassinate the first lady and the Supreme Court Justice.

"The technician explained to me that this type of a gun isn't available to regular citizens, so identifying the owner, is very important." Patrick encouraged Dan to respond.

"Second amendment doesn't cover it?" Dan asked.

"If you have it, then yes, but it's not openly available for purchase," explained Patrick.

Patrick realized that extracting more information from the research facility was useless and he must let them work at their own pace. But he wanted more information about the rifle from Dan, who could reveal more information regarding this issue. The fact that the investigation linked the gun to Israel was not a good thing. The fact that *Zikit* might be an Israeli assassin-for-hire petrified him.

"Israel exports those rifles all over the globe," Dan replied.

"Who sold you this rifle?" pleaded Patrick.

"A few third world military countries, South America, the Balkans, and Asia. It's easily possible that one of them could have found itself in the United States via smugglers for the right price!"

"OK, why smuggle an Israeli rifle when you can purchase a professional sniper rifle right here in the states?"

"True, in my opinion, there are a few reasons: first, you want to blame someone else and sabotage the evidence. Second, the user was an expert using this kind of weapon," replied Dan.

The information struck a sensitive cord with Patrick. The involvement of an Israeli-made rifle connected to the assassination was another clue to the executioners.

"We are in the same business, Dan. . .we should not keep secrets from each other!"

"Once I'm not the only one who knows, it's not a secret anymore," Dan replied.

CHAPTER 15

Langley, Virginia, 8 a.m.

Patrick, after much persuasion, received a green light from the Secretary of Defense to let Jamila, Farouk, and their son enter the United States as refugees and start a new life as FBI informants.

On his almost daily call with Dan Eyal in the Washington Israeli Embassy, Patrick questioned if there was any trace of the rifle used for the terror attack.

Patrick knew that it took great professionalism. Snipers were always awarded for their work in the military.

"I assume the sharpshooter must have been an ex-military soldier trained professionally to use a telescopic sniper rifle like this from a long distance," Patrick said curtly.

"I hate to tell you that's just the start, and that's assuming the target was missed," Dan said.

"Are you insinuating that if the shooters missed their target, they will try again?" Patrick asked.

"Precisely!" exclaimed Dan.

"So, whoever wanted the President dead will not stop until they succeed," Patrick said.

Patrick was comfortable with the conclusion and he needed to bring this to his forum.

The window shutters of Patrick's office were pulled down due to the glare of the early morning sun—a seven hours' difference from the President and the defense secretary on Air Force One. As usual, he was one of the only ones in the office this early–the best time to claim private time with a glass of bourbon.

The door to his office was closed with a "do not disturb" sign he stole from a hotel hanging on the doorknob.

A sharp knock on the door startled Patrick out of his deep thoughts. He hoped it was the coffee and bagel he ordered.

"Enter!" he called loudly and his assistant walked in and put the briefing notes on his desk and turned to leave.

"It seems that everyone is in a bad mood around here lately." Patrick shook his head as she hurried out of his office.

The first paper to attract his attention read, *Three unidentified men were shot to death in an apartment leased by Hassan Abu Shikri.*

"Bingo!" he rejoiced. The second briefing read that the building landlord was brought into FBI headquarters for questioning the previous night. He wondered what he missed.

Patrick zoomed out of his office. He was not sure if his boss was informed of the situation since the office was locked and he was not around. His assistant scoffed when she saw him rushing out.

Patrick jumped in his car and floored the gas pedal without waiting for his personal driver to join him. The driver would have used the siren to clear traffic so they could reach FBI headquarters faster.

He assumed that the landlord's interrogation would take place at headquarters. He parked in the underground visitor's spot and went up, showing his badge even though he'd been there hundreds of times before. He headed directly into the chief agent's office, watching him through the glass wall. The agent signaled Patrick to come in while he was on the phone.

He hung up as Patrick entered the office.

"Wow, what a surprise? You can't miss a good show, ha? Right, Patrick?" he snapped.

Patrick heard the sarcasm in his voice but ignored it. He knew there was no reason to fight over this. Daniel, the chief agent, was a scumbag, but unfortunately he was the best FBI agent on this case.

Patrick didn't want to lose time patching pieces of information together to create a full picture. If it was the landlord of the apartment where three dead bodies were found, the FBI would be still analyzing the garbage cans around the city for information, so not a great discovery to be proud of, but certainly a good lead.

"Where is the landlord, Daniel?" asked Patrick.

"Come with me," he said laconically and smiled with satisfaction that only a FBI agent would understand.

Daniel, the chief agent, was short with a protruding belly and short legs. His bold skull shined like a newly-polished Cadillac after a thorough cleaning.

They walked down one flight of stairs to the interrogation room, looking inside through a one-way mirror. The poor landlord, confused and looking displaced, didn't know what hit him when he was roused from a deep sleep the night before and brought in for interrogation.

"No, I don't know this guy," he answered as the investigator showed him a photo of Hassan.

"But he signed the lease," the investigator said, louder now. "How can you not remember him?"

"The name is correct, but it's not the person who signed the lease!" the gaunt, 70-plus year old landlord replied furiously.

"So, can you explain what he looked like?" he insisted.

"Well, that was six months ago, and he paid in cash for the entire year," the landlord stated.

The investigator pulled the rent notice that Hassan saw the night before and showed it to the landlord and asked, "If he paid for the entire year, what's the rental notice for? Can you explain that?"

"Renewal!" exclaimed the old man and he choked, coughing. "What did I do wrong?"

The investigator offered the man a bottle of water and the landlord took it.

"Six months in advance?" The investigator raised his eyebrows in surprise as he stared at the landlord.

"It's normal. I do this all the time since I have a long waiting list and want a commitment up front."

"How did he talk? Did he have an accent? What nationality did you assume he was? A Middle Easterner, perhaps?"

"Do you mean if he was a foreigner? Oh, yes, yes, he was but not sure what kind of an accent he had, though," he answered immediately. "He limped!"

"He limped? Left or right? Which leg?"

"I don't remember!" The landlord cried, looked desperate.

They showed him the faces of the victims murdered in the apartment and asked, "Do you recognize anyone?"

"No," he replied.

"We want to play for you a recording. See if you can identify the accent you heard, please."

For the next half an hour, the man listened to voices with several accents as he nodded his head and murmured, "No, no, no. . . wait a minute, go back, is this German?" he asked.

"It's close, but it's Russian. Is that what you heard?"

The man shook his head. "I'm not sure!"

"Listen again." The investigator pressed a button and a Middle Eastern accent audio byte played.

"No, no, it's more like the Russian to me, but again, it was six months ago. You arrested me eighty minutes after the shooting. Am I being accused of anything?" he asked, concerned.

"You are here for questioning. You are not under arrest. But we would appreciate any detail you could share with us. Even if you think it's not important, please try!"

"No, he just limped. The man who signed the lease was a little darker and had short, curly hair," the landlord described the man as best he could to get the investigator off his back.

"Think hard. Birthmark? Tattoos?"

"Oh, yeah, one of them, a short, muscled man, had a tattoo on his forehead!"

"Describe it!"

"It looks like anchor with an arrow."

"A ship's anchor? Can you draw it?"

The landlord took the pencil and paper on the table and scribbled something on the paper.

"How big was the tattoo?"

"Just like I drew it, about the size of a dime," exclaimed the landlord.

Then they brought a facial composite expert to draw a sketch of the man and drew a tattoo on his forehead.

The composite didn't resemble anyone on record.

"Perhaps the facial recognition computer can fix that?" yelled the investigator.

"It will take time to match the results to the FBI facial recognition data!" replied a data technician at headquarters on the speaker phone.

"Am I accused of anything? Did I do anything wrong?" The landlord repeated.

"NO!" The investigator snapped. "You are not accused of anything; we rushed to save your life from someone who might have wanted to keep you silent."

"Why?"

"Since you apparently have seen one of the suspects in our inquiry."

"Am I in danger?" he asked, sweating with fear.

"Right now, you are a target. We don't know how many people are involved, and it's not safe for you to go back to your home. You are exposed, and we must now keep you in a witness protection program with temporary relocation for you and your family. Do you understand?"

The investigator seemed exhausted and put both hands on the table to drive the point home.

"For how long?" the landlord asked with a soft voice, so low it was barely heard.

"We don't know. We're working as fast as we can. Is there anyone else you're close to? Family? Anyone this killer might target?"

"I live alone. I have no family."

"Can I see the bodies?" asked Patrick and Daniel nodded his head.

"The bodies were sent to the forensic department."

"'They must have an untold bloody story to tell,'" Daniel quoted one of the forensic scientist's sayings.

"Who are they and why were they killed?"

"More importantly by whom?" asked Dan.

The investigators didn't expect the landlord to answer any of their questions, and he didn't.

"So, from this photo, can you identify the man who signed the lease?"

"No, I told you that! What does Hassan have to do with the murder?" asked the landlord, angry and confused.

"The three dead people in your apartment were killed by Hassan. He is the main suspect, unless you've seen anyone else around the unit?"

"Ask the neighbors!" The landlord threw up his hands in frustration.

The investigator, frustrated, shot back, "Don't worry, they are in the other room!"

Patrick was watching through the one-way mirror and concluded that there was one less issue to resolve.

"The victims were not identified as Middle Eastern or Iranians, even though everyone was eager to pin them to those nationalities," Patrick stated to the second agent and to Daniel.

"This has totally upended the investigation. We were leaning heavily on that theory," the detective replied skeptically.

"Someone is steering us in this direction. Have you heard of the terror group called Soldiers of Allah?" asked Daniel.

"Of course! They claimed responsibility!" snapped the agent.

"Don't put your money on the claim. It's old news. We don't know where the claim came from, its origin and the video reveal nothing so far," said Patrick, holding the news about the video information he got from the Mossad for a later time.

The agent nodded his head, and replied, "There is a lot of misinformation floating around, more and more shows up constantly."

"Like the District Heights woman's rape?" asked Daniel.

"Yeah, we are trying to find a connection, but we're concentrating our efforts now on finding the man who pulled the trigger!" said the agent.

"All shots were taken by one professional foreign agent, someone who trained for this job for a long time," Patrick speculated. "And we have no clue who that man was!"

"Dead end, no new conspiracy theory!" confirmed the investigator. "Until we identify the dead men and capture Hassan, we can't move forward!"

The forensic science team sealed the apartment to prevent any crime scene contamination. After the scientist combed the unit with a toothbrush, and collected hair samples, skin tissue, toilet- and sink-trap water samples, they examined and tested the DNA of every organic cell tissue.

Eventually, the Criminal Justice Information Services division (CJIS), the Special Identity Unit (SIU), the investigative and Operational Assistance Group (OAG) and the National Crime Information Center (NCIC) took over the identification of the victims. Patrick wouldn't miss those dead assumed-to-be agents when the only link connecting them to the assassination was Hassan Abu Shikri, who worked in the building where the shots originated.

The photos were distributed to all Western intelligence agencies for assistance in identifying the men.

"The NSA used photo recognition of all the visitors who entered the country in the last three months," said the agent.

"We must find this motherfucker Hassan!" Patrick shot back.

"Finding Hassan is a priority," Daniel concurred.

"He holds the solution to this riddle," concluded Patrick. He wished they could hack Hassan's cell phone.

"We are not sure if he owns a cell phone. We didn't find cell phones among the victims either," the detective said, as if he read Patrick's mind.

"Finding Hassan could be even worse. He doesn't make any calls and he can't be tracked; NSA tracks millions of calls an hour," added Daniel.

"Every minute that passes is critical. If he disappears, it will delay the investigation and complicate things—" Patrick could not complete his sentence. The agent interrupted.

"I know, both of our agencies' reputations are on the line, first for not preventing the assassination attempt and, second, for not being able to find the people responsible right away, but we are working on it!" promised the agent.

Chapter 16

April, Verskoy District, Moscow, Russia

A merican embassies around the world were put on security alert by the Secretary of State in the event of more terror attacks, especially embassies in countries considered adversaries to the United States, including China, Russia, and radical Muslim countries in the Middle East and Asia. Everyone was spying on everyone, clashing and leaving trails of death behind them, in an ongoing cat-and-mouse cycle of espionage. They all wanted a piece of the action to hurt the United States a little more, some openly and some behind an Iron Curtain.

"Good morning, Katarina!" the American Embassy guard greeted the woman entering the building.

It was an exceptionally cold day for mid-April, and she was all bundled up. Katarina inserted her ID into the card reader and passed the security gate with a wide smile.

"Good morning," she replied with a flirty tone and swayed her hips, walking like a model on the runway.

The guard chuckled and enjoyed the show.

Katarina always reported to her office on time, no matter what.

Security procedures were tightened due to the recent assassination attempt, and everyone was checked coming in and going out of the embassy. Employees understood and cooperated with the Marine checkpoint working with the security officer to scrutinize everyone, including the Americans, but not Katarina.

Agents checked on random local employees after they left the Embassy grounds for any inconsistencies in their routines or behaviors, and to see if they were contacting any foreign agents to exchange information.

For the last three months, Katarina was followed, and her weekly Tuesday routine attracted the security officer's attention. Agents noticed the same man appeared to be there on the same day each week, getting off the bus at the next station after consolidating bags. Then he walked to his housing complex 10 minutes away.

This time, he didn't consolidate any bags and just simply walked off and vanished for the last time. The Tuesday routine of collecting information from the embassy was terminated, and left many questions unanswered. Agents took hundreds of photos of Katarina and him exchanging documents on the bus. They looked so innocent, like father and daughter. "The lesbian" and "the old man" were their confidential code names.

The CIA planned to spread disinformation to see where it would end up. Katarina was watched to spot anyone else who was spying in the embassy for the Russians or another foreign agency.

The upgraded security measures immediately sent a signal to all covert agents involved to take shelter underground. Katarina therefore terminated the routine document exchange with Dima, and that was the last time she saw him. CIA agents knew where Dima lived and waited for an opportunity to break in. However, they knew that Dima wouldn't stay at that address long.

Katarina kept her lifestyle discrete. In Russia, a gay lifestyle was a violation of the state law. But her more significant secret was her asset to the CIA, spreading disinformation. She played both sides, and her closed-circle cell operators were the only ones who knew it.

South of Russia and China, a CIA double agent disclosed a list of American agents' networks in their country and they eliminated them one by one. They left no trail, and put all agencies on alert mode. Since that time, the double agent vanished from the face of the earth without a trace.

The NSA and the CIA invested billions in high-end technology, satellites, drones, and listening devices to spy on everyone they suspected was an informant. They relied on submarines and spy ships disguised as fishing vessels, such as the *Liberty*, which was accidentally attacked by a formation of four Israeli Mirage jet fighters in a 1967 conflict in the Middle East war. *Some bad times,* Evan thought.

When she got home, Katarina called to her dog to greet him as she always did.

"Hi Poopoo!" she called in a charming voice.

Usually, the dog came to her, wagging its tail in anticipation of a nice walk or some dog treats. This time the dog cowered in his corner basket and refused to leave. It was early evening and her apartment was dark. She turned on the lights and saw a gun muzzle attached to a silencer, aimed toward the middle of her torso.

"Whoa," she cried in surprise as she froze in place.

"Shut the door slowly, Katarina, and don't make any foolish moves!" Evan spoke with a funny American accent.

She obeyed Evan's command and locked the door behind her.

Evan noticed her figure, encased in a tight leather mini skirt and black leggings. Her Western boots were probably bought by a colleague in the embassy using his Amazon account. It was a great look.

"Nice boots, not a cheap gesture considering that Russians have to work all month for such a pair!" he said sarcastically.

"They are covered with snow mixed with dirt and didn't get the respect they deserved today," she replied in the same tone. She stood next to the door as the dog cowered with his tail between his legs. The dog approached Katarina slowly, knowing something was wrong with this picture.

She bent to pick the dog up, but Evan made a noise and she froze again. "Sit on the chair over there!" he commanded, leading her to her dining set in the corner of her kitchen.

The apartment was warm and cozy. She felt warm in her short coat. "Can I remove my coat?" she asked in English.

"Yes, very slowly," repeated Evan sitting and watching the show.

"Who are you?" she asked.

She removed the coat and exposed a tight silk blouse that accented her firm breasts.

He ignored her question and shot back, "It won't work, Katarina. I know you are lesbian, so you can't seduce me. You might have been giving some services around the embassy in exchange for information. . .not sure what you would do for Mother Russia, but I want to know who you worked for and what exactly was your mission?"

Evan broke into the apartment with the aid of one of the embassy tech gurus. First, Evan searched the apartment for bugs, cameras and weapons. He was sure Katarina was unarmed since those were not allowed in the embassy. A quick enjoyable frisk confirmed it.

"Are you enjoying yourself?" Katarina snapped in disgust.

"It's my job!" Evan replied.

"What else is your job?" she asked.

"Depends on my results," he said.

Then Katarina went silent, as she watched Evan moving his eyes along her thighs, her breasts and finally, to her face.

"Nice place, Katarina. I am not sure the Embassy is paying you that well. . .this prestigious district, not far from your Bolshevik mayor, it's not bad!"

"You will be surprised who is paying for my rent," she said sarcastically with a nasty smile.

"I am sure you will tell me sooner or later," Evan said.

Evan pulled a few photos from his jacket and put them on her dining table. She took a quick glance and looked back at Evan, who was still pointing the gun at her.

"Who is that man?" he asked, sounding like a jealous boyfriend.

She cocked her head slightly, staring at him in a funny way. "You are losing your cool. But I know you're an agent, not a killer."

Her body language disclosed to Evan that she was not threatened or stressed by him. She was totally calm and comfortable. That surprised Evan.

Apparently, she knew something that Evan didn't. Being a lesbian, she trusted the liberal Americans more then she trusted her own comrades in the Kremlin. She knew that she couldn't hide in the closet for too long while all the doors of opportunities shut down one by one. It was the United States Embassy that offered her a job as an administrative assistant, and the Russians saw the opportunity to recruit her to spy for them. Perhaps someone assisted her in getting the job. That was not disclosed in any of the material Evan had on Katarina.

She informed the security officer in the Embassy to make sure she had an open back door she could use to escape. Russian intelligence agents—or at least she thought they were Russians—offered her immunity from prosecution of her lesbian lifestyle in exchange for information from the American embassy. She reported the contact with the agents and immediately went on a misinformation program, especially regarding the American military plans and movements, and the President's cabinet schedules. She also identified American CIA agents operating on Russian soil. This, of course, lit the alert light that the Russians might know something about the attack.

"This is Dima," she answered softly after a short silence. "He is the Russian agent whom I told your agency I am collaborating with."

Evan pressed further, "OK, who is Dima working for? Is this the guy you transferred all the intelligence information to? What was the purpose of the information and what was it used for?"

Katarina shrugged. "He is an analyzer, a small fish, not important. He was hired by a third party on the side for some cash, not serving the FSB agency that he works for full time," she replied.

Evan tried to make eye contact and asked, "And Dima hired you for the information you transferred, correct? I presume he transferred the information to the FSB?"

She nodded and then shook her head. "Yes and no. Yes, he transferred to someone and no, I am not sure it's his intelligence agency, the FSB, Mr. Harris."

Evan remembered that he didn't introduce himself. "How did you know my name?" he asked.

"We're both working for the same agency, Mr. Harris."

For a few seconds, he sat motionless and Katarina remained silent. Something about this stylish, confident woman told him that someone in his agency misjudged her and should never have put her on the agency's assassination list. *Or maybe there is something else, someone is playing me, or us,* Evan thought. *Katarina is probably the key to untangling the possible plot.* He suspected that someone misled him, perhaps they wanted to see him trapped by his own agency, burned of his identity, or killed. *Is Katarina part of this plot?* Evan, impressed by her confidence, smiled and lowered his gun to see where this might go.

"I knew you were coming, but didn't know when," she added without waiting for Evan to respond.

"Working for the same agency?" he murmured and stood up and slowly walked behind her, inhaled her perfume and whispered in her ear, "Who are you Katarina? You seem to be quite a woman. To me you are an enigma, a nice looking little Russian spy dictating the conversation and the agency we are both working with, who might not know what you're hiding."

She was silent and immobilized, waiting for his next move, then without any fear she turned to him face to face.

"Dima was a double agent himself, understand?"

"Really? Tell me what you know?"

"Dima works for the Russians as I told you," she said. "He also works for another group headed by someone who calls himself The Chameleon. All correspondence leads to the United States."

"Chameleon?" Evan's mind raced as he tried to figure out how the name Chameleon fit in the puzzle. He yawned, as the jet lag made him feel tired and a little fuzzy and he took the other seat next to her. She noticed.

"It was easy for me to choose sides; it is my own country that betrayed me. . .my homeland is my adversary!" she said, agitated.

Evan didn't ask for a reason to believe her. He felt she was genuine; he learned her profile even with the missing information before accepting his mission and thought she even might be an asset if he used her correctly. He knew that the embassy treated her more like a human being. She knew who Evan represented, because she knew a thing or two about the American spy agencies and their operational methods. Evan cryptically felt that something didn't add up in both their minds.

"Evan, I know the FSB will try to kill me when it's all over, they will have no use for me."

"Or the CIA!" He cleared his throat and stared at her.

"Or The Chameleon!" she exclaimed dramatically "Did anyone see you come in?" she asked, concerned. Evan shook his head.

"No, unless your apartment was under surveillance. Why?" He was curious and approached the curtained window and looked outside.

"Look!" she pleaded, "I have nothing to lose. I am not the person you think I am. . .my job was to find out from Dima who is he working for, and have him lead me to the organization he reports to in order to find out what they are up to and why." She gasped breathlessly.

Evan pulled the window curtain open a little more to find the street quiet with little traffic.

"I hear you," he said.

"So, you came to kill me without knowing who I am? You know why?" she asked.

"I am sure you will tell me," Evan replied.

"We are both supposed to find out who Dima is connecting with. I guess he trusts me; he thinks I am a loyal comrade working for the Russians. He doesn't know that I don't believe a word they promised me."

Evan listened to her explanation and covered his mouth, coughing.

"I understand that he works for a proxy, a third party, but they are not stupid enough to expose themselves, all we need is one thread of inf-" he started.

"In your country, there are people who spread disinformation. There are a handful of people who know I'm a double agent. One of them was the vice president and his Chief of Staff who helped me get the job in the embassy. Dima works for the Russians, but the information I was supplying him with was not for the Russian FSB, it's for insiders here. . . probably someone in the Russian embassy in Washington," Katarina explained.

"But people in Washington know all the information you gave him." This puzzled Evan.

"True, and that's the whole point, it's fake you know? And they probably know that by now!" she said, excited. "This is why I am ready to call it quits and flee, you caught me at a bad time!" She gasped and shrugged.

Katarina thought she had to convince Evan to cooperate with her to complete the mission he came for and pretend that he killed her. Someone in Washington would be satisfied. Then they'd make Evan kill Dima, then assassinate Evan to erase any trail of the operation in Moscow under the noses of the FSB.

"The only thing important Dima might know is a clue or two about who The Chameleon is. Evan, report that you killed me. Make up the story and let's see what happens!" she pleaded. "Then, I'll help you to find Dima, tonight!"

"If you are suggesting that Dima has a connection with someone who knows The Chameleon, that perhaps is connected with attack on the President-" Evan started.

Katarina cut him off and exclaimed, "Exactly, or perhaps he will lead us to The Chameleon himself!"

"Keep going!" He wanted her to keep talking.

"I am running a small mission in an even bigger mission, as I said, you probably were not informed!"

"Who is your direct contact in the states?" Evan asked, furious.

"Marcus Barbour, Patrick Stevenson, and in the embassy, Bob, chief of security," she sighed.

"Fucking assholes!" he growled. "What's the purpose of all this?" he asked, feeling suddenly betrayed.

"They probably don't know, and that's the purpose of my mission. They want me to find out if there is a mole in Washington!" she exclaimed and took a few steps to her pantry and got a few premade pastries, juices, and fresh fruit from the refrigerator.

"You look like you're starving!" she exclaimed, and quickly arranged a few things to nibble on.

"I guess I won't kill you. At least not for the time being." Evan smiled. He was pretty hungry, after all.

"Someone wanted me dead. I am done supplying information. Maybe I was used by both sides and one side said 'enough.' You have to believe me!" Katarina pleaded.

"So what you're saying is that there is a connection between your mission and the murder of the FLOTUS."

"Yes, it was an assassination attempt to kill the President right after the inauguration ceremony and has nothing to do with the military decisions of the former President."

"Who would benefit from the President's death?" Evan asked.

"That's exactly what I need to discover!" She knew that Evan already had chosen a side. They were both comfortable to collaborate with each other. She watched Evan empty the snack tray in silence.

"I admire your mission and am pissed off I was not to be part of the coup," he said angrily. "What information were you able to gather, and where can we find Dima Petrankov?"

"I picked up information by manipulation. Dima knows more than he was telling me. I think your President is under attack on many fronts, and no one in your country knows when or what will hit him. I informed Marcus and Patrick that perhaps there is something brewing for the President's Saudi Arabia trip, but I'm not sure," Katarina explained.

"Give me specifics," Evan said.

"Dima asked for the confidential trip information, including the President's itinerary, flight specifics, and security procedures. The assassins who tried to kill the President, will try again," she said.

"Well, the President is flying to Saudi Arabia, I think, today or tomorrow, I lost my sense of time, and you are suspecting that there is an assassination plot against him in Riyadh?"

"Yes!" she exclaimed, "I fear so!"

Something in her body language told him that she knew more but was not ready to discuss it. *This might be her survival wild card* he thought, *she didn't totally trust him yet.*

"Well, now that you are telling me all this, perhaps someone didn't want me to join the President on his trip. Is it to save me or keep me away from the presi-"

"Or wants you dead," she whispered harshly.

She cleared her throat and pushed her blond hair back, exposing her smooth, white neck. He inhaled her scent a few minutes ago. *Keep it professional*, he reminded himself.

"I am feeding Petrankov disinformation with some real news. It's just a question of time until the people he is working for realize that I misled them. I found out that they got the list of our agents in Russia and China. Why were you sent here?" Katarina asked.

"One wants to kill you and another told you I am coming, and they don't know each other," Evan scoffed.

"Yes!" she said.

"It's a puzzle, someone is playing with both of our heads, perhaps all the heads in Washington together!" Evan said, trying not to fall into a trap someone set for them both.

"Some of our agents were discovered, and left the country in a hurry. The embassy changed the security rules." She looked disturbed and wondered if she was on the list.

"Yes, you are definitely in danger!" he exclaimed sadly.

"No one needs my services anymore, and I am a liability for them. I'm dead man walking!" she scoffed.

Evan scowled. "One question remains unanswered. How do I know it was not you who gave our agents' list to the Russians?"

"I don't know any!" She frowned. "My mission came directly from Marcus and Patrick through Bob. The vice president and Frank Dabush gave their thumbs up!"

"I am furious. Your mission was to spread disinformation and only four people knew about it?" Evan raged.

"Five with Bob, but yes, out of the four, I believe two wanted to kill me and two wanted me out of the country escorting you when we were done!" Katarina moved around restlessly. She stood up and walked back and forth from her kitchen to the dining room not more than twelve feet away. Her apartment was a tiny, 400-square-foot unit in a condominium complex. It featured only two windows, one in the dining room and the other in the small bedroom, both facing the street. *Perfect for a single woman and a dog*, he thought.

"What the fuck are you talking about?" Evan asked angrily. He didn't expect this change of plan and felt like a helpless decoy. Evan used his cell phone to look at her CIA profile. Katarina gave him her password to enter her profile, which was incomplete. Perhaps someone had removed important pieces of information from the database. He saw her ties to the Russian intelligence community marked as "double agent." The file had photos of her destinations, her contacts, and the information transfers.

Evan realized that perhaps he was her insurance policy. He wondered while examining the apartment, now seeing the two suitcases and her dog cage, as if she was going somewhere for a long time without any intention of returning.

"Did you hear the Bible story of 'Bilham,' the messenger who was sent by the king of Moab to curse the kingdom of Israel and then instead he blessed them? This situation resembles that because I came to curse you and instead found myself blessing you!"

She rolled her eyes.

"I'll tell you everything if you help me to get out of here fast!" she pleaded. "Now do you believe me?" She raised her voice and moved forward to be closer to him.

"We need to trust one another. I usually don't fall for a beautiful woman, and if you double cross me, I'll kill you!" he promised.

"You see, I know how the CIA operates, I am not the one you are looking for. I am the one who was supposed to find the mole in the embassy and extract information from Petrankov. This came from Marcus, no one else knows, perhaps only Patrick. They agreed to send you here with the idea that you would find the truth. If they lose you, no big deal, I am concerned that Dima will vanish," she reiterated.

Evan was surprised. "How can you prove what you are saying? How do you know I am not part of their game?" His face disclosed his dismay.

"The Soldiers of Allah for example!" she exclaimed. "Perhaps the Soldiers of Allah group is fake? Perhaps it was created by the Russians, to shift the blame of the assassination onto the Islamic world and let Islamophobia take it from there. Did you ever think of that?" She pouted.

"Did they claim responsibility?" Evan asked.

"Yes, it broke in the international news despite the fact it was censored. . .this all happened while you were traveling here, but that is not the issue," she said sarcastically.

"What's the issue then?" he asked. "What do you know about the Soldiers of Allah?"

"This is what I was investigating as I extracted information from Dima. I know that they are Russian Muslims, perhaps Chechnyans. I work directly for the CIA director Marcus Barbour and Patrick, with no middleman. Just like you!" She scowled.

"Like me?" He sounded surprised and slammed the table.

"Yes, you work and report directly to the President and are missing most of the important information they already know. I report directly to Marcus, he trusts no one nowadays!"

She stopped walking back and forth and tucked herself next to the window, looking carefully outside as if she was expecting something or someone to show up.

"So get me out of this maze," Evan said.

"From what I've gathered so far, someone wants to make the attack motive about revenge and blame someone else. Someone who doesn't exist!"

"You mean revenge and retaliation connected to the drone attack by the former President?" Evan tried his luck connecting the dots. "What could they possibly gain by the retaliation attack?"

"Nothing, that's not the point again!" She was frustrated. "That's what the attack planners want you and everyone to think," she said.

Evan grimaced and started to understand where Katarina was leading him.

"Got it!" he finally said.

"Bravo!" replied Katarina and looked at her watch. "We need to complete the investigation and see who masterminded this catastrophe."

Evan was amazed at what Katarina discovered so far, confirming they needed solid proof before the situation exploded into a global conflict beyond anyone's control, and unleashing a doomsday scenario.

"Is Russia involved in this?" Evan asked.

"Perhaps not at all, maybe it was all faked to make you believe it was Russia!" Katarina was furious at what she believed was a smart sabotaged plot. Only a mastermind could erase all tracks and disappear into thin air.

"Has the name Hassan Abu Shikri come up in your communications?" Evan asked.

"No. Why?" Katarina responded, her eyes narrowing.

"I want to know. . .I was on his trail. We are looking for Hassan Abu Shikri. He may be tied to all this!"

Evan tried to remember every detail surrounding the car explosion near the mosque. He didn't remember much of anything. He was in the hospital in Alexandria, Virginia, for three days under heavy guard. His memory came back, but he didn't remember any details from the explosion.

Fading memories of lying on a stretcher were all he could remember. He didn't remember being unconscious on the frozen ground until the paramedics arrived. He barely remembered that he fell when the wailing ambulance drove him straight to the intensive care units. Patrick figured after the assassination attempt at the mosque that perhaps it was a Muslim connection to his investigation, perhaps the thread he was looking for, but it still didn't lead to the next point in the international connect-the-dot puzzle.

"Do you know the punishment for being gay in Russia?" Katarina asked as she nervously looked at her watch again. She looked outside her window once more and it was already dark with ample streetlights illuminating the street. The light penetrated the apartment through the curtains and cast shadows on the floor.

Evan ignored her question. He knew gay and lesbian people were not welcomed in Russia.

"Dima Petrankov might know more than I think, because other than the Russians, anyone else working with Dima remained a mystery; usually an agent knows only his mentor to avoid the spread of information, but when it comes to Dima, he served in a few positions," she said grimly.

"We need to pay him a visit soon!" exclaimed Evan.

"I have one clue and-" she started to say.

"Well, I understand you are worried and ready to leave. I saw the suitcases in your bedroom. Take me to Dima Petrankov tonight," Evan insisted, despite the fact that he was on his feet for almost 24 hours.

"I have one clue and I thi-" Katarina froze.

Rapid fire bullets smashed the apartment windows on the third floor and pierced the adjacent walls and ceilings. Plaster and smashed mirror shards fell to the floor.

Evan pushed Katarina to the floor and covered her up with his body. The dog had to fend for himself, barking hysterically and running from room to room looking for shelter.

Then, the quiet came.

The angle of the bullets seemed to indicate they came from a passing car on the street below.

Katarina tried to say something, but Evan put his palm on her mouth and with his finger he signaled, "Shhhh, quiet."

He was not sure if that was just a warning shot or an unprofessional assassin doing a bad job.

"Someone doesn't like you," whispered Evan.

"Maybe, someone doesn't like you either!" she answered sarcastically and pushed him off her.

"Someone might not like that fact that I am here," he whispered back.

"You might be surprised; it could be the same people who tried to kill you at the mosque!"

"Makes sense, it seems to have become a bad habit," he replied, and thought that the last time he pinned someone down to the ground due to a shooting, it was the President himself on inauguration day.

He got up from the floor and carefully peeked through the shattered window glass as cold air blew in. Evan was making sure that his shadows wouldn't reveal his location just in case someone was still watching.

He could not see anything on the street below. If there had been a car, it vanished. He examined the adjacent building and figured that it could not be the location of the shooter. His cold blue eyes combed the street and he assumed that they would come back to finish the job.

Katarina waited on the floor and then crawled to the window and stood next to Evan.

Perhaps they are on their way up to the apartment, she thought.

"We need to get out of here!" she commanded. "We are both in danger!"

The fact that someone might know about his visit to Katarina bugged him. Only a small group of his colleagues and the President knew.

"Is there a second means of egress in the building?" Evan asked and cleaned the debris from his suit and tie and tucked his shirt back in his pants.

"Yes, let's go!" answered Katarina and started fast to collect things up as she could.

Evan pulled her hand with a tight grip. "Stop, we are not on vacation; they might wait for us somewhere."

She was calm and not traumatic or in a state of a panic.

Evan was convinced now that Katarina was telling the truth. Dima Petrankov would have to wait for a better time to be questioned, that is, if they got out of this night alive.

His instincts told him not to push away a second thought that perhaps it was just a trick, but the bullets were real. Too much to think about under pressure and they sought the safety of the embassy.

"What about my dog?" she asked.

Evan was relaxed and encouraged her, unfortunately, to leave the frightened dog in the apartment.

"Just as you are, no dog," Evan exclaimed and grabbed her by her hand again.

She released herself from his grasp and hugged the dog that seemed to know it was a final goodbye. Endless tears flooded her eyes as she gave him a last look.

"C'mon, let's go!" he whispered loudly.

She opened her apartment door a crack, and found the hallway empty. Evan pushed himself forward with his gun in his hand.

"The only way out is the front building doors or the garage where I parked my car," she said as they left the apartment.

Katarina thought it was a blessed coincidence that Evan appeared at the right time. "God? Destiny?" she murmured.

"Russian agents don't miss," said Evan skeptical.

"It was an assassin for hire!"

Evan raised his eyebrows and scanned her figure once more.

CHAPTER 17

The next day, Patrick drove to the FBI forensic labs in Quantico, Virginia, where the three bodies were examined for identification and cause of death. Determining the cause of death was essential to identify the type of weapon used for the killings and to identify the victims and why they were killed. The autopsies were carried out by a medical examiner assigned to the crime investigation.

Patrick, with advanced notice from Daniel, the FBI Chief in D.C., met with the forensic pathologist in charge of the autopsy, a young physician named Mel Cohen. who graduated from Boston University. He immediately demanded to see the bodies and glean as many details as he could.

Dr. Cohen led Patrick to the morgue. "We took DNA and fingerprints to compare our reference samples with the national DNA database for identification," he explained.

The basement was quiet, empty, cold, and creepy. The lights were pale, but Dr. Cohen was comfortable in this environment.

"Anything match?" asked Patrick, eager for a breakthrough.

"Not that I know of," exclaimed the pathologist. "We are waiting for the national lab report."

In the morgue itself, the pathologist opened three drawers, exposing three bodies in white body bags, clearly showing the identification tags at the base of the bag.

The tags revealed only numbers, not names. Dr. Cohen unzipped the zippers and exposed the bodies for Patrick's review as he explained the autopsy details.

Each one had a small anchor tattoo on his forehead, a symbol of a gang member of an organization like the MS 13, and exactly as the landlord detailed in his FBI interrogation the night before.

"They look like Iranians," Patrick said. "Can the DNA tests determine ethnic identity?"

"I am asked this question occasionally," the doctor replied, as he put on his medical gloves and gave a set to Patrick. "DNA geography is important in our counterterrorism; we want to know where they came from and what their genetic origin is."

Dr. Cohen spoke in a monotone manner, and was almost boring to listen to. Patrick figured that it was tough to make a pathologist enthusiastic enough to reveal everything they knew; they assumed a visitor would understand all their professional lingo.

"Ancestry companies do offer details of-"

"It's admixture!" exclaimed the pathologist "But if we go this route, I am confident to say that based on a meaningful cluster of similarity, meaning the average of all three deceased bodies, they are not European-Americans."

Patrick chuckled at the answer and the pathologist looked puzzled. *What did he do wrong?* he wondered. Then he said with confidence, "We don't have the world DNA database, so we can't generalize their origin, if you want me to guess further I can say off the record their origin is mid- to far- east Asia, Mongolia, Tibet, or Northern Russia. A genealogist can answer better," he sighed.

"Is Chechnya in this category?"

"Sure, you can put it in the mix," Dr. Cohen said, amused, as if they were playing a guessing game like charades.

Then, the pathologist went over the dead bodies again. "This one had a broken nose, and this one had knee surgery."

"Hold on, this one with the knee, what's the issue?" Patrick thought he had found something.

"He had a broken knee, perhaps an accident?"

"Could he walk?" Patrick pressed the issue and stared at the pathologist resetting his eyeglasses.

"Sure, but he probably limped on his left leg."

"Does the bureau have the report yet?"

"It's in the process, we got the corpses last night."

"I want to see his entire body!" Patrick demanded, and the pathologist removed the body bag and exposed the pale corpse. Patrick took notes. "Height, weight, curly short black hair, flat wide nose and short forehead," he said as he was going over the details for later review. He opened the dead man's mouth and found two gold teeth in the lower jaw.

"The gold teeth replacement is typical to Kurds and the Kavkaz area," said Patrick, confidently. "I saw many of them in my visits to Afghanistan, North Iraq."

"The Kurds?"

"Yes, it's more popular in those areas than in Europe or America, where porcelain tooth replacement is the more popular method," he explained.

Patrick took a few photos with his cell phone, and turned to leave, but not without one last question, "Dr. Cohen, did the lab match their DNA to semen found connecting to the rape/murder incident?"

"You mean the young woman from District Heights? No, it's too early. I'll make a note of that."

Patrick exhaled, raised his hand and waved the patholo-gist goodbye and drove back to Langley. He was excited for the information he got even before the FBI had a chance to hear and review it.

Chapter 18

Andrews Air Force Base, three miles east of Camp Spring, Maryland

Three months after the assassination, the Presidential motorcade made its way onto the tarmac, with the President ready to embark on his historic trip as promised in his campaign. He preferred this over the short flight on the Presidential helicopters from the White House lawn.

The President planned this trip on the brink of the new cold war among the three superpowers, as the adversaries enjoyed watching from the sidelines as the extreme Islamic Jihad slammed the United States time after time. He brewed over this concept during his campaign, back when he was still just a candidate. He promised not to surrender to the world Jihadi governments and to impose economic sanctions on those who did not align with the domestic policies, stirring up a mess with the world affairs.

"I need to be traveling right now like I need a hole in my head!" the President scoffed, "That's a bad joke."

"Well, that was your campaign agenda, Mr. President!" added his special Middle East convoy, Greg Williams, who joined the trip at the last minute.

"Evan? Where is Evan?" the President asked, probably forgetting Evan's excursion.

"He is leaving this afternoon for Moscow!"

"Oh, yes!" the President remembered. "I'll miss him!"

The limousine stopped at the foot of the plane's stairs and the men exited the car and escorted the President along with Secret Service agents toward Air Force One.

A bunch of reporters shouted random questions. The President broke from his group and approached them as the secret agents ran to keep him at a safe distance. He raised his hands to ward them off.

"Mr. President, what is the purpose of your trip?"

"The real purpose of the trip is to convey to the world to leave us alone and we will leave you alone. Mess with us, and we will mess with you," he said, stoically.

The reporters started shouting again but grew quiet as the defense secretary stepped forward.

"To keep the moderate Islamic countries on our side without the threat of being abandoned. The President's policy of nuclear umbrella protection will work!"

The secret service agents gently guided the President to move on and take no further questions.

Just before they settled in, the President entered the cockpit and greeted the crew, who were busy preparing the plane for its long journey. As he sat down and buckled his safety belt, the attendant asked if he could offer them refreshments prior to takeoff.

"We are good," replied Greg Williams.

Then the President joked, "I changed my mind from a liberal President before the elections to whatever I need to be now to get the guilty parties what they deserve!" he swore, but as memories of his wife resurfaced, he became sad and quiet.

Although the President refused talking about the incident and never mentioned his wife's name in public, he refused to acknowledge that he needed professional treatment for his trauma. Rufus Barker decided to show his strong side in front of the media and appear mentally strong in public, and fit to serve the American people. He knew sooner or later though, if he did seek therapy, it would be leaked to the media and reporters would turn this fact into a nightmare for the rest of his first term.

Occasionally, he had night terrors, dreaming about his wife shot dead on the Capitol Hill grounds. Time after time, he woke up in the middle of the night, took his tranquilizers and went back to sleep. It was a private matter, and he wanted to keep it that way.

"The liberals will challenge you!" Greg warned.

"The liberals didn't lose their loved ones!" replied the President firmly. "No President started his first term with such a shitload of issues!" he added, frustrated.

"GWB, our forty-third President and 9/11," exclaimed Alvin, the Defense Secretary.

"Yeah, we should examine what George W. Bush did and learn from it. . .anyway, no one from his family was a victim in this attack. For me it's personal," exclaimed the President.

That was exactly where the military and the top brass were concerned, and the President might rush to conclusions just to find a suspect to unleash the wrath of its military might to annihilate some country, somewhere.

"Ignore the first few reports Mr. President. The hints, clues, and disinformation that we're hearing has required a new strategy," said Alvin. He knew the President was reaching a boiling point.

"We will create joint Middle East peace talks, and keep coalition forces headed to Saudi Arabia and Israel. The combined military forces will be a unified front against the aggression and expansion of the Iranian regime in the Middle East," the President ordered.

"The Russian-backed Iranian proxies (that might also be backed by China) are the biggest problem now," declared Alvin. Greg Williams, sat amongst them.

They all preferred the old, liberal Rufus Barker, who would have busied himself more with domestic issues and less with Russia's and China's worldwide intentions.

It was early April, a calm, beautiful day with perfect weather and clear skies. Some of the more than 100 journalists, agents, and other cabinet members and service crew entered the airplane from the rear door. For the journalists, it was simply another Presidential trip that needed media coverage.

As Colonel Dan Elliot, the Air Force One captain and his copilot, Major Clarence Levine completed the pre-flight checklist on the exact replica of Air Force One, a Boeing 777X parked on the other side of the airport. Already onboard were 100 Marines fully equipped and combat-ready to protect the President at any time and as the CIA required.

The new flying White House had two decks (the Boeing 747 had three) and was a technological upgrade with the most classified systems that any head of state could desire. The defense secretary, a tough African-American man over six feet tall and a bouncer's muscled frame was a former Navy Admiral who successfully ran operations in the Middle East and Europe.

The plane was equipped with an operating room. The President's personal physician, Dr. Rintler, stood ready with his medical team on board. In addition, the plane was equipped with the most advanced anti-missile attack technology and used flares and countermeasures aimed to intercept Air Force One in midair. A large, illuminated red alert would activate upon such an attack. Finally, the vessel sported protection in case of a nuclear attack. It had a nuclear explosion capability that protected its inhabitants against nuclear radiation and the shock waves that accompanied nuclear blasts.

The military used the code name "Doomsday Plane" for the twin Air Force One, which would to be on alert for any possibility that might require it in an unfortunate event. The "Doomsday" Air Force One started its two Pratt and Whitney engines then taxied north to the active runway threshold of runway 01L.

The cockpit crews admired the impressive state-of-the-art glass cockpit, but the pilots demanded analog instruments as a secondary backup system.

Another important technical addition was the midair fueling capability, which could keep the airplane airborne indefinitely. The cabin door closed on schedule at about noon, and Colonel Elliot switched his radio frequency to 121.8 MHz to contact ground control, which directed Army 1—its code name—to the runway. Air Force One's twin (Army 2) was already waiting for the President's plane to take off first; and when it did, Army 2 took off and kept 10 miles behind the President's aircraft.

The flight to Riyadh generated tremendous pressure on the CIA, and they checked and approved the flight plan to ensure that they wouldn't be forced to land in a hostile environment in case of an emergency. Unlike a commercial plane, Air Force One flew with its transponder shut off to avoid detection as it cruised at 40,000 feet.

A formation of four F-18 Super Hornets took off from the USS George H.W. Bush carrier, the strike group patrolling the eastern Mediterranean Sea. They intercepted Air Force One and split into two pairs to escort the two planes in. The Super Hornets were fully equipped and ready to intercept any airborne or groundborne threats. Crossing a chaotic environment like the Sinai Peninsula with hostile groups such as ISIS, Houthis, and other Jihadi terror groups fighting the Egyptian army meant enemies were all around, and they needed special measures in place. As they neared their destination, the captain banked the aircraft to the right, heading south crossing land through Egypt to fly 100 miles along the Suez Canal, and then turned left thirty degrees, to fly directly into Riyadh. A few hours later, while descending to 30,000 feet above the Mediterranean Sea, the crew saw the sun rising over the rounded horizon, a spectacular scene that painted the sky in bright hues. The sea below flickered with a spectacular reflection of the rising sun.

"Bardawil Lake is on the left," declared the captain as the plane approached the Sinai Peninsula.

"My second time over the fertile Nile delta on the right," replied the copilot, seeing the many local fishing boats heading back to their ports after a long night of fishing deep in the Mediterranean waters.

Twenty minutes later, over the town of Suez, the captain engaged a controlled descent approaching the Saudi air space, and cried out with surprise, "What the hell. . ."

Captain Elliot, although he was thoroughly trained for an attack was unprepared when he heard the loud noise: The red-missile attack alert light flickered wildly as it chimed with a high-pitched wail.

"Is it a malfunction?" asked the copilot, while Elliot quickly examined the entire instrument panel.

"We are being attacked; missiles launched," said the captain, with a voice as steady and controlled as he could muster.

"Engaging laser electronics systems," Levine answered quickly and turned on the missile radar scrambling system. The F-18 formation leader confirmed on the radio and maneuvered his formation to deploy its flares and redirect the missiles.

"Missiles approaching fast from the left," the captain declared and instinctively disengaged the auto-pilot. He banked the plane to the left in a sharp thirty-degree turn and dropped the nose directly into the approaching missiles' paths, hoping the plane would survive the maneuver. The copilot immediately turned on the missile defense and electronic jamming systems and watched the two missiles speed up. He engaged the flares and together the laser system to draw the missiles away from the aircraft. The missiles kept their path toward the President's plane, which was not as maneuverable as the jet fighter.

"Wait a couple of seconds." The captain heard the F-18 leader on the radio. "Three, two, one. . .break now," he thundered.

Elliot pulled the yoke all the way to his chest, causing the plane to change its dive to a quick ascent with full throttle. He knew how to handle himself with the G-force and hoped everyone else was safe.

"Hope we survive this maneuver," he murmured to himself as the intense, three-G-force pressure on his chest briefly stopped his breathing. He tensed his muscles and squeezed his stomach in before exhaling forcefully. He inhaled again, and held his breath; he knew that a regular passenger plane airframe could never survive more than two Gs; however, Air Force One was structurally designed to maneuver at four

Gs. Elliot kept the plane from slipping into a higher G, since three-G-force is equal to the forces experienced on a roller-coaster and do not generally cause emergency situations for the passengers.

"It's obvious that the attack was aimed at the President," Elliot grumbled.

The F-18 pilots received the same missile alert indication as Air Force One and dispatched an automatic distress call in the emergency frequency. The jet fighters scanned the skies for possible new threats, and they noticed the dust "poof" on the ground that was produced by the missile battery launching yet another set of missiles.

The "poof" disclosed the location of the battery and the F-18 locked on the missile battery radar to launch their deadly accurate air-to-surface missiles in retaliation. The jet fighters' pilots didn't ask for permission to engage and destroy the targets. Any future political consequences would be cleaned up by the Secretary of State to prevent any further diplomatic crises and military conflicts.

In a coordinated maneuver, the F-18 formation split into two pairs. The first pair of jets tried to attract the missiles directed at them and the other pair dove to destroy the four SA-6 surface-to-air missile launchers, NATO code name, "Gainful."

"Someone really likes us!" the captain said sarcastically as he watched the attack on the ground.

"Advancing missiles!" reported Levine with a calmness he might have during routine training and not in a life-and-death situation.

The 50-plus year-old missiles were probably available to terror groups via black market armament brokers. Right after the fall of the former Soviet Union, military surplus flooded the market and brokers could make fast cash as long as supplies lasted.

"Some shithead disclosed our route and schedule. How the fuck did they know where we are?" roared the frustrated captain as he scrambled the plane in the air per the jet-fighter leader's directions.

"Emergency procedures," declared the captain and continued to command loudly as the copilot acted to function in automated mode.

"Target destroyed," reported the formation leader.

Elliot was busy bringing the airplane under full and steady control. The copilot started an emergency protocol procedure and looked for a place to land.

The twin Army 2 plane behind them received the emergency code and notified the Pentagon and the vice president. The CIA headquarters in Virginia also learned of the current drama and kept its content confidential in the network.

The situation at 30,000 feet was still considered active and dangerous. Considering the situation, the Sixth Fleet automatically went into combat alert. His aviators were seated in the cockpit waiting for instructions to ready for immediate take-off if needed.

Two additional fighter formations received the command to takeoff equipped with three drop-tanks full of fuel and smart bombs to finish the job against the ground targets. They were instructed to fly ahead of Air Force One's path and identify other missile launcher threats and destroy them, no questions asked.

"Resume normal flight navigation," declared Elliot as he stabilized the plane.

"What the fuck happened?" screamed the President as he recovered from the ordeal. He liked to be buckled in his seat during flights regardless, and fortunately was not caught by surprise. His office was in turmoil, practically everything was on the floor: papers, stationery, coffee, and some folders.

The purser made it to his office and opened the door without knocking. He saw the defense secretary on the floor recovering from the maneuvers.

"We were being attacked!" he said in distress.

"How is everyone in the cabin?" asked Rufus when he saw the horrified face of the purser helping Alvin to his seat and buckle his belt.

"Under control!" he said with slight anxiety in his voice.

"We succeeded in sabotaging a few missiles," the captain's voice was heard in the cabin. "We are being escorted by the Sixth Fleet squadrons; it's not over yet, stay buckled up. Sorry about that."

"Fuck! Not again!" Elliot howled and engaged all the flares stored in the wings and threw all the countermeasures he could due to a dozen smoky missiles that were launched all at once.

Two missiles were diverted away by the fighters, successfully preventing a direct hit and avoided a catastrophe in midair. Three other missiles could not make it to Air Force One's altitude, even though they were effective up to a 46,000-foot ceiling. They fell back to the earth a minute after launch and exploded in a large cloud of smoke and fire seen for many miles.

"Missiles launched!" warned the Squadron leader.

"Holy shit!" screamed the copilot in exchange.

Two missiles flew perfectly straight up toward the plane. The proximity fuse in the missile ensured an explosion close to the target, which would have caused catastrophic damage and blown the plane apart in a million pieces. A jet fighter escorting the AF-1 took the hit too. The near explosion shook the President's plane violently but could take the hit and continued its leveled flight.

"I see no parachute! The pilot has sacrificed his life for the President!" Major Levine stated in deep sorrow as he fought to regain control of the plane.

The second missile was seconds from reaching its target only to be intercepted by a second Navy Hornet whose pilot also died protecting the President's plane.

"What is that noise?" asked Major Levine.

The jet engine's RPM and the nozzle temperature dropped down as the turbines stopped indefinitely. "Engine failure!" announced the captain. "Start crash-landing procedures!" he commanded.

Debris from the close proximity missile explosion became lodged in the AF-1 engines, which immediately caused a major fire and malfunction. Both engine's red fire alert lights were on, and flickering annoyingly. The metal clanking sounds of the disintegrated compressors' destruction was heard in the cabin and it horrified its passengers, who saw the fire from their windows.

"Engines out!" cried the copilot trying to revive the engines "Restart procedure failed!" He sounded hopeless.

"Prepare for an emergency landing!" said the captain.

The captain cut off the fuel supply and immediately engaged the fire suppression system. At the same time, he dumped the fuel to reduce the plane's weight before a possible crash landing.

Another piece of metal hit the windshield, cracking it and causing a possible flight failure and death for all onboard.

"Fucking shit, it's crazy!" rumbled the copilot.

The cockpit became a cacophony of alerts as they all went off at the same time. The crew ignored them and instead focused on stabilizing the aircraft.

"Switch to emergency frequency 121.5 MHz." the captain ordered.

"Roger!"

"Do not place a distress call yet!" the captain yelled back, controlling the airplane from rolling upside down.

The copilot, busy with his own emergency tasks, didn't hear the last statement and proceeded to announce the emergency call.

"Mayday! Mayday! Mayday! We are going down! Repeat, we are going down!" the copilot exclaimed, breaking the confidential code of AF-1's location.

Without power, the procedures went into impact alert. The first order of business was to control the plane's descent and look for a suitable landing site. The cockpit crew didn't have the time to inform the cabin crew or the President on the situation and their intent to crash land in Sinai. The captain assumed that his passengers were in a state of panic already, and knew the situation was dire.

The cabin pressure lost, oxygen masks dropped from the panels above the cabin. Army 2, about 10 miles behind, was directed to climb to its maximum service ceiling and head west into Egypt. The order was so that Army 2 could outflank the area waiting under the Cairo Air traffic control tower radar for instructions until the threat was eliminated. No one was sure how many missiles still existed, but they all hoped it was an isolated incident.

"We are going to lose the airplane," Major Levine stated calmly. "We are deep into Sinai center, let's try to land in Sharm El-Sheikh."

"It's too far," replied the captain. "Going back to Bir-Gafgafa is out of the question as well. . .we won't make the turn," he said nervously.

"The only option is an abandoned airfield in Bir-e-Tamadeh, heading 020 degrees about 40 miles." The copilot hid his panic, and tried to concentrate on navigating the plane.

"The airfield is not in our system!" replied the captain.

"Believe me, it's there. It's in a main highway junction. My grandfather practiced there with the Israeli Airforce more than 40 years ago, and I learned his maps." He convinced the captain to trust him.

"Let's ask Cairo for instruction!" suggested the captain and knew it was a blank shot.

"It's a waste of time, trust me!" the copilot admonished.

"Concurred," replied the captain. "After you!"

Captain Elliot stabilized the plane into a steady descent and locked on to the copilot's new navigation instructions heading 020.

"There is no other alternative, captain!" replied Major Levine while checking the damage from his window.

"We're at 22,000 feet," stated the captain.

"We are gliding over the Mitleh pass. Perfect. We are on the right path!"

"Descending 2,000 feet per minute at a speed of 280 knots will keep us in the air for 11 minutes and cover a distance of 35.44 miles," confirmed the captain, based on the copilot's estimate.

"Roger, we need to keep it in the air a little longer!"

"We are a little short of the 40 miles though!"

The captain indicated the approximate landing site location.

Elliot lowered the rate of descent to make the range reachable and keep the landing speed optimal so they wouldn't overshoot the runway.

"Engine fire extinguished," reported the copilot. *One thing less to worry about,* he thought.

"Roger," replied the captain as he looked back to see the trail of black smoke left behind the wings.

"I'm sure everyone sees the black smoke that's pinpointing our position!" Major Levine was concerned.

"Let's land safely first!"

The emergency hydraulic system generated by the Ram Air Turbine system (RAT) kept the plane's controls operational.

Major Levine combed the horizon and stated, "I am trying to identify the airfield."

"Roger, we have only one shot at this!"

The crippled plane responded, and Elliot knew that its landing would be the only chance he had to test the plane's emergency systems. He hoped the landing gear was not damaged and would operate successfully.

The copilot was still looking for a sign that they could land the plane safely.

"Any sign?" asked the captain.

"Still looking, we must be close now!"

"Concentrate, major, we have the President on board!"

"I'm concerned with the runway conditions!" the captain said, concerned.

Neither pilot had any other options to consider. At this point they were not sure if the landing location was suitable for a heavy jetliner landing, however, it was too late to change direction.

"True, it's been a long time since it was used!" added the copilot with concern in his voice. "There is no better way, captain!" he exclaimed.

The chances of surviving a crash landing was slim. They knew the drill. They just needed to keep everyone thinking positively.

"Steady as she goes." The captain kept the plane gliding as he waited for the copilot to signal as soon as he saw the runway.

"Should be somewhere around there!" the major pointed out.

"You have no ATIS information data, major. No control tower or ILS approach system. . .just find it!"

Captain Elliot kept the President informed of the options and their decision to land. No one questioned it. "Everything is under control. It's alright. We'll land soon, so prepare for impact!"

Frequent sandstorms covered the beaten asphalt strip with patches of sand layers, some blending with the aerial surrounding topography.

"There it is!" shouted the excited copilot. "Eleven o'clock low, sharp!" he continued, pointing in that direction.

"The runway is in sight. You were right, major!" The captain sighed in relief.

Although hard to see in the distance, an experienced pilot knew what to look for. The runway blended in with sand and mature desert foliage.

"Speed steady. . .we'll land heading north!" confirmed the captain.

"You see the asphalt-shaded lines on the sand?"

"Very clearly, major!"

The airfield taxiways and runway were clearly visible and it was obvious that the desert claimed ownership a long time ago. Only a person with hawk eyes could spot the abandoned airfield from a distance. "Seems the runway heading is about 300," said Elliot, locking on the airfield five miles away on its left.

The plane glided east and Elliot needed to turn 120 degrees left into the runway just at the right time, the right altitude, and the right speed. His brain analyzed the data fast with the copilot assisting with the reading.

"We are a little too high and fast," said Major Levine, and the captain started a light side-to-side maneuver to lose altitude and speed so that they could land properly.

"Flaps 40!" Elliot ordered and added, "Gear down." The emergency hydronic system did not disappoint, and the plane lowered its speed as it was intended.

"Brace for impact!" Elliot declared when he completed the wide left turn.

He was determined to align the nose with the Sadr Al Haytan, a wide, two-lane highway, and bank slightly to the left onto the runway.

After he crossed the 'Al Hassana' highway, about 500 feet above ground level with prevailing winds blowing from the Northwest causing a slight crosswind, he curbed the airplane nose on the center of the runway and prayed.

"Four hundred feet," declared Major Levine. "Three hundred. . ." He continued its reporting with the cockpit annunciator, "165 knots!"

A quick look from the cockpit window and one could see deteriorating barracks and buildings, five underground hangars, scattered around the base. The blazing desert sun had no mercy on the skeletal remains of this airfield, which once was an active Israeli Air Force base after the Six Day War. The ghostly scene was the only historical witness of the peace treaty between Israel and Egypt and its demilitarized zone.

"This is it," Elliot said. With very little time to recover, the captain tried to keep the nose steady on the center.

"One hundred feet," Major Levine announced.

The plane hovered low above the runway as it crossed the threshold, spreading clouds of dust that engulfed the plane and creating a vortex behind it. The right landing gear touched the hard surface first with a loud screech that shook the plane violently, and blowing out two tires with a loud explosion.

Elliot tried to bring the left gear down without losing the center of the runway. He controlled the twist by activating the ailerons while the nose gear was still up in the air. The captain forced the elevators to drop the nose down faster and activated the spoilers and the brakes to slow and stop the aircraft. *Wow, how the thrust reversers could help now*, he thought.

They quickly passed over a thousand feet of runway and he had no idea what the remaining distance was before they would crash into the sand dunes that lay ahead. If he could, he would extend his arms and feet out of the cockpit to stop the airplane. The "long landing" indicator alert would signal the cockpit crew of the situation.

At 120 knots on the ground, the pilots looked for a miracle to stop the plane. Major Levine spotted objects on his side of the runway: A series of dusty deacon aircrafts which were left as a souvenir by the Egyptian air force after the Six Day War and were never cleared by the Israelis. The deacons were situated along the runway, which was not wide enough for the 199-foot wingspan crossing the edge of the 180-foot wide runway on both sides.

"I see the Deacons. It doesn't get any better than this," the captain said sarcastically as the plane started to shift to the right side due to its blown tires.

"Be careful," Major Levine alerted Elliot, but he could not avoid the collision. They didn't have the luxury of keeping the airplane safely on the center of the runway and stop it on time.

Suddenly, as they thought that they were hitting the deacon airplanes, the worst situation became their immediate reality: without warning, the front gear collapsed due to a ditch on the runway. It dropped the nose violently down onto the hot asphalt, and caused the entire plane to shake out of control. The nose scooped the sand, pebbles and bushes in front of the cockpit, and shattered the already damaged windshield into small pieces that sprayed the cockpit with the force of a tornado. Luckily, the layer of sand softened the friction between the plane's nose and the asphalt, in effect, lubricating it, and preventing it from sparking a fire.

The thousands of windshield shards peppered the pilots, who were trying to stay focused on the plane's controls, and tiny drops of blood appeared on their faces. The heavy plane skidded for 200 feet, twisting to the right in an endless rightbound circle as the right wing hit the deacon planes.

As the right engine hit the ground, the impact sheared it off from the wing, and caused a major leak in its remaining fuel tanks. The wingtip scratched the runway and caused sparks that started a fire that spread fast into the cabin. The plane skidded another 50 feet, dropped off the runway, and came to a complete halt after it impacted a high dune.

"Shut off everything and get out!" Elliot scramed as he unbuckled himself.

As smoke began to fill the cabin, the crew members immediately assisted the President, the Secretary of Defense, and the passengers in evacuating the doomed plane quickly and safely, using the only three remaining functional emergency slides.

The center fuel tank threatened to explode at any second as the flames grew closer.

"Get the President!" ordered the crew cabin manager as he pulled a stretcher from storage.

"He isn't moving!" replied a steward, who looked around to find the President's physician.

The President was supported by the crew while the physician checked the his vital signs.

One steward supported the President's back and accompanied him on the emergency slide. At the bottom of the chute, another crew member helped to get the President onto the stretcher and away from the burning plane.

The physician ran after them, panting as he watched the big black cloud rising behind them. The President was overcome with smoke inhalation, as were many others onboard.

"Jump, jump!" yelled the cabin crew, as they pushed everyone down the slides at the same time the President was evacuated.

"All out!" reported the cabin manager to the captain.

"OK, we will search the cabin one last time. You go on. Evacuate!"

"We are staying with you!" he replied and asked the two flight attendants to stay with the cockpit crew and check the cabin.

The last passengers slid to safety, although some had to be forced to jump. The captain and his copilot were only slightly injured, and along with three other senior crew members ran through the smoky cabin to make sure no one was left on the doomed aircraft. Then, without warning, the center fuel tank exploded with a loud boom, and immediately killed Captain Elliot, his copilot, Major Clarence Levine, and the three cabin crew members who stayed behind to search for passengers.

Seventy-two other passengers of Air Force One survived. Thirty-two were injured, mostly from smoke inhalation and broken bones. The President was in critical condition. The silence that came after the ordeal was amplified only by the crackling, burning fire that broke the stillness of the desert.

Chapter 19

F or about three months, Hassan hid in motels around the District Heights area, and tried to blend in. He used the cash he got from the dead agents for food and necessities. He wondered how he got the courage and expertise to successfully kill all of them, a personality trait that he didn't know he possessed and one he somehow didn't regret. It was them or him, and he chose wisely.

"Where to?" asked the cab driver who picked him up.

Hassan hesitated a fraction of a second and the driver took a quick glance through the back mirror.

"Reagan Airport," he replied.

Air Force One took off at the same time and flew overhead as the cab made a U-turn and zoomed south to Reagan National Airport. After a short ride through the light traffic in the Capitol, the driver asked, "Which airline?"

"American," he replied automatically, since that was the airline that brought him to the U.S. when he landed here the first time.

Hassan's thoughts drifted as he tried to come up with a plan. It was three months since the assassination. He was distressed and emotionally drained and not in the mood for a social conversation.

"Nowhere to go, nowhere to hide," he murmured to himself, feeling depressed.

"What?" asked the driver.

"I'm not speaking to you!" he snapped.

He wondered if any random Muslim group would agree to assist him, but first he'd have to find out how to connect with them. They called themselves the Soldiers of Allah. Hassan remembered the three agents he killed and wondered who they really were?

He was a small fish that was recruited without consent for a mission he wanted no part of. He wondered if the video of the rape and murder had made it to the media and spread his portrait in key points throughout the city. So far, and to his knowledge, it was not displayed in public or broadcast by the media.

The money and the old prepaid minutes of a flip cell phone he bought on the black market could help for a few weeks, perhaps months. *Then what?* he wondered.

His photos were shared with many intelligence agencies around the world. He was sure that not only the governments were after him, but perhaps private agencies who competed for the 5 million dollar price on his head as well. Even if he was caught and offered full cooperation, he still knew nothing about the plot.

The cab headed south on Highway 395 and signaled to merge onto the George Washington Memorial Highway headed to the airport. When the cab stopped in traffic on one of the bridges that spanned the Potomac river, Hassan grew tense.

"It's crazy nowadays!" exclaimed the driver.

"What's wrong?" Hassan asked curiously as he watched the traffic.

"There are so many roadblocks. The cops are still looking for some escaped terrorist connected to the terror attack," he replied nonchalantly.

"Oh, really!?"

"Are you late for a flight?"

"No, just waiting for a friend!" Hassan lied blatantly.

Concerned over crossing the police roadblock, Hassan thought fast as he weighed his options. He was not ready to spend his days and nights in the basement of the FBI, inside one of their interrogation rooms.

"Continue on 395, avoid the airport entrance and then exit to route 1 south to Alexandria," he instructed the driver.

"Oh, OK, what about your friend?" the driver asked.

Hassan ignored the question and planned the destination he had in his mind for a while, the Iranian mosque. *They probably assumed that I would never dare go to the place where a bomb almost killed Evan Harris,* Hassan thought to himself.

He pursed his lips, and his eyes darted everywhere to spot any followers. He asked the cab driver to stop behind a six-story corner building.

"Stop at the corner, please!" he said while wondering why he had not seen more roadblocks, especially leading to the Capitol exits.

"How much do I owe you?"

"$38.00."

Hassan pulled a $100 bill from the pack of cash and handed it to the driver.

"Do you want change?"

"No, keep it."

He exited the cab, and looked into the distance to the same spot where Evan's car had recently exploded. He saw the parking lot of the state credit union building that was secured by a police car with two police officers in the front seat. The formation was standard police protocol when there was violence.

"Shit, they are probably monitoring the mosque too," he murmured nervously. He secured the backpack on his back and walked in the opposite direction. *Perhaps making a detour and approaching the mosque from the back door is a good idea,* he thought.

The distance from the corner of the building to the entrance of the mosque was about thirty feet. He wondered if he could cross the distance without drawing the police officer's attention. They might suspect that something was wrong if he walked straight from the cab into the building or worse, if he came from the back. He was sure they saw him exit a cab, walk up the street, and move around the back of the buildings. At this point, if he showed up it would send a signal that he was trying to smuggle himself into a mosque. "Shit!" he cried in frustration and a cold spasm crossed his spine.

"How stupid am I?" he murmured.

Then he froze. The police car started to move slowly to exit the parking lot, toward the main street with full-blown emergency lights on.

They saw me! he thought and crumbled on his spot, his heart racing.

Instead, the police car zoomed up the street without looking at him at all. He waited to make sure that they were not coming around from another street, and then he rushed the distance and entered the front lobby.

He sighed with relief and thought that the officers probably decided to take a lunch break, reminding him that he'd gone quite awhile without food or drink.

He pressed the chime and waited.

Oh, shit, I have the gun on me, what a moron! he thought in a panic.

Chapter 20

Puteyskiy Tupik Street, Moscow

Evan and Katarina weighed their next steps cautiously. Not sure who fired the shots and if the building was surrounded or not, they knew that exiting the building from the front door would be a death sentence.

Time was against them, but the darkness of the night was an advantage in hiding their escape route.

"You know the building. How can we get out of here?" asked Evan.

"Let's go down to the underground parking garage, I am sure they will come back," she said confidently.

"I am sure they are in the building already!" he said and checked his gun.

Katarina led the way and Evan lingered after her, watching his back to meet any attackers with bullets.

"I should have explored the building better!" he said.

"It's too late, you have to trust me!" Katarina replied.

Evan liked her confidence. He did forget rule No. 1 in his profession: Have one door to enter and 10 doors to exit.

"Is there more than one way to get out?" he asked as they walked to the elevators. He was trailing just behind her quick footsteps. "No stairs?"

He mentioned that he preferred the stairs but got no response. She was too busy focused on her plan.

It was a modern, seven-story mid-rise building with one main, guarded gate. The main entry was on the narrow Puteyskiy Typik Street, the unique architecture was a combined entry with an attached 15-story building, probably with its own independent emergency egress and elevators. It also had the same guarded entry around the corner that was still under construction.

Katarina was not sure if it provided access to the street from her lower building but they'd surely find out.

"We'll see!" she replied, pressing on the button, and ignoring his request to walk down the stairs.

In the elevator, Katarina took off her boots and tore off the heels. Apparently, she was an athletic woman and moved her body swiftly like a cat. *Very smooth,* he thought. If she would have meowed, Evan would believe she was a real cat.

"We're going to the garage!" she said, pointing to the stairwell when they exited to the lobby.

The move from the third floor via the single elevator and then switch to the stairs to the underground garage was smooth and they already were confident that they were secure. However, the attackers had different plans.

Katarina moved fast toward the rows of parked cars, but suddenly, a side door opened and two men with official black suits and matching hats drew guns and pointed at them from a distance.

"Stop!" they yelled in Russian.

Two bullets fired and echoed loudly in the enclosed area, hitting a parked car that activated its blaring alarm system.

"After me," she cried loudly. But Evan didn't wait for a permission and shot back at the Russian agents. He missed his first round of shots.

"Shit, I knew they were already in the building."

"There's more than one team," replied Katarina and drew a small handgun that Evan missed when frisking her. He took note of that.

"The shooting from the street was to force us out of the apartment while the second team was waiting for us to show up!" she said, bending down to use the parked cars for protection.

"It makes sense!" Evan shot back as he did the same thing and, in the interim, looked for the Russian agents to see if they decided to pop up elsewhere.

The pair had no idea how many attackers were trying to track them down, but they only hoped that the gunshots would not summon the entire police force.

"Where are we going?" he asked while firing back two shots.

The second Russian bullet hit the concrete wall in front of Katarina and when Evan shot back, they took cover behind concrete columns.

"To my car, damn it!" she replied angrily.

"OK, get in, start the car. I'll hold them back!" Evan exclaimed as he shot again.

Katarina started her car, and at the same time, two other agents stormed the garage from another door that blocked their exit to the street.

"Shit!" cried Katarina. "We are trapped on both sides."

Katarina was helpless for a fraction of a second until Evan commanded, "Reverse and get out, I'll shoot at them as you drive, OK?"

She floored the pedal, reversed and turned the car at the same time, showing a racing driver's skills while the tires screeched leaving black marks of the concrete floor. She switched gears and pressed the gas pedal once again with all her might. *Removing her heels was a smart idea,* Evan thought, *she knew what to expect.* The two agents in the back started shooting sporadically and emptied their pistol cartridges into the running car. Miraculously, they didn't hit their targets.

"I'm not sure who they are, but they're a stubborn group of assholes!" she hollered, moving the steering from side to side trying to navigate the way out.

"Sooner or later we will find out!" replied Evan and pushed his torso out of the window to return fire and at the same time, he pulled out his second gun to shoot the two agents in the front of the car blocking the exit.

Katarina ignored the bullets and directed the car toward the upper level ramp and from there out to the street.

Apparently, the Russian agents prepared for this mission carefully and Evan noticed the two agents in the back getting into a car and following them out of the underground garage.

Evan concentrated on the agents in the front that were now targeting Katarina head on. His CIA and military training skills kicked in as he shot one in his pelvis and the other in his upper left shoulder, sending them both on the cold concrete floor, neutralized but not dead.

"Good shots!" Katarina cheered.

They passed the wounded agents driving at top speed up the ramp as one took his last chance to stop them. Evan shot him, this time in his chest, sending him back to heaven to meet his creator.

The car behind them tried to stay in the race, a UAZ 469 Hunter, a light, all-terrain military, Russian-made 4x4 vehicle. They were forced to compete with the *Lada Grenta*, a popular Russian compact car and by far more maneuverable in city traffic.

The security guard arm crossed the garage exit horizontally, and the parking attendant signaled them to stop.

Instead, Katarina pressed on the pedal to increase the speed, and crashed through the wooden arm and sending shards of shredded wood into the street.

Katarina made a sharp right turn onto Puteyskiy Typik Street, ignoring the attendant's screaming and cursing as he ran after her. She approached the usually heavy traffic of Zemlyanoy Val Street that loops through the center of Moscow heading north, then cut into the embassy grounds.

"Where are you heading?"

"The embassy, of course, dummy!" she replied sarcastically and stared at the back mirror.

The small vehicle showed resistance once Katarina drove it into the street without slowing down. The screeching tires left dark smoke and burned rubber in its wake. Soon after, the two found the traffic was lighter.

"They will still follow us!" She saw in her rearview mirror.

It was a crazy chase, looping through the center of Moscow with all its governmental and cultural buildings around. On the highway, they drove close to each other, moving from lane to lane, and occasionally exchanging shots and cursing at everyone around them.

After she passed the National Center of Contemporary Art, Katarina cut and turned right onto Barrikadnaya Ulitsa Street, a one-lane road that was under construction. With no choice, she drove on the other lane opposite the traffic as Evan looked back to see if the UAZ Hunter was still obnoxiously close behind them.

She carefully chose to exit the highway next to the TDC Novinsky shopping mall, to try and lose the attackers. She navigated around the Moscow Planetarium back onto the highway before she exited and headed south toward Bolshoy Devyatinsky Lane, leading them directly to the embassy's main gate.

"Thank you for the tour!" Evan tried to be funny and admired her control of the vehicle.

"Oh, you are welcome, it's free you know!"

For a moment, it looked as if they might have lost their followers, but as they approached the embassy gate on the right, Evan noticed the agents' car turning onto the same street. Fast.

Huge solid square concrete structures, each weighing a ton, were located between the street and the embassy to keep suicide car bombers at a good distance away. Two security booths were located at the main security gate, one on the left, –a smaller one–and one on the right. Beyond the electric steel arm, there stood a 12-foot tall rolling steel gate. The area was lit up by exterior light fixtures and state-of-the-art monitors recorded all activity.

The Lada stopped just inches from the gate arm. Two Marines armed with automatic weapons at the ready, approached the vehicle. Evan immediately got out of the car and showed his badge to the soldier. The second Marine aimed his M-16 automatic rifle at the Russian agent's car as it entered the site and collided with Katarina's car.

They all aimed their weapons at each other, all frozen on the spot. The Marines were a little confused and were not sure who was whom until they recognized Katarina.

Any stupid move could result in a massacre. "We want the woman," called one of the Russian agents in a heavy accent.

"Identify yourself, sir!" commanded the first Marine who approached the Russian in a couple of steps with his M-16 directed at his chest.

The marine identified Katarina and gave Evan a thumbs up, seeing his badge. He told Evan and Katarina to move beyond the arm gate and stay on the Embassy property line.

"I am a government official and she is under arrest," the agent said confidently, and showed them a badge from a distance.

"Are they real?" Evan asked the guard.

"I can get you an authentic police badge or any badge for a ruble!" He laughed.

"I can't do that, sir, she is staying here!" the marine replied politely as he raised his rifle muzzle higher with an intimidating move. The second marine was just a step behind as backup.

"Call the embassy security officer!" demanded Katarina.

Evan and Katarina stepped back slowly and passed the gate arm into the embassy domain, an open backyard, although the 12-foot tall steel gate kept them from entering the building.

The Russian pulled a badge and came closer to the guards to reinforce their identity and said, "We are the Moscow police and this woman is a murder suspect."

The Marine shook his head and said, "It's midnight, no one is authorized to extradite her to you now. You have to wait for tomorrow and return with an arrest warrant." The Russians had no control over the situation.

"Without an arrest warrant, sir. . . the woman is now protected by international law beyond this gate."

"They are lying; there was no murder," Katarina yelled back at the official in Russian and added a juicy curse only a Russian would understand.

Evan and Katarina let the Marine handle the situation but were ready to act in case the situation escalated. They didn't know how far the Russians were willing to go with their demands.

"Holy shit!" She finally gasped for air and whispered to Evan, "I think they are referring to Dima, who else would they want to kill and blame me?"

"I hope it's not true, Katarina!"

The second Marine made a phone call from the booth. After a short conversation, while they were still all holding their guns and standing firmly on the ground, a well-suited gentleman came out from the building and cautiously examined the explosive situation.

"I am the embassy security manager, put your guns down, all of you, before someone gets hurt!" he commanded.

The Russians agreed to unarm themselves.

"We must take custody of that woman!"

"You have to leave the premises, right now. You are on American sovereignty," replied the security manager.

They stood frozen in place, and exchanged angry glances. Finally, they realized that they were not authorized to escalate the situation or they'd cause a major diplomatic breakdown. The attackers slowly backed up, got back in their car and disappeared into the night without a trace.

CHAPTER 21

After an accelerated six month training program when they arrived in Israel for treatment, Jamila and Farouk were persuaded to have an additional short training session while awaiting for an assignment. This new training meant to train the couple to assimilate within Arabic-speaking communities to spy on their society for information leading to future terror planning cells so they could prevent those attacks.

Given the importance of the situation, a boost to recover information from the Muslim societies, Gad suggested to transfer the married couple/new Mossad agents to the CIA, and to be supervised by Patrick.

The CIA and FBI agreed with the idea thinking that authenticity worked well, and it was more than they had in their existing arsenal.

"It's another set of eyes and ears we don't currently have!" said Patrick excitedly.

"Think as they will. They will be outlet agents, Patrick," cautioned the director.

"It's worth the risk, chief!" Patrick replied.

"They are still foreign agents, and we should keep an eye on them as well!"

"I would take the chance and I trust the Mossad. After all, we've collaborated on many successful missions," Patrick put his best cards on the table.

"Yeah, I know about your mission in North Korea. Remember? Great job!"

"Well?"

"OK, Patrick, on one condition!"

"And it is?"

"This is confidential, just you and me. They report to you only, no one else. . .I guess I don't have to tell yo-"

"Thanks, I know my job!" Patrick cheered up and thought he scored a hard point.

Patrick arranged for Jamila and Farouk to enter the United States as refuges with their son. Indeed, they would start a new life in the United States.

Patrick planned to greet them personally and not to waste too much time before explaining their assignments.

It's more important to let them settle, take a week or two to acclimate, and then start working, he thought.

Infiltrating religious centers and tracking down information in suspicious communities who don't welcome newcomers was a challenging and dangerous task. Patrick didn't coordinate this with the FBI, and it wasn't the first time. The CIA, even though separate, didn't like any outside involvement, and assumed that new, unidentified faces with real refugee stories would grant them authenticity.

"Now you owe Israel a free F-35 squadron," yelled Marcus as he laid eyes on Patrick. He started to like this idea more and more with time, and he also liked the new thought of having the Israeli cyber department infiltrate key political figures to spy on them.

Four days later, the Mossad agents entered the United States via a CIA private jet and landed at Andrews Air Force base. Customs and immigration agents assigned for the special event greeted Jamila's family, while a translator joined them at the last minute and explained the process to them.

Patrick introduced himself as special aid to personally assist them. The couple dressed in their traditional Muslim clothing, a hijab for Jamila and an abaya over her regular clothing; and Farouk in an ankle-length white thobe and checkered black-and-white kufiyah with a black rope band on top. Jamil, their son, was an exception. He wore regular children's clothing, as he preferred to be like all the other children that surrounded him.

The personal customs and immigration process was speedy and in less than half an hour, they were in Patrick's SUV with a driver to transport them to their new home. A social worker and a landlord representative to certify them for public housing greeted them in fluent Arabic and showed them the two-bedroom unit overlooking the Potomac River in Northeast Alexandria, Virginia. The apartment was stocked with necessities, fully furnished and move-in ready. Jamila inspected the cabinets and the two bathrooms.

"This is your room Jamil!" She sounded cheery and satisfied. The child's room was sunny and bright, and the walls were painted with Disney characters, and action hero posters were taped to the inside of the door and one wall, above a small desk.

"Are there any other Muslims here?" she asked the social worker.

The social worker, a new graduate from Georgetown University, was pleasant and answered immediately.

"Oh, yes. In Virginia, we have a large population of Muslims from all over the USA. You will feel at home here, though every start is hard."

Jamila examined her young face, "Where is your accent from?"

"My parents are from Egypt. I was 10 years old when we relocated here, and I love it." She seemed genuinely positive and content. "Can we sit and go over a few things?"

"Sure, what next?" asked Jamila when Farouk and their son were in the child's room, admiring the artwork and making sure not to detract from the process.

The landlord's employee asked Jamila to sign a few certification forms for public housing vouchers and Jamila asked, "Am I signing away my life?"

"No, it's the procedure for the government to pay your rent to the landlord," the young woman explained.

The three women sat at the glass dining table hovering over forms, rules and regulations.

Patrick walked in and asked, "Everything OK, guys?"

"Perfect," they answered positively.

"Jamila," Patrick got her attention and spoke slowly so she understood. "These good ladies will take care of you, show you where to shop, and where the mosques. You and your husband will get a fixed income in cash, cell phone, and credit cards you can use for transportation. I'll be a step away from you. Call me if you need me!"

Patrick hoped that the program would work. He put his weight and reputation behind this. He didn't want to compete with the FBI on who is the best at this and actually it was not the CIA's job to spy on domestic neighborhoods, but Patrick felt ownership and therefore decided with Marcus to keep this confidential.

"Thank you, Patrick, sir!" she replied.

Patrick left the complex with mixed feelings. He just needed to hope that they will do what they were trained to do. After all, freedom is not cheap.

"Let's get out of here," he barked at the poor driver who didn't know what had just happened to Patrick. Stress, he figured, as he started the engine. "Where to?"

"My office!" he said and sank into deep thought. *How long do they need to adjust before hitting the mosques?* he asked himself. *Which major Iranian religious centers in D.C. and in Alexandria should they start with first?* His head was spinning. He realized that Jamila and Farouk would need explicit directions and daily assistance with their covert activities, and he needed to assign someone to them. *That person must be an immigrant posing as a friend or a relative who works for the agency,* he thought.

The drive was uneventful, and before Patrick knew it, they arrived at the main agency gates. Even though he was well-known to the guard, he asked for identification and validated the ID in his booth.

The gate opened up and the driver pulled up in front of the main building entry. Patrick got out and walked to Marcus' office.

"Is he in?" he asked the assistant, who gave him an affectionate stare.

"He is waiting for you!" Her voice was soft and flirty.

He opened the door and saw Marcus having a phone conversation with someone.

"Sure. . .OK, I got to hang up now. . .*ciao!*" He slammed the phone down. "Fucking asshole!"

"Who was that?" Patrick was curious.

"Frank Dabush!"

"What did he want?"

"Forget it, it's not important. . .but you know?" Marcus hesitated and frowned. "He thinks he is the President's Chief of Staff, not the vice president's, and he's barking orders at me!"

Patrick asked again, "What did he want?"

Marcus inhaled and exhaled slowly and said, "He is intervening with our investigation; he said the vice president is pushing him for results."

"Bullshit, Tom wants results but would never give us direct instructions, it just doesn't work that way!" Patrick retorted.

"Anyway, how did it go with your immigrants?" Marcus asked as he got up to stretch.

Patrick took a seat on the couch as Marcus walked to the bar and asked Patrick to join him. He poured glasses of bourbon on the rocks and handed one to Patrick and sat on the armchair next to him.

"It went pretty well!"

"We should hold the assumption that Hassan is believed to still be on U.S. soil," said Marcus, sitting comfortably.

Patrick noticed that Marcus' office had bare walls that were very boring. There was no style or personality. Everyone brought favorite photos or paintings to hang on the wall. *At least hang up the President's portrait, for God's sake*, Patrick thought. Then he paid attention to his boss and replied,

"I'll put those people to work right way, chief! Their wartorn Syria is sympathetic, at least."

"Let's hope so," concluded Marcus.

The undercover spies trained their son to forget they ever lived in Israel; they trained him never to mention it. They forbade him to speak the few words in Hebrew he learned in the Kibbutz for the sake of their mission and their personal freedom once they had completed their assignments.

The FBI suspected that Patrick might be using international spies, and questioned him whether or not he used one of their agents to do the same job. Patrick kept his silence and collaborated with the FBI without disclosing his plans. He felt they were at his discretion.

Gad, keeping the Mossad ownership on his agents, asked to keep an eye on them. "If my theory is right, perhaps someone from the inside will try to neutralize them," he said to Patrick. But he refused to arm them for self-defense. This conversation took place on the phone when Patrick was on his way to Andrews Air Force Base.

"I'll watch them. No weapons!" Patrick insisted.

"Don't forget it's a loan!" Gad reminded him.

"Don't worry, Gad. Who the hell would know that we infiltrated your agents in mosques?"

"I don't trust anyone, Patrick, and that's why I've survived all these years in this business!"

"Got you, sir, you have regards from my. . .how do you say it? *Kodkod*?" he chuckled.

They both laughed hard when Patrick repeated the Hebrew nickname code for a top commander. It meant head. Since Gad knew that Marcus didn't like him much, he often called him the "Hydra spy," referring to its many arms spread around the world. That was just an inside joke between the two.

Patrick disclosed the conversation and Marcus changed the subject.

"Also, I want to discuss the Mossad theory that they suggested to you–that the assassination was not political and was a spy ring involving a foreign country."

"A plot you mean?" Patrick said. "Everyone who shoots a President is political!" Patrick chuckled. "We need to review our idea of the Evan and Katarina assignment; something's fishy there, no doubt!" he exclaimed.

Marcus closed his eyes and rubbed his head in frustration. He got tense just thinking about the idea that something might go wrong with their internal investigation of politicians in Washington.

"We need a motive. . .Why? What are the pros and cons?" asked Marcus.

"I hope Evan and Katarina bring a clue or two. . .but do you have any ideas who might benefit from this? Should I prepare a list of people, with your permission, to spy on? I will have Katarina suggest who to add to the list, whoever she thinks might be fair to check." Patrick sighed deeply.

"If this goes public, we are dead." Marcus was skeptical of the idea to spy on Washington without the Supreme Court Justice. *If they know, the entire world will know,* he thought. He could do that on a foreign soil, like Russia, where they were investigating a Russian mole in Washington.

"We just lost our mole in Russia; they asked the Interpol for help to find him!" Marcus said.

"They do to us what we do to them?" Patrick declared.

"Well, I'm not sure what Katarina has unearthed, and the mole named 'Chameleon' that the Mossad intercepted. . .his communications might be a complete hoax!" Marcus replied.

Patrick emptied his glass and put it back on the table with a bang. "Sure, it might be, just as I think the Soldiers of Allah taking responsibility for the assassination was a hoax as well."

Marcus sighed. "If we want to survive this mess, we need permission to spy on people an-"

"No one will know." Patrick cut him off trying to convince Marcus.

". . .and permission from the defense secretary."

"And he is probably dead now somewhere in Sinai!"

"I agree that we are in an emergency, but we also need to work smart, Patrick!" Marcus groaned. "Dima Petrankov might play us with the Russians and his contacts he is working for on the side. Hopefully Evan will dig in with Katarina, find him, and bring him here!"

Marcus was still skeptical, but he shrugged it off.

"Let's go with the flow," suggested Patrick as he checked his watch. It was already noon and the bright sun sent glaring beams through the office window.

"Let's think about it, Patrick." Marcus was restless and selected his words carefully, "Katarina's assignment must be kept confidential and Evan must judge for himself what's the best for us and our country. I trust him!"

Patrick noticed his boss' stressed out body language when he clenched his teeth "Me too. After all, it was Frank Dabush himself who recommended that Evan check our Russian connections and prove that Katarina was not double crossing us."

"I haven't heard from Evan since he left," Marcus said tersely.

"He was a good agent before Rufus snapped him to serve as a bodyguard!"

Marcus took the empty glasses and placed them in the sink, then stood next to Patrick.

"You know, when you repeat a story many times it becomes true."

Patrick struggled to understand the statement. *What did his boss mean?* Then he tried his luck and shot back, "Do you mean the disinformation about the Soldiers of Allah?"

"That's exactly what I meant, someone repeating the information and feeding the media with the conspiracy to confuse the public." Marcus sat down.

"This was meant to confuse you and me, Marcus. It's just background noise." Patrick was confident and snapped his finger.

"I like the way you think, Patrick!"

Patrick appreciated the complement and felt the strong support from his boss.

"This is why we think that the entire thing is orchestrated here in Washington, a mole, right here in our agency or in the cabinet. . .not sure yet."

CHAPTER 22

Bir e-Tamadeh, Sinai Peninsula

The Army 2 plane hovered above the airfield and was instructed to drop the Marine paratroopers about half a mile southwest of the abandoned airfield where the topography was leveled without any major obstacles.

Landing with their full armament, the troops would join the survivors on the ground, hoping the President survived the accident and would save them all from the imminent upcoming insurgents' attack.

NSA satellites directed to this area found no insurgents present, but they did see ground activity. It was a dangerous mission, given the fact that there was no early intelligence data and information to share with the troops.

All they knew was that Sinai was infested with Jihadi insurgents, a deadly threat that could easily ignite another major war in the Middle East.

The Pentagon decided to parachute in the marines without consulting its regional allies–Egypt, Israel, and the Saudis. They were not concerned with the mayday communications between the President's plane and the approach control center in Riyadh.

The delayed landing of Air Force One in Riyadh was questioned by many who were connected to the same frequency. Therefore, a rushed statement was issued by the White House

Press Secretary that the airplane was forced to land for refueling and should resume its journey soon. The Pentagon knew that they couldn't keep this a secret forever. Many foreign Intelligence satellites were directed on the approximate point of Air Force One's route to find clues about the President's actual location. The Pentagon's and the CIA's control of the situation was crucial.

The F-18 fighter jets circled the airfield low and ready to respond to any aggression or threat. The pilots reported any movements on the ground and recycled their formations to keep jet fighters in the air nonstop.

The burning fuel cloud from the doomed plane rose fast, and signaled the crash location that could be seen for miles. Sure, it would attract Jihadists to the area, and they needed to be on the highest alert to fight for their lives.

After a few minutes, when no apparent danger appeared, the order to drop the paratroopers was given. Army 2, lowered its altitude to 10,000 feet and slowed down to 150 knots. Army 2 was instructed after it completed its mission to head to Israel and land at Hatzor IDF Air Force base, also known as Wing 4.

Another formation escorted Army 2 to its new heading. The Pentagon did not take any chances. They simply didn't know what they were up against. Israel offered help and were refused by the Joint Chiefs of Staff, who had taken temporary command.

It was 8:00 a.m. the following day, the day after the departure from Andrews AFB, and almost 13 hours after takeoff. Marcus Barbour was informed immediately by Vice President Tom Phillips about the grave situation the President was in. He was requested to assist the Joint Chiefs of Staff to come up with a plan to rescue the survivors from the center of one of the most hostile places on earth.

"It's no secret which airplane was shot down, and the communication is spreading like wildfire," Tom reported to Marcus. "We don't want to disturb the network of smugglers and the desert residents, most of whom just want to keep their normal way of life away from the Jihad wars everywhere," he replied grimly.

ISIS, Al Qaida, and other notorious Jihadists representing the Islamic radical factions would take this opportunity to eliminate the "Big Satan" which probably would be the biggest victory they ever dreamed of: Bring the Americans down to their knees. "They would not pass up this opportunity!" exclaimed the vice president.

Not knowing exactly who was in charge on the ground to plan the withdrawal, the vice president, now the acting President, commanded to join forces for the rescue. They were informed that the President wouldn't last long without being treated immediately in a state-of-the-art hyperbaric oxygen chamber.

Once the survivors were moved into the abandoned barracks, the medical team immediately helped the President with his symptoms. He was dizzy and had a hard time breathing. He groaned in pain with every breath, and he appeared to be suffering from chest pains.

Since Army 1 was destroyed, it was impossible to save any medical equipment and supplies, not to mention food, blankets, and pillows. Army 2 dropped those supplies off along with the troopers. The Army 2 crew emptied the aircraft of everything that would help the survivors, especially oxygen tanks to help the smoke inhalation victims. The paramedics parachuted down with the soldiers and landed safely. They were immediately directed to help with the most critical patients.

Dr. Rintler immediately inserted the oxygen tube in the President's throat to prevent his airway from swelling further and stopping his breathing. "The President's condition is grave and could go either way," whispered the physician to his colleagues.

Intensive care was a priority for the next couple of hours. Only the MV-22 Osprey aircraft that could take off vertically and fly as a regular plane was able to accomplish that mission and bring the President and a few other critical care survivors to the aircraft carrier for full treatment. Any failure to do so would result in casualties.

The Sixth Fleet was equipped with those airplanes for a quick response and two were dispatched with a medical team toward the abandoned airfield in the Sinai Peninsula. The physician did everything he could do to ensure the President would stay alive. His 50 years of experience in the medical field was certainly put to the test.

Dr. Rintler's college colleagues retired long ago but he took the President's care as a mission. "Angels are protecting the President," he said, administrating a sedative so the President could relax. As someone who had many medical emergencies during his life, the doctor knew that nature always took one path and the angels diverted to another. Now they collided as the President battled for his life.

Right after Army 2 completed the mission, it changed course and disappeared on the eastern horizon toward the rising sun to its new destination, Israel. The picture from above drew a disaster area and the backup captain reported the scene to his superiors. The healthy people helped in many ways and organized the scene, since they didn't know how long they would have to live there. A few roamed the desert around the airfield dunes to find any info about the surrounding area. Soon, the sun would heat the landscape and things would get nasty.

The critical situation was disclosed to the acting President. He dispatched his cabinet and the Pentagon to find a quick solution to bring the survivors and the soldiers back home. A couple of scud missiles were fired from North Yemen by the Houthis backed by Iran, which reached their maximum range and fell miles away–short from their intended target. That meant that insurgents had already heard the news and knew the approximate location of the troops. The company commander was concerned that this would serve as a warning, and that this would be the start. An assault on the President would spark a regional conflict or, at worst, a global war, when the Marines would have to take the bullet for the President.

Thirty-six-year-old Major Jeffrey Ahmad resembled a superhero from a Marvel movie, and was dressed in all his equipment ready for combat. He gathered his company for instruction and reminded them that their prime duty was to cover the President at all costs. He was informed via his satellite radio that two MV-22 were on their way to protect the area and keep it clear from insurgents.

Ahmad performed a fast, motivational ceremony with the troops as they shouted slogans together. At the end the Marines called *Semper Fidelis*, which meant "always loyal," before he assigned them to key strategic points around the abandoned airfield.

Using a GPS map, Ahmad and his two petty officers climbed to the highest dune nearby, on the north side of the still-burning Air Force One wreckage. They used their binoculars to discover that the airfield had four connecting access roads, outflanking the airfield from the Sadr Al Haytan highway. At the same time, they could see the exposed underground concrete hangars without the camouflaged nets which once used in the past to host the Egyptian jet fighters before the Six Days War in 1967. Now, the hangars served as shelters for the President and the other survivors awaiting the rescue troops. He knew the Osprey aircraft would be vulnerable to SAM missile attacks from the ground while on its way, making landing very dangerous without full ground and air protection. Dust and desert conditions were the plane's enemy as well.

From the aircraft carrier currently sailing the Mediterranean Sea, it should take about 30 minutes to reach the area, and Ahmad took the information under his consideration and calculated the risks of such an operation. Thoughts swirled in his head. Controlling the area for a short time was possible, however, but not for a long time. Despite the rising temperatures, his spine shivered from anticipation.

The petty officers split into two groups. Each group covered half of the area circled by the airfield. They were equipped with automatic weapons and grenade launchers, blocking the approach access roads, while Major Ahmad situated himself with a few soldiers in a strategic, high point location so they could alert the others in case of approaching insurgents or the need for additional orders. Tensions exploded among the troops. It was too quiet for a peninsula known for its many military incidents such as killing hundreds of Egyptian military personnel and worshippers in mosques each year. Within a short time, the Marines managed to cover the area.

The searing sun burned from above. It continued its lazy rise and promised no mercy as the heat and humidity rose. The survivors waited in an underground hangar, which was hospitable. In the event any additional scud missiles would be launched, they felt secure hiding in it. The major under-stood the safety of the President, that the head of state was his responsibility.

Major Ahmad communicated with Dr. Rintler periodically to check on the wounded. He also knew that in a direct attack by hundreds or perhaps thousands of insurgents, he would quickly lose the upper hand. He depended on the Sixth Fleet strike force, which stood ready to dispatch its operational landing troops when needed.

The pentagon approved the rescue operation in stages and the troops were onboard the landing carriers on their way to the Sinai coast west of Al-Arish. While en route, they waited for final approval to land on the beach.

The armament used by the Sinai Peninsula insurgents was diverse, and included anything they could smuggle in from the black market under the eyes of the Egyptian military. Most of the weapons were manufactured mainly by Iran. The Iranian regime stirred the area into a whirlpool of blood and fueled local conflicts, one against the other, and all against western countries.

Major Ahmad was an experienced combat officer who served in Afghanistan, and he personally understood the challenges involved since he was a Muslim. If he was ever caught by any of the terror groups roaming the area, he would be beheaded for cooperating with "Big Satan"—the infidels—and he had no plans to do so anytime soon.

An approaching sound of a rotor aircraft was heard in the distance and Ahmad's radio came alive.

"Major, three white pickup trucks are fast approaching from the north," the lieutenant reported.

"Thank you, lieutenant, stay tuned!" he replied as he looked through the powerful binoculars. What he saw made him tense up immediately. As two low-flying aircraft appeared from the north, the three pickup trucks on the highway were about to turn right into the long ramp leading to the airfield.

"Code red!" the lieutenant yelled, assuming the insurgents were preparing to shoot the Ospreys down.

The Pentagon intelligence viewed the Ospreys' path and reported that it was clear and authorized them to fly low. No one knew about the approaching trucks on the threshold of the airfield. At the same time, the lead pilot of the MV-22 communicated with Major Ahmad, who ordered his soldiers to light a flare to mark the President's location so they could land as close to it as possible. The two MV-22 pilots were not aware of the drama below and started their approach into the field toward the smoky target. The insurgents from the three pickup trucks got off quickly and spread into the northern dunes, which were also the paths used by the aircraft to approach the landing site. He expected an attack and prepared to defend himself.

"Hold your fire!" commanded Major Ahmad. "They do not appear to be hostile, although I'm am not sure what their intentions are!" he shouted in the radio.

"Major, I can see clearly they are equipped with RPG rocket and grenade launchers. Those could bring the aircraft down!" he yelled back.

The pilot didn't get any instructions from the ground and he tried to call Ahmad again. "Yes, you are covered, land at your own discretion, sir."

The planes landed, raising dust clouds with their extremely large, spinning rotors. Immediately after and without delay, Dr. Rintler and the crew loaded the President and the defense secretary on board the first aircraft along with three other critically injured survivors.

The second MV-22 loaded victims based on their injuries' severity. Major Ahmad was busy watching from the top of hill as the planes loaded people on board. The lieutenant called him in a panic, "Commander, about two dozen pickup trucks are quickly approaching from the same road!"

As the first two pickup trucks seemed friendly and arrived with no marks, carried no flags, and no banners, these new trucks were full of them, signaling their affiliation with their favorite terror group.

"Holy shit," roared Major Ahmad and took a deep breath. "This is a fucking war!"

It seemed as if they knew the area perfectly and they identified the first two pickup trucks as if they were siding with their enemy. Two precise RPGs blew them out of the ground, and started a major fire. The last pickup trucks from the long line got off the road, in an orchestrated plan. They took positions in front of Ahmad and surrounded the first group of unidentified insurgents with about 200 men. They were lightly equipped but had deadly intentions. Ahmad figured from the equipment in their possession that they probably all used the same smugglers.

"The situation on the ground is dangerous. Loop around low and head south first to outflank the insurgents," instructed Ahmad.

"Roger that," the lead pilot replied. The plane cautiously headed south first, then turned north and the second plane followed right behind him.

Ahmad let out a big sigh, seeing the planes moving away and toward safety.

RPG and grenade explosions sprayed the air, and marked the beginning of the attack. It looked like major combat erupting between the insurgents, with the first group of insurgents fighting the second group in heavy fire exchange.

Two anti-aircraft missiles were launched and targeted the two Ospreys.

"Scrubs 30," (slang for fly 30 feet above ground) yelled Major Ahmad to the Osprey pilots. "Two STA on your way!" he shouted louder, watching the trail of smoke that the missiles left behind.

"Jink right low!" (outmaneuver) commanded the lead pilot to Dash 2, the second aircraft pilot. Both quickly lowered their altitude and tried not to hit the ground with their enormous blades.

The two missiles approached at 600 meters per second, their radars homing in on the plane. They missed their targets by a few feet and continuing their flight east toward the mountains below.

"Bravo Zulu," the lead pilot reported for a performance well done, then added dramatically, "The President, the defense secretary and Greg Williams from the special convoy to the Middle East are on their way to H. W. (USS George H. W. Bush)" Major Ahmad sighed with relief, again knowing that his job would be a bit easier from this point on. "Roger that, good job!" he said.

The lieutenant watched the aerial episode that lasted a few seconds, and when the planes were at a safe distance, he combed the missile launch spot and reported, "We are under attack by insurgents; one unidentified group is helping us fight what appears to be an ISIS-affiliated group. Other than my company, we have about 50 survivors trapped here waiting to be evacuated."

Chapter 23

Sinai Peninsula

Major Ahmad reported directly to Tom Phillips and the Joint Chiefs of Staff an update about the situation on the ground. He also reported Dr. Rintler's grave prognosis of the President's condition as well as the status of everyone else on the ground, which got worse by the minute. It was an all-out war against time for the survivors.

"We need support, sir!" the major pleaded in a raspy voice into his satellite communication phone.

His face and nostrils were covered with dust and he realized he didn't eat or drink anything the last few hours. The events followed one after another and reminded him how valuable time was.

"Well done, major!" Tom congratulated Ahmad on evacuating the President from the gates of hell. "We are working on it, the Joint Chiefs of Staff are on the line."

"Not sure how much time we have, sir!" Ahmad was composed but his tone signaled urgency.

Ahmad evaluated his options of counterattack and knew that military aid would not come that fast. He thought that if the important people were out of danger, his troops would be like sitting ducks. Someone would calculate the risk of the abandoned troops versus a regional war with the adjacent countires.

"A few small groups started to fight each other!" he reported back. "I'm not sure who they are and what the purpose of the fight was between them."

"Major, this is General McLaughlin!"

The major recognized his top commander's voice. He continued, "Our satellites are monitoring the situation, major. There are insurgents looking as if they are fighting to protect you!" His voice was persuasive and relaxed. He tried to reassure that the army did not leave anyone behind, dead or alive.

"I see, general, but the question is if they are done fighting each other, would they turn to attack us?"

Trying to second guess the general was impossible. *It's easy to fight with a keyboard and a plasma screen, and give instructions from air conditioned rooms while the real combat fighters are the officers in the trenches,* Ahmad thought sarcastically.

"Just like you, I understand the Middle East mentality. It's all about who will be credited to annihilate you, but for the moment, let them fight, we have our troops in the Sixth Fleet ready to be deployed if necessary!" General McLaughlin said confidently. "We are debating whether we should inform our allies."

The fighting got intense when a small, unidentified Islamic group and a large group of insurgents ran from the hilltops, changed positions, and began shooting like maniacs.

"We are communicating with the Sixth Fleet commander. Stay tuned!" said the general in an authoritative tone. "We will patch you in soon!"

Tom let the general assume command and reported to him directly while he tried to secure democracy. He called the attorney general a close friend. The vice president trusted that he could navigate the legal maze on how to obtain control while the President was still alive, but couldn't lead the country under attack due to his illness.

The phone rang at 1:30 a.m. and the attorney general picked it up, feeling it might be connected to the hush-hush situation somewhere in one of the corners of the world.

The voice on the other end of the line confirmed just that when he recognized the VP's voice.

"Tom, where are you?" he asked tiredly as he tried to wake up.

"In my office at the White House. Why?"

After a short discussion, the attorney general cut Tom off in the middle of his sentence.

"OK, I got it. . .get the current security cabinet in there ASAP. . .under the 25th Constitutional Amendment the cabinet can elect you to be the 'Active President' until Rufus Barker can resume his power."

"Good, we need to make it official, plan to be here by 3:00 a.m."

"You owe me, old friend!"

"Count on it!" said the vice president, sounding exhausted.

He hung up the phone and called Frank Dabush, his Chief of Staff, who picked up immediately.

"Frank, 3:00 a.m. sharp, West Wing office, call the following people to attend an emergency meeting!" he exclaimed.

"OK, I'm ready," Frank said without understating the reason for the meeting and asked, "What should I tell them?"

"It's confidential!" he said. "Call Marcus, CIA; John Duke, NSA; Homeland Security Secretary; Josephine Lambert; and the Secretary of State, Scott Cody. Have Alex on standby for further information."

Frank pushed away the naked woman on his bed. He met her at a bar just a few hours earlier and she whined as he started to dress.

"It's fucking 1:30 a.m.," she complained, angrily.

"Dress and get out!" he growled in disdain. "C'mon, move it, now!"

Frank gave the stranger a dirty look and heard her say "Fuck you!" drunkenly before she immediately passed out.

An empty bottle of Beluga vodka on the floor was the only witness of the wild party last night. "But the party is over," he murmured to himself.

A service cart of leftover food sat next to the sleeping woman. Frank took it and slammed it into her face, but luckily for the woman, it hit the bed. He grew violent and short-tempered.

"Get dressed. I don't have much time!" he yelled, as he pulled $1,000 from his wallet.

Money talks, and it certainly did in this case. The minute the woman saw the cash, she dove for it.

"Fuck you and fuck your fucking boss," she murmured ignoring her panties on the floor.

"Take your panties with you!" He tried to hold her hand and she pulled back with a loud moan.

"Why don't you wipe your face with it, *Don Juan*," she snapped.

Frank was stunned. Next time he would choose his companions better. He laughed out loud when she slammed the door behind her.

He opened the door. "You left your panties on the floor!" he yelled at her as she disappeared down the corridor. He locked the door, then called security to make sure she was in a cab as quickly as possible.

"Fucking whore!" he whispered and smiled at the same time.

It was remarkably amazing for someone his age to still party like he did. "I'm old enough to know what I'm doing and young enough to do it twice" was Frank's motto, and he used it whenever he met a young woman at a bar.

Frank was always proud about his ability to hold a large amount of alcohol before passing out, claiming he inherited it from his heavy drinking parents, but that was not true. "If you don't drink, you can't socialize. You don't socialize, you can't mingle and so on," he learned in Washington.

The first call he made was for room service to bring up a gallon of hot black coffee, which he gulped to sober up as quickly as he could.

Close to 3:00 a.m., a few limousines popped up out of no-where and approached one by one at short intervals by the West Wing entrance at the White House. Security was given short notice of the invitees to the special emergency meeting. The vice president greeted them with a heavy, grim face, given the fact that he might end up as the next President if they didn't figure out the right next move. The limousine drivers were escorted to the press conference room and entertained by Alex and Frank after the VP's door was shut down after them.

The office was furnished with two identical light cream Victorian sofas, a simple round wooden coffee table, and wall-to-wall beige carpet. The VP's desk was situated at the end of the room with two armchairs on either side. A couple of Hudson River school style oil paintings hung behind the desk, and a portrait of George Washington also hung on the wall.

"What's up?" some asked with weary eyes as they all greeted each other with questioning looks.

Tom pointed at the credenza and then went to grab some coffee and refreshments, motioning to the guests to do the same. The window shades were pulled down to prevent anyone from spying on them.

Tom then began the meeting. "It's now 10:00 a.m. there. . .a few hours ago, the President's Air Force One was shot down by SAM missiles over the Sinai Peninsula. It crash-landed and we have some casualties. . ."

"The President?" the guests murmured in shock, not wanting to ask the most crucial question of all. Tom continued, "The President is in critical condition and is being transported via Osprey to the USS George H.W. Bush carrier in the Mediterranean Sea. Alvin Nelson, our defense secretary, is also injured from smoke inhalation but is in stable condition. Both are currently unable to assume command!"

The news shocked everyone in the room.

People asked questions about the President. "Attack by who?" they asked in unison. "How did it happen?" another asked. "Why?" snapped the last one before Tom shut them down.

"The President's condition required immediate hospitalization for smoke damage to his lungs. I spoke with his personal physician, Dr. Rintler, who urged me to transfer the President to the nearest hospital in Israel that specializes in such conditions."

Tom raised his hand. "I know. . .I hope he is in good hands as long as he's flown to Ben-Gurion University hospital in Be'er Sheva." Tom mentioned the hospital in detail as Dr. Rintler confirmed it with him an hour before.

"Why not transport him to our VA hospital in Hamburg, Germany?" asked John, the National Security Adviser.

"It's too far!" exclaimed the others.

"Besides, the Israelis are the best at these sorts of injuries from the vast experience with constant wars. I trust them!" Tom said.

Tom cut off the chatter again. "Our agenda is to one, protect the President on his way to Israel; two, activate Amendment 25 of the Constitution; three, select a military response to the attack of surface to surface scud missiles from Yemen; and four, rescue the company left behind with the remaining of Air Force One survivors and destroy the remaining airplane fuselage and its secret components."

The attorney general took the helm for a moment and announced, "Gentlemen, it's obvious that the President can't operate and make critical decisions on what the vice president mentioned briefly. The President needs to be replaced until he recovers fully."

Tom examined the faces and checked if the info sank deep into their awareness.

"We are under attack," the attorney general continued. "I have the liberty to ask this forum to vote to activate the amendment under emergency to elect Tom as acting President."

"Who are we fighting?" asked Scott Cody, Secretary of State.

"It's a linear war. We have no clue!" Tom answered.

"We are examining a few avenues. First, the Iranian Revolutionary Guards, a new group called Soldiers of Allah," said John Duke the NSA director and Marcus on behalf of the CIA concurred.

"Let's vote!" called Tom and the forum raised their hands.

"All yeas, no nays!" declared the attorney general.

"Good luck, Tom!" said one.

"We are here if you need help!" claimed another.

"Don't hesitant to ask for help," they all concurred and wished Tom luck in his new role.

Tom didn't anticipate that in such a short time after his inauguration that he would have the country's future on his shoulders. He was still horrified from the assassination attempt on inauguration day when he was sworn-in under attack. He trusted Frank Dabush to be his loyal helper, to keep him focused.

"Gentleman, this meeting, the President's condition and his location must be kept confidential," said the acting President as they prepared to leave his office. As the new day started, bright lightning broke through the clouds, following loud thunder. Then the rain came.

"I hope this storm will clear my storm away," Tom mumbled and closed his office door after the forum.

Chapter 24

Alexandria, Virginia

A couple of days after they entered the United States, Jamila and her family joined as full privileged members in the Iranian religious center. Their son started preschool at the facility, letting Farouk and Jamila spy on their own countrymen without any guilt. They would not be considered good Samaritans.

Hassan hoped that the Mosque will shelter him and guide him since he had no clue what to do next.

He changed his mind, preventing himself from not attending mosques, but it had been three months since he visited one and he was sure that some of them were subject to repeated visits from federal agents. Perhaps it was safer now.

He entered the building and lingered in the lobby, breathing heavily and feeling strange, unattached.

"Shit, I don't feel good," he mumbled to himself and pressed the door chime. The pressure on him was enormous.

The door opened, and the bearded cleric greeted him with a shiny, round face, and a big fake smile.

After a short glance, he realized that the man in front of him might be a fellow countryman and asked, "What can I do for you, my brother?"

Hassan liked the softness of his voice and got a little more comfortable despite the fake smile on his face.

"My name is Waleed Shahatat." He hesitated as he quickly gave the name of his childhood friend.

"Pleased to meet you. If you need help, Waleed, you are in the right place." They shook hands and tapped with their right hand on their chest for friendship, a brotherhood welcome. They walked past the hall into the building and right into the Imam's office, and Hassan sat on the same seat Evan sat on a few weeks before.

The Imam examined Hassan's face. The young student looked a bit dazed and confused, or at the very worst like someone who was having a miserable day; definitely not a person who would assassinate a sparrow, much less a President.

"Are you feeling alright?" asked the Imam with compassion in his voice. Hassan nodded his head and looked at the Imam as if he was silently pleading for help. The Imam immediately was aware who Hassan was, based on the description and information Evan Harris left with him on his visit.

"Tell me you didn't do it!" the Imam said skeptically as he raised his eyebrows.

Hassan shook his head and said softly, "No, I didn't. I was framed, suckered into it, I have no idea how. One thing led to another, and every step I took, I was deeper into this shit!" His face was gloomy.

Evan's business card was still in the Imam's drawer and he pulled it out, then changed his mind and decided to put it back, murmured, "This can wait."

"Waleed is not your real name, isn't that right, Hassan?"

Hassan was not surprised that he'd been recognized and nodded his head "yes."

"I am Imam Afshin Shiraz," the elder said. "What is it exactly you want me to do? In a place like this, we must be careful and honest, you understand?" He paused and sighed loudly.

Hassan was sitting tensely, but his shoulder pulled forward with emotional reaction to what the Imam said.

"We are not allowed to help or shelter anyone against the law, especially fugitives. The entire world is looking for you. The authorities have visited and asked many questions. I am sure they will do the same in every mosque in the country; they have the resources, Hassan. We are protected under the constitution's privacy protection act, but in your case it's against the law."

The Imam felt mercy for the troubled young man who was drowning in the murky swamp of terror organizations, their manipulations, and their exploitation.

Hassan was silent, listening, and holding his head with both hands.

"What options do I have? I have nowhere else to go!" he cried.

He put his backpack down and pulled his gun out from behind his back.

The Imam and the cleric tensed silently as they watched Hassan remove the bullets from his revolver and put them on the table.

"You already know that I am the one they are looking for," he said with a trembling voice. "I am nothing but a victim," he paused. "It's a tight ring of terror, bigger than life. I have no control in it. They marked me. I'll do what you need me to do. I'll leave it up to you!" Hassan hoped his honest plea would help him.

The Imam was not convinced, and was not sure how Hassan would react with a gun in his possession.

"Did you kill the three people?" the Imam asked.

"It was self-defense!" Hassan cried.

"From FBI reports, it was a very professional self-defense, my son."

The Imam pulled Evan's business card out again and called the number. The phone rang, and the answering machine came on, so the Imam hung up. It was a major decision to make, *should he call the police? Should he call the FBI? Should he be loyal to the country that gave him asylum? Or should he be loyal to his religious followers who probably thought the right thing to do would be to help Hassan?*

Then, the Imam felt a strong belonging to his own race and religion. He signaled his cleric to keep the whole thing confidential.

"We can help you with legal advice," the Imam reassured Hassan.

"You mean lawyers?" Hassan tensed.

"We have a new refugee family that just came from Syria. They are nice people. I will ask them to host you for a couple of days until we find out the best way to help you, but in the end you will have to turn yourself into the FBI, but at least you'll protected by the law."

The Imam used his charm. He knew better than to dance in two parties at once. Meanwhile, Hassan thought for a moment then shook his head.

"Who are they. . .how can I trust them?" he asked, disturbed.

"This is the best advice I can give you so far. The outcome depends on your next steps, as long as you don't have any issues with the law, you will be safe," the Imam said.

Hassan reluctantly agreed. His chest felt heavy, and he was not sure how to feel about the Imam's advice. *The Imam might benefit somehow from turning me in*, he thought.

"I see that you made up your mind," concluded the Imam, paving his way to the solution.

He is pressuring me, Hassan thought. The cooperation with the FBI could help and might be more important to the mosque.

"Fuck, yeah!" Hassan growled in frustration and slammed the table with tears in his eyes.

The Imam wanted to prevent hate crimes against his mosque, and knew how to navigate between his feelings towards a young Muslim fellow, and his loyalty to the authorities. He did what he did, but not without remorse.

The Imam picked up the phone and dialed a short intercom number and asked in Farsi, "Is Jamila there?"

An unidentified voice on the phone asked him to hold.

A new woman's voice emerged on the intercom speaker, "The new family?"

"Yes."

"She will be here in an hour to pick up her son, what should I tell her?"

"Tell her to come and see me!" he replied as he met Hassan's gaze.

The weapon was still lying on the table and they sat in silence, watching each other, and asking themselves unanswered questions.

"Tell me your story," the Imam finally broke the silence, "The truth!"

Hassan started to talk quickly without blinking. When he began talking about the gray van and the murder of the girl from District Heights, the Imam could not keep quiet and jumped right in.

"There were videos released by the FBI that showed you raping the girl and killing her, so how could you deny it?" The Imam's face grew red as he leaned closer to Hassan.

"I had a gun to my head!" Hassan yelled.

"Did you kill that girl?" the Imam pressed.

"No, I didn't, they did!"

"Who are they?"

"Iranian agents, it was all orchestrated and. . ."

"It's a no-win situation!" he stopped Hassan.

"I am trapped, don't you see that?"

"Yes, you are in deep trouble, my brother, and we can't hide you," the cleric stated and promised to himself to discuss this with the Imam privately.

"Look, Hassan, you will be safe with Jamila," promised the Imam.

"Immigrants from Syria just got here today," added the cleric.

"Staying here you will put the entire community in danger!"

Hassan stood up, and prepared to leave the room.

"I'll leave then," he said defiantly and went to the door.

At that moment, the door opened, and an Islamic woman entered and looked up at the Imam.

"Are you looking for me?" she asked curiously.

A minute later, Farouk joined her. Both froze in their places.

Chapter 25

Washington D.C., White House

The day after the President's departure, he fought for his life in the blazing hot weather in Sinai while the acting President ordered Frank Dabush, his Chief of Staff, to call for an emergency meeting. The National Security adviser, John Duke; the Pentagon top brass chief of naval operations, Admiral John Wilcox (known as 'Skinny'); and the CIA director, Marcus; with Patrick, his deputy, assembled in the Roosevelt room for an emergency meeting regarding the situation on how to handle the rescue operation of the trapped survivors in Sinai. Army General McLaughlin, known as 'Mackey' joined via video conferencing. Secretary of State Cody joined a few minutes later, entering the room panting and drying his head from the rain.

It was late at night with drizzling rain that increased the melancholy mood of the town. The White House was very tense and Tom Phillips tried to keep the team focused and cohesive. The cabinet members were used to reporting in upon request to any emergency call by the active President.

The foggy situation and the deluge of information landed on their desks and hit them without warning. It needed to be scrutinized to give clear instructions to the Navy and the ground forces.

"So, this is the situation," Tom Phillips said at the end of his briefing as he looked at the grim faces sitting around the long mahogany conference table.

The Roosevelt room, next to the Oval Office in the West Wing, was gloomy despite the ambient feeling the interior designer tried to achieve with a false skylight in a windowless space. A painting of Theodore Roosevelt riding a horse hung above the fireplace.

"The Sixth Fleet is ready!" reported Admiral Wilcox as he shoved an unlit cigarette into his wide mouth.

"Are we trying to gain control on the ground?" asked General McLaughlin. "We—"

"No. . .we are looking to evacuate Major Ahmad and his troops," Tom said. "Not looking for a full-blown war!"

"Exactly," concurred General McLaughlin.

"Any intervention, sabotage, or hacking from any foreign nation?" asked Secretary Cody.

"Not that we know of, other than a lot of misinformation out there. We are monitoring our satellites, which revealed some movement in the Sinai Peninsula, mainly small groups," answered the NSA director as she looked at her laptop for live streaming information.

"What do you recommend? I mean to bring them all home. We don't have too much time!" Tom shot back as he tried to get his top military brass to react.

"First, we need to make sure the superpowers know that we are not asking to start a war in the Middle East, secondly we need to inform Egypt and the rest of the surrounding Middle East countries that this is a rescue operation and that they need to stay out of our way." Secretary of State Cody was more concerned about the international state of mind and diplomatic chaos to untangle it and keep the world calm.

"Forget it, Mr. Secretary!" scolded General McLaughlin. "If you want to rescue and evacuate our people just do it, ask no one permission, and just send our military to act!"

"Agreed!" confirmed Admiral Wilcox. "Take an example of the Israeli raid on Entebbe, Uganda; they operated in silence, swift, and daring, before anyone knew who the attackers were, their C-130 was full of hostages and already back in Israel!"

"Gaining quick control over the situation will prevent other superpowers from taking advantage. We must act fast, I agree, but is our military ready?" asked Tom Phillips. "I don't want more casualties!"

"Look, I understand we are vulnerable, and our troops have their backs to the wall, but," Cody didn't complete his sentence as Admiral Wilcox interrupted him.

"We are not vulnerable, sir, we have the largest military power in the world, and you are the active President. It's your call to activate us to act or not!" stated Admiral Wilcox. Then in an act of arrogance, Admiral Wilcox moved his cigarette to the other side of his mouth and returned a dirty look directed at the Secretary of State.

"I hear you, admiral," replied Tom vaguely. "This is not Uganda, and the hostages are not Israelis. You cannot draw a parallel line here, since the news that we might send the entire Sixth Fleet is real, while no one believed the Israelis would make the 3,000-mile flight."

Tom shrugged and let out a silent moan. His stomach muscles tensed and he tried to hide his discomfort.

"Are you all right?" asked Cody, concerned. The rest glanced in silence.

"Yeah, I am OK, just a sharp pain in my lower back but it's gone now. Go ahead, gentlemen."

"Sorry, sir, for your discomfort, however, if the secretary of defense was here, we would wrap up this plan in no time," General McLaughlin insisted, aiming his statement at Cody, who rolled his eyes, while Wilcox was dying to light his cigarette.

"Yes, but right now he isn't here, and both of us are able to make rational decisions, so as of now, I temporarily take the defense secretary role as well to make as quick a decision as we can!" scolded Tom and frowned.

"With both the President and the defense secretary in an Israeli hospital, it's easier to plan for the rescue of the remaining troops and survivors," replied General McLaughlin, ignoring Tom Phillips' discomfort although he sympathized with him.

The tension in the room was palpable. For a moment everyone sank into their own thoughts. Tom in his first major military role thought that he had to make them create a reasonable and responsible action plan. The key was to work together, and he scolded his brass.

"Gentleman!" he emphasized. "Each one of us has an opinion, we should unify our front. Yes, Marcus?" He pointed at his CIA director.

"True, not minimizing the survivors' and the troops' lives, both the President and the defense secretary are in Israel in the same hospital wing for treatment of their critical conditions, and the hospital is heavily guarded," confirmed Marcus.

"It needs to be kept out of public," Patrick said confidently. "We tried to keep the entire crash landing confidential, but I am sure many intelligence satellites confirmed it," he added, concerned.

"OK, if the plan is to go in, then what? How long will it take to come up with a reasonable plan with no casualties?" Tom asked.

The general and the admiral stared at each other and murmured a few words between themselves, then General McLaughlin lolled his head forward slightly. "Let's give it a shot before I fall asleep," McLaughlin said with confidence, "Three days!"

Wilcox nodded his head, even though he knew the active President would reject the plan from the get-go.

"Three days?" Tom was surprised. "By that time, we will have World War III, and you guys right now are contradicting yourselves. In three days, the entire world will be out there chopping each other to pieces to be the first to crucify us. . .where is the 'silent, swift, and daring' crap, like the Israelis you guys just told me about?" Tom moaned again and tightened his lips.

"Understand, it's a very complicated mission given the fact that they are surrounded by fanatic Jihadists from all over the Middle East—" McLaughlin was rudely cut off by Tom.

"You have three hours to come up with your recommended mission plan. Plan and advise carefully, I will not veto any reasonable plan, I understand the cost and that we might endure a few casualties. General, we are at war without waging one, is that clear?!" Tom concluded.

Silence settled in the room. Everyone was staring at their iPhones, going over emails, and messages they had ignored during the meeting even though half of Washington was asleep.

"I just received a text that SSM fired toward our survivors, they exploded nearby, probably they were launched from Yemen," said Marcus, reading the report he got from his CIA agents.

"Someone is spreading the news, you see?" claimed Tom decisively.

"How do they already know it's from Yemen?" asked Cody.

"The Houthis rebels from Yemen, the only ones who might dare to attack us, sir, they are Iran's proxy, fighting the Sunnis in Saudi Arabia," added Marcus.

"Where is the fire? You will see Iran traces, never missing a good party in the Middle East, perhaps they stirred the entire assassination attempt, I'm wondering if Donovan, the assassination inquiry chairman, considered this venue," Tom was anxious as he wondered if he should retaliate, but not before having Saudi Arabia confirm that missiles were launched from Yemen.

"We'll know in 10 years," snarled Cody, apparently, he didn't have a good reference from Saudi Arabia.

"For the first step, sir, I'll call the Navy to order the Sixth Fleet to land troops into Sinai and create a beachhead as defined by the U.S. FM 100–5, Operations protocols. The operation would be seizing and holding the beachhead to gain access into the peninsula until other military forces from the Army or Navy could join in." Wilcox finally got the courage to start the military action plan and put his wet, chewed-on cigarette on the table.

"How long should it take if decided?" encouraged Tom to keep going.

"Two hours from your command to engage!" Wilcox threw the ball back to the active President's court.

"We are not equipped to rush 150 people with the equipment you have on board your Sixth Fleet!" objected General McLaughlin. "We may ask the Israelis to send a few C-130s, which are more appropriate then the Ospreys we have available now."

"Like the Entebbe raid?" scoffed Tom again and shook his head as a negative gesture. "Can't we be more original?"

"No, we can't involve our allies. Doing so will cause a negative reaction among the Muslim world, especially Egypt, and that obviously will spark a war that will suck us all in."

" 'A few C-130s' you mentioned are Israel's entire squadron," laughed Patrick who knew them from his close friendship with his colleagues overseas. "Can we fly ours from Hamburg?"

"Understood! But Hamburg is a few hours away and the Ospreys are right there in the middle of the conflict," Admiral Wilcox replied. "I am trying to think outside the box."

"My agency with the intelligence officers onboard the fleet will immediately intercept hostile communication lines using our entire gamut of equipment and redirect our spy satellites," Marcus explained. Patrick nodded his head in agreement and added, "We should start a cyber-attack with all who might electronically interfere with our operation!"

"Good thinking, Patrick!" Tom exclaimed.

"At the same time, we will prepare our Super Hornet jet fighter squadrons to destroy the missiles launched in Yemen once they've been confirmed." added Admiral Wilcox.

"We will provide you all the target information via satellite imaging," Marcus said, "and of course, will confirm it's the Houthis."

"We need the current position since they are a moving target of motorized launchers," growled the admiral, igniting a small feud.

"We know our job, admiral, stick to yours, we know they might be bombed!" Marcus scolded.

"Sorry, I didn't mean to be sarcastic, Marcus!"

"It's OK, we are all tense and looking to get this done!" Marcus replied.

"Do you have the equipment to bring the boys home?" asked Tom and directed it to the admiral.

218 • WILLIE HIRSH

"We have a Marine squadron of CV-22s, Ospreys on board the H.W., and suggest navigating at dark," McLaughlin responded.

"How many sorties you need?" asked Tom.

"If you remember we had a similar rescue operation in South Sudan and the planes were hit heavily and returned with severe damage, but we got back home," McLaughlin replied, but Tom was impatient, and the general was fast to complete his theory.

"Twenty-four troops and thirty-two civilians man two aircrafts for the survivors and five aircrafts for the troops, and we have on board only six of them," McLaughlin analyzed.

"That means that one aircraft will have to return, and the last troops left on the ground will be vulnerable." Admiral Wilcox did the calculations. "Well, we just need to bring one aircraft to the beachhead and return right away to save time."

"That make sense," Tom concurred.

"We should start immediately to interfere with any Jihadists approaching the area, and destroy bridges, roads, supply facilities, and command centers, but not necessarily in that order," Admiral Wilcox continued.

"So, we will have a plan in twenty minutes!" Tom cheered up after analyzing the small "think tank" he assembled. He made his first major decision as an active President and nodded his head, feeling victorious.

He stretched his arms forward and declared in a simple word pointing his finger to an imaginary point on the wall mimicking captain James T. Kirk from the fictional *Star Trek* franchise. "Engage!"

CHAPTER 26

Sinai Peninsula

On the other side of the planet, Major Ahmad and his Marines counter-attacked the few Jihadists who could not wait to regroup with their allied tribes to better their chances to annihilate the Americans–'their wet dream' as Major Ahmad used to say.

It was a race among the Jihad groups, a race about who would be the first to credit themselves with the destruction of the American infidels.

General McLaughlin wasted no time. He communicated the plan immediately to his officers and personally discussed the rescue plan with Major Ahmad.

"Hold on until dark; we are landing our task force on the ground there. Prepare a safe landing site with goosenecks at 0900 your time zone."

"It's eleven hours!" thundered Ahmad.

"Yes, eleven hours," confirmed the admiral. "We will provide you with umbrella protection in the meantime. Major, our jet fighters will patrol the skies 24/7 to eliminate threats starting in thirty minutes. Use our standard communication frequency."

"Roger that! Out!"

Tom, without allowing his sudden health issues to interfere as the acting President, controlled the operation as the commander-in-chief live from the situation room. He didn't permit the smallest detail unchecked or unturned and didn't allow the background noise to distract him.

Frank Dabush was there to assist his boss with all his requests, but Tom kept everyone not in the "think tank" out of the military operation plans for now.

Tom was advised by his top brass that in modern warfare, an invasion like the one in the Sinai Peninsula was called 'linear warfare' and would be performed by unidentifiable forces, without uniforms, flags, decals, or notice.

"No!" Tom thundered over the idea and coughed, grimacing. "America will not operate like thieves! I'll advise the Egyptians only after a successful beachhead landing is completed."

"Agreed," Admiral Wilcox concurred. "The Egyptian government has no control of the insurgents in Sinai anyway."

The fleet planned to launch an attack, using precision airstrikes, launching cruise missiles, or drones as needed to protect the beachhead area, the stranded survivors, and the Marines.

The chief of naval operations promised everyone that the military knew how to turn the wheels and get the Americans out of there safely, and as soon as possible. But in his heart, he prepared for the long haul, unless he would be allowed to have the Sixth Fleet invade the peninsula. He assumed that this would not happen without the Egyptian government approving it first. But politics do not blend well with military operations. Soldiers want a quick victory and prefer the politicians clean up the mess afterwards.

He remembered as a young high school boy the humiliation of the American hostages in Teheran, and after that he volunteered and joined the military, just to make sure that America never would kneel to terrorists, again.

The nonstop fighter jets formations buzzing around the doomed airfield had permission to shoot anyone they identified as a threat, no questions asked. Rules of engagement were put on hold and were left at the discretion of the soldiers in the battleground.

The assumption the generals agreed to was that nighttime would be the most dangerous time. The fanatic insurgents would try to sneak in through the cover of the night into the underground shelter to attack the survivors.

The major and his officers prayed that the Pentagon knew how to evaluate the ground conditions. The Navy had never been in such a rough situation before. Ahmad hoped that everyone learned the results of operation 'Eagle Claw' performed by the Delta Force when two Helos collided trying to rescue the American hostages in Iran. *At least we performed well in evacuating the President,* Ahmad thought.

"Task Force 61 of the Mediterranean Amphibious Ready Group was put on alert," announced the Admiral.

The task force consisted of three amphibious ships with their landing crafts, and the Marine ground forces could move ashore by sea and air in amphibious assault crafts for an emergency evacuation mission on short notice. Even before the order to land on shore, the ships were ordered to close the gap to the shore closer to El-Arish, a town on the north shore of the Sinai Peninsula.

At first, the Pentagon issued the command to destroy the Houthis missile launchers in Yemen with aid from allied intelligence agencies. Then Tom Phillips changed his mind in order not to accelerate the brewing conflict. Satellites were diverted to the area to spy of activities. Unfortunately, most foreign intelligence satellites were also diverted.

The precise beachhead point was chosen fastidiously to be five miles southwest of El-Arish, a secluded, flat area. After hearing the troop 'invasion theory,' and protocols from the Chief of Naval operations, it was in the military's hands to execute while Tom watched all the details from the situation room in real time.

"I wonder how the Egyptians will react once they know we landed on their turf?" Cody wondered.

"I am sure they know our intentions, there is a full-waged war going on just under their noses. It's a mess down there!" grumbled Marcus Barbour, the CIA chief.

Patrick chuckled, "It's naïve to think the world is not watching us. Let them have it!"

"Granted, let's leave politics for later, it will be my responsibility to deal with the political outcome," said Tom and closed his eyes for a brief moment due to another stomach spasm. He opened his eyes and saw the Sixth Fleet's rear admiral's grim image on the large video screen.

"Sir, Rear Admiral Lansley online!" Patrick reminded Tom and he nodded.

"Oh, good morning rear admiral!" Tom called, sounding cheerful despite his condition.

Rear Admiral Art Lansley, close to his sixth decade with forty years on Navy ships, changed to a polite smile and greeted the cabinet with, "Good Morning."

It was 5:00 a.m. D.C. time, and noon in the Sinai peninsula.

"We see a lot of activity on the ground, sir!" the rear admiral stated. "We are ready with the operation to land in El-Arish. It will be a miracle to be able get them all out alive," he said gravely.

"Don't give me this negativity, rear admiral, we are deep in this shit now. We need to get in and out ASAP before everyone wakes up!" Tom thundered and coughed slightly, gasping for air. "Make it happen!" he growled and curled his lips.

Marcus was sure that some terror states might participate and finance this operation behind a curtain of deception. *Then time becomes the most important commodity,* he thought. Tom was right to scold the rear admiral for his lack of motivation. For the enemy, it was a religious mission, and they didn't care if they had to die for it–they were educated from birth to give their lives to be a Shahid.

We just need to kill them just as they become radicalized, thought Tom and replied to the rear admiral, "If the flight to carry the President with an Osprey worked, it will work with our survivors!" Tom scolded the fleet commander and the rear admiral was fast to answer.

"It was before anyone could be organized; It was risky but the condition of the President, based on his physician's assessment, well-deserved the risk. End results–we're good but the situation on the ground is much different now. I would prefer a C-130 transport there," he claimed. "Our communication with the troops is in trouble!"

Admiral Wilcox nodded his head and stared at the screen, seeing his fleet commander helpless as Marcus intervened.

"We have our five-satellite MUOS constellation in orbit," stated Marcus.

"Clarify; what do you mean with your statement?" asked Tom, signaling that he was awake and paying attention.

"These have global tactical satellite communications capability, which are designed to work like a cell phone network in space. It's secure, high-speed communication for our troops around the world," added Marcus. He was proud of his knowledge of the systems to explain them before someone else could jump in to explain it in better details. "This helps us communicate with ground forces at all times." He had to put the punch line all the way to the end.

"OK, communication is important, what is the rescue plan?" asked Tom again. "The rear admiral is looking for answers!"

"Our nearest C-130 is in Hamburg!" said Marcus, blandly repeating what everyone already knew.

John Duke, the NSA advisor, cut in and added his two cents, "Before we used 'beyond line of sight' capability to communicate mission data using a high-speed Internet system," he said in a monotone voice that drove Tom crazy.

"Not sure what you are talking about, John? We need to transport 170 people in one shot! Let's discuss this on a smoke break and get back in five. Looks like the admiral and general need their fix," said Tom with a hoarse voice to ease the tension in the room. Everyone chuckled.

They went to the West Wing dining room next to the Roosevelt room. Tom looked through the bullet-proof windows into the Capitol's empty streets at this early morning hour and wondered how the area would look in the next few days if something went wrong with this little war he was running. He trusted his top brass with limited warranty. *Always ask questions,* he used to say. *Sometimes ask the same question again in a different way; one of the answers will be the correct one, pick and choose and act.*

Puffing smoke rings in the air, they kept discussing the situation and then got back to the meeting room where the rear admiral was still on the screen.

"I see you had a smoke break yourself, rear admiral," said Marcus.

"It was an opportunity, sir!"

"Battlefields have become even more challenging and the war games more complex. Each soldier is the general on the ground and he needs to know what to expect beyond the next hill, the next target, where the enemy forces are trenched, and where friendly forces are positioned. Reliable lines of communication that provide data and voice communication could keep everyone on par, on the same page, and prevent combat error such as a squadron attacking its own forces on the ground due to lack of identity," the fleet commander advised.

"As we all just discussed and agreed, due to time constraints, we need to use the Ospreys tonight," decided Tom.

"The plan is simple; the Ospreys will land on the agreed point with extra fuel, medical supplies, food and water. The beachhead must be established and secured first; survivors will be flown from the airfield to the beachhead to minimize the waiting time between sorties. Seriously injured people will be flown to Israeli hospitals and the less injured will be treated on the way by our paramedics and fleet physicians. 'Dark flight,' no navigation lights. Be careful. Good luck!" The admiral took a deep breath.

"I give my full consent," Tom replied with a thumbs up, simply without intention to elaborate on the matter. "Wake me up in couple of hours; I must sleep!"

CHAPTER 27

At the present time, without any connection to the events that unfolded over the last couple of days, the USS Ross, a Sixth Fleet ship, docked in the Israeli port of Ashdod to assist with logistics. The issue was that this rescue operation must be done on the same night, and the ship was not dispatched to assist yet.

South of Tel-Aviv, about an hour's drive away, was another struggle–to save the President's life. The secretary of defense was in a stable condition and breathing on his own. He looked like he was bitten up and bore light scratches on his face and his left arm was in a cast, but he was aware of his surroundings.

The President was connected to a breathing machine under anesthesia. His lungs would eventually fully heal with medication and inhalers that he'd have to take for the rest of his life. The smoke damage to his lungs scarred them permanently and he would always be short of breath as a result. He would have to quit his two-pack-a-day smoking habit if he wanted to live, and only time would tell if surgery might have to be performed in the event the President lost his voice. It was early in the evening before the scheduled beachhead landing on El-Arish in the next couple of hours.

Tom Phillips decided—along with the President's family— to bring the President back to the United States for treatment once he was in stable condition. Once he left the hospital, he would need follow-up care and return immediately to the emergency department if they felt that his condition worsened after his discharge from the Israeli hospital.

Dan Eyal informed his boss, the head of the Mossad, to arrange all the necessary procedures to accept any injured survivors from Air Force One or the military operation planned for tonight, just like they did when Israel prepared for war.

The Israeli prime minister was informed through his secretary of defense of the upcoming event. He prepared his Army, the IDF, for a military strike in the event the operation escalated and Arab countries mistook the rescue operation for a new joint attack by the U.S. and Israel. The communication was encrypted on their private lines.

"I didn't get an official request!" said the PM. "Don't forget everyone will think that we are landing on an Egyptian sovereignty without permission while you put the IDF on war alert."

The phone woke up Tom Phillips from a deep sleep less than an hour after he went to bed. "Mr. Vice President, it's the Israeli premier on the line!"

"Damn," he growled, trying to clear his head from the fuzziness and drank the glass of water always kept on his night table. "Let him wait," he murmured.

Tom finally picked up the phone with a lethargic hand, and overheard some loud discussion and concern that the Middle East was on fire.

"Look, I want to help the Americans, but I must clear this with President Batsisti; he will understand," the premier said loud and clear. "He might think we are together on this and cancel the peace treaty under pressure of the Arab League of Nations and his citizens!"

Tom heard what he heard and was not in a mood to be lectured by anyone with only two hours of sleep the last day.

"This is not a case to discuss in advance."

"Tom, would you allow someone to invade California without permission?"

"If you want to help, can you communicate with Batsisti?"

"OK, as long as you are OK with that ill will, just brief me with the plan."

Thirty minutes later, all leaders were on the same page and their armies were on standby.

Immediately, Gad called Patrick and Marcus. "My PM spoke to your VP a moment ago and you are clear."

At 9:00 p.m. local time, the Sixth Fleet was on the move, and launched the force to land on the beach. Six Ospreys landed on the beach waiting for a signal from Major Ahmad preparing the goosenecks on the runway for safe landing.

At the proper time, a formation of F-18 Fighter jets lit the sky with flares. The Ospreys took off and landed one after the other, with soldiers loading the civilian survivors first.

"Open your eyes lieutenant!" Major Ahmad instructed on the radio. "It's too quiet!"

"Roger, Major. We see movement and not sure what's going on!" his metallic voice was heard clear and confident.

"What movement, lieutenant?"

"The two groups fought against each other–there's new talking!"

"Shit, that's not good. We need to get out of here."

The Ospreys landed without navigational lights in total darkness. A marine major general with a perfectly ironed desert camouflage uniform jumped from the first craft, dusted himself off and coughed lightly.

Major Ahmad approached the craft and saw the marine general straighten up and salute. Apparently, he was the squadron commander and a veteran pilot.

"Major Ahmad, the commanding officer, sir!"

"Good evening, major, what's the situation?" he asked with a dry voice as it was not clear to him, then he noticed the survivors emerging from the dark, some supported with makeshift crutches limping to the crafts and others supported by the flight crews.

"Turn off the blades' tip lighting!" he continued as the marine pilot signaled to that and asked the rest to follow up.

"That better?"

"Amazingly the insurgents are not firing at us, we had fights here all day, the blades could mark our position, sir."

Noise of jet aircraft hovering above created an illusion of comfort and pride. "Perhaps that helps," the pilot said.

"We have about seventy survivors; some need medical attention and one hundred Marine troops on the ground."

"How many troops?"

"One hundred."

"Copy!"

Ahmad cleared the situation as the survivors moved swiftly under the huge rotors whirling above.

Major Ahmad kept the lieutenant and chose the most skilled marines to act as the rear guard for the force to take off and wait for their evacuation with the next flight as planned. "I need the best men with me," Major Ahmad said, watching the planes take off and disappear in the darkness.

"It will be a very challenging hour!" replied the marine sergeant next to him, a 22-year-old from Kansas.

"We have to hold a h-. . .get down!" Ahmad screamed when he heard a familiar whistle sound.

"Forty mike-mike," yelled the sergeant (Forty mm grenade).

The first grenade exploded a mere twenty feet from them and they dropped to the asphalt like a bag of sand.

"Take shelter, stay together," he screamed as a deluge of bullets were sprayed by automatic weapons.

"It's coming from there," the first lieutenant said and pointed to a certain direction.

"Damn this sand, unbelievable," groaned the sergeant next to Ahmad and the lieutenant.

"We are not the blue noses, sergeant!" said Ahmad.

"What's that?" asked the sergeant and his eyes searching for the next surprise. He was tense since it was his first combat operation, unlike his officers who already served in Afghanistan and got involved in fighting insurgents. They stayed calm somehow.

"Blue noses, our buddies who served above the Arctic Circle."

"Yeah, good time to joke, major."

"The fucking goosenecks are now a problem!" stated the major and called on the communication for the jet fighters hovering above to destroy the target and protect the team stayed behind.

"RPG over there!" yelled the lieutenant. "Mayday, we are under attack here!" called the major.

The lieutenant grabbed the grenade launcher from his sergeant and aimed at the point he mentioned and pulled the trigger.

They exchanged fire with insurgents situated on one of the hills overlooking the airfield. Their images were clear on the horizon line, despite the darkness.

"Do you see them, lieutenant?"

"Yes, clearly, lacking one-o'-one in military school."

"Bold Eagle Leader, insurgents on the north hill half a mile from us, attacking!" Major Ahmad exclaimed.

"Copy, Bravo Foxtrot, target on site, Bold Eagle Leader."

"Bold Eagle Leader, we are engaging the attacker, we will be in distance to point the area with our laser beams," he responded.

Jets sounded maneuvering above with after burner flare behind.

"Let's engage the bastards!" called the major and the group moved toward the hill in the dark side of the field.

A formation of two Navy Super Hornet jets appeared above them from out of nowhere. One jet fighter lit up the sky with flares and the major and his lieutenant marked the location with laser beams.

A few cluster bombs exploded on the hill and smeared the area with high dust cloud.

"Bravo Zulu!" exclaimed Ahmad. "Let's go guys, let's finish the job!"

Seconds after Major Ahmad and his company stormed the hill, taking advantage of the dust and confusion to kill the remaining insurgents, the enemy's few survivors fled for their lives using the same dust cloud to escape and leaving their weapons and boots behind.

"Thank you, Bold Eagle Leader, marvelous job there!"

"You're welcome, major, your bird is entering the area. Good luck."

The last sortie from the Osprey landed at the same location about three minutes later, evacuating the remaining troops as some bullets whistled around with no targets. Worried that insurgents still watched and waited for opportunity, they took off with open doors, and aimed at the dunes below.

On the other side of the planet, General McLaughlin called the vice president.

"Mr. Vice President," the General said calmly, "Major Ahmad on the radio. Sorry to wake you up again, sir, I thought you may want to know-"

"What now?" he asked, grumpy and dazed from lack of sleep.

"Full successful operation. They are all safe, sir!"

Chapter 28

The three dead men killed by Hassan were examined using every possible means to identify them, including a facial recognition database used by NSA, scars, medical and dental records, watches, jewelry, even the shoes and clothing they were wearing, their origin, labels, etc., but nothing matched existing records.

The tattoos were examined and sent to every agency for identification. Only professionals would leave no trace when they were gone, but "every corpse has a story to tell" the pathologist had told Patrick.

"There are no dots to connect!" exclaimed Patrick to his boss in frustration. "This is a well thought out operation, and there must be a foreign government behind it."

"NSA stated that the fingerprints did not match the records or the FBI database," replied Marcus.

"I examined the bodies, not a happy scene," said Patrick to Dan as they situated themselves in a coffee shop on the same avenue not far away from the nearby Israeli embassy, ordering lunch and cold drinks.

"The rifle serial number was under the scrutiny of the lab to track its path. I think they hit a brick wall," Patrick said as they both sat and waited to order.

"Right now, we have to look elsewhere. If they get back to us good, if not, we have to search other avenues," Patrick repeated what Marcus told him and Dan concurred.

Dan was listening in silence. He knew that Patrick and his boss, Marcus were under a lot of pressure.

"So much shit has gone down since the ceremony, it makes me wonder when this town was so busy? The FBI's lack of knowledge of the full picture is stressing everyone out!" Patrick sighed in frustration.

"What's the progress of Gordon Donovan's federal inquiry?" asked Dan, who was not familiar with American protocols.

"It's like a court, Dan, Donovan subpoenas everyone in D.C.," laughed Patrick. "He didn't ask me to testify yet, but it's coming. Every police officer and agent at the time of the ceremony was invited to testify before his congressional panel."

"Including politicians?" asked Dan, surprised by the way Donovan ran the inquiry and gave him credit for that.

"Sure, the VP Chief of Staff, White House Chief of Staff, most of the President's cabinet-"

"Really, I didn't see it on the news," said a surprised Dan.

"Depends on which channel you are you watching," Patrick coughed loudly. "He is investigating the event thoroughly and confidently." He wiped his mouth with the napkin and sniffed. "The cold is still here!" he stated and smiled.

Marcus Barbour dragged Patrick to conference call after conference call. One with the acting President and his Chief of Staff, and one with the FBI. The NSA office was demanding progress results after seeing it all move too slowly.

Patrick's cell phone rang. He signaled Dan to listen and pressed the speaker and put full volume but not before making sure no one in the coffee shop could hear the conversation.

"Mr. Stevenson, it's Dr. Winston from The National Institute of Standards and Technologies Lab in Boulder, Colorado."

"Hello, Dr. Winston, I have with me Dan Eyal from the Israeli embassy who is familiar with the rifle if you have any questions."

"Oh, yes. Hi, gentlemen," he replied politely.

The man paused for a moment, thinking about how to break the news. "We could identify only three letters and two numbers on the rifle, and its origin is still a mystery. We think we would be able to expose the rest using the electron backscatter diffraction method and also using an electron microscope to examine the atoms of the metal, but it's a puzzle and will take time."

"What have you got so far?" asked Patrick.

"The first three letters were IMI which meant 'Israel Military Industries' and that we know and was easy. The other two numbers were nine and eight located in the sixth and seventh of twelve serial number spots. "

"Well, that's a good start," Patrick encouraged the scientist.

The information was wired to Gad straight from Patrick's phone and the Mossad started their own rifle tracking journey. Since it was manufactured a long time ago, the rifle had exchanged many hands, and some carriers were not alive to tell their story. Many arms brokers were from Israel, mainly retired Army generals, and made quick profits selling surplus Israeli inventory to some of the sleaziest firms from the gutters of third world countries. Dan suppressed the idea that an Israeli weapon was used to assassinate the President's wife. The news might evoke chaos in the entire world. It was just the same atmosphere as it was after 9/11 when the world waited to see what the American response would be. He felt guilty, in a way, but could not control a gun once it was sold to another entity. The NRA would say, "guns do not kill people, people kill people."

Patrick felt like déjà vu investigating the Iran-Contra affair during President Reagan's second term.

An hour later, still in the coffee shop the cell phone rang again and it was an overseas call. It was Gad, the head of the Mossad and he started talking without greeting Patrick.

"Israel sold 2,500 AK-47s, known in the Middle East as *Kalashnikovs*, with 3 million rounds of ammunition plus 50 IWI Galil sniper rifles, the same as the one used in the assassination attempt. They were sold to the Columbian Government which transferred them to a group called 'UAC,' a paramilitary and drug trafficking cartel helping the Columbian President keep his post. It was a legit transaction, a quick search shows that the group does not exist anymore; however, its leader was still operating individually with drug and human trafficking and trading or selling their weapons illegally to the highest bidder."

"Good stuff, Gad, all we need is to find this guy, so we don't need the lab info anymore. What is the leader's name?"

"I didn't tell you his name, yet. I am sure you will have more accurate records of the man we called in our agency *el pequeno*, which means 'the little jackal.' Julio Esperanda is his real name."

"Were any other similar rifles sold anywhere else? Otherwise it's just a guess," claimed Patrick who didn't want to waste his resources.

"We have no records, but that does not mean similar rifles were not sold to others. We have many military weapons stolen from our storage by our Bedouin community who sell them in auctions . . .Oh, yes, by the way, Esperanda, he is still alive." Gad's quick chatter sometimes got lost in translation and Patrick had to focus.

"Where can I find him?" asked Patrick.

"That's for you to find out," replied Gad. "We can only tell you that it's a very high probability that the gun in your possession came from a Columbian drug cartel and entered the United States probably through your open border policy."

Despite the seriousness of the situation, Gad managed to put a smile on Patrick's face by hinting that he would be opposing open borders. *After all, Israel is surrounded by walls everywhere,* he thought.

"Thank you, Gad. . .appreciate your help."

Dan was impressed by the fast information that Gad presented.

The phone rang again, and Patrick pressed the accept button for the second call. The FBI director was on the line with a gloomy tone of voice.

"Pat, Frank Dabush's car exploded into a million pieces!"

"Holy shit!" Patrick cried loudly. "What the hell happened? Is he alive?"

"Yes, thank God for that."

Chapter 29

Alexandria, Virginia

J amila recognized the man in the office sitting there with his gun on the table. When the Imam saw the child, he immediately removed it and shoved it into the drawer.

"Jamila, meet Hassan!" He pointed in Hassan's direction. "I would appreciate if you could host him for a few days."

"Sure," she said calmly. "Our house is your house, Hassan!"

Farouk, her husband, was still suffering from his back wound, but repeated his consent after his wife and Jamil, their son, giggled innocently.

Hassan glanced at his host and felt strange, his conscience told him not to trust them. Was it the way they looked at him, or the cold shoulder the husband showed?

"Is it OK, then?" the Imam asked, and Jamila and Farouk answered together, "Oh, yeah, yeah, of course!"

After a short introduction, Jamila said without blinking, "Let's do it tomorrow, since I need to prepare the room." Then, she asked to leave to do errands.

After she and her husband left the room, she grabbed her husband's elbow.

"Do you know who this guy is?" She was breathing heavily in a panic.

Farouk nodded his head and kept quiet, letting his wife lead the way.

"Yes, I got a chill when I saw him!" he replied.

"I am scared, Farouk. This guy looked very dangerous, did you see his eyes? How he looked at us?"

They moved quickly out of the building. Jamila held their son.

"Yeah, it's like the FBI is looking for us and not the other way around."

"What a small world!" she exclaimed.

Farouk could not stay quiet when his wife was excited and nervous. "Jamila, don't you see how fortunate we are? Look at it on the bright side of all this!"

"Which bright side?" she shouted and pulled his arm again.

They stopped walking and they stared each other on the sidewalk by the mosque.

"If this is the man the FBI is looking for, our assignment is completed don't you see? We are free to live our lives!" Farouk was the one to lead now. "It was a good call to postpone it for tomorrow, we should call Patrick right away!"

Farouk dialed the number and before he had a chance to say anything, Jamila grabbed the phone from him yelled into the speaker.

"I have your man!" she said as her husband froze.

"Are you sure we are not making a mistake turning in now?"

"What? Did you change your mind? You are confusing me, Farouk, I thought you would be happy. What about our lives, our family, Farouk?" She sighed and looked at him with anger.

Patrick was listening to the conversation in Arabic and the possible dilemma they both faced. He could not miss this opportunity he thought and asked few times in loud voice, "Where is Hassan? Jamila, talk to me!"

"Stop, Farouk, you forgot who wanted you dead in Syria? Your own people!" she confronted her confused husband.

"He was invited by Imam to stay in our home for a while, I told him to come tomorrow," she said, talking in her broken English as Patrick listened.

"Tomorrow is too late, where is he now?" Patrick got impatient.

"Um. . .in our mosque!" she replied quickly without divulging the location. "We just came from there," she added.

"OK, I see your location, don't move, I'll send a police car to pick you up. Don't go back and keep walking like everything is normal!"

A few minutes later, several police cars shot into the mosque parking lot, surrounding the building in silence and blocking the escape routes and entrance to the lot.

Jamila and Farouk were in a police car a block away as she realized that there were children in the preschool class. "Thank God I pulled my own son from there today," she praised Allah.

Patrick joined five minutes later and let the FBI detective lead the arrest as he watched from a distance with his handgun ready to fire.

The detective with a few special police squads engulfed the building and blocked all exits and monitored all the windows. Then he rang the doorbell. The camera swiveled once more watching a few fully guarded officers swarming the porch.

The Imam was in his office with Hassan and had no idea of the drama evolving outside. His intercom rang and the Imam picked up the phone "We are surrounded by the police," the cleric said in a panic.

The Imam pulled the window shade up, and both saw the police force prepared to swarm in.

"Open the door for them," he replied to the cleric.

"You called them!" thundered Hassan in anger. He shook like a leaf trying to figure out what to do. He looked at the Imam, and was ready to hit him.

"No!" the Imam sounded apologetic trying to calm him down. "Probably Jamila and her husband did," he added fast with eyes wide open and totally petrified to see how quickly Hassan turned into a monster.

Then Hassan jumped on the Imam and pushed him from his chair. He pulled the handgun from the drawer and inserted the loose bullets into the cartridge, then he grasped the Imam's neck tightly and pulled him toward the prayer hall.

"Tell him to lock the door!" commanded Hassan and the Imam called loudly for his assistant to do so. It was too late. The detective pushed the cleric and stormed into the hall and as his force split into two groups, each controlled one side of the building.

Hassan aimed his gun toward the Imam's head, still grasping him and called for the cleric to get closer to act as a human shield.

The detective and his team used remote control model-sized vehicles with cameras to check on the situation inside the prayer hall.

Hassan shot the vehicle and two more were sent into the hall. The shots frightened the children in the classroom and they started to cry out loud.

Hassan took his two hostages into the classroom and saw it was full of crying children.

"Hostages. Full of children!" called the detective in his communication ear piece.

"Be careful, do not act before we are ready," his boss replied.

"Hassan might be dangerous," intervened Patrick from the distance.

"Hello, Patrick, you *are* here, *ha!*" the chief detective asked sarcastically.

"Relax, Daniel, I am not here to steal your show. Ok? We called you after all, right?"

"OK, what do you know about your suspect, is he armed? Dangerous? Easy to talk to?" asked Daniel.

"I know as much as you know, after all you interrogated his former employer. Don't forget, we need him alive," Patrick said as the detective in the building confirmed the presence of hostages.

Patrick acknowledged, hoping that the top FBI detectives could control the situation.

A few new voices entered the network, giving instructions, but with no progress to report.

Inside, Hassan got into one classroom with two dozen children and barricaded himself, ready to fight for his life. That's not what he planned for himself when he came to this country; he felt pity for himself and there was no one to talk to who could help him diffuse the situation. He was nervous when the police showed up and he acted irrationally.

"Can you communicate with them, I mean Hassan?" asked Patrick.

"We are trying to obtain communication!" Daniel responded.

"I hear children crying," the detective reported, calmly monitoring the next remote-control car entering the prayer hall, then he added, "I guess they are in the one of the class-rooms. Call the paramedics and prepare for battle."

"We called the entire hostage response team. Wrap your cell phone with your extra shirt and throw it into the mosque, once it's done, we'll try to call them."

246 • WILLIE HIRSH

"I can't do it from here, try someone else from outside, break the window!" he suggested.

"OK," replied Daniel and instructed another detective situated on the lot to do that.

Hassan clenched one child's arm and asked all of them to sit and be quiet. A shattered window froze him as he thought the police squad had broken in. He saw the blue shirt and wondered, *What the hell they were doing? Are they throwing smoke grenades to force him out?*

"The children are terrified!" the Imam complained to Hassan.

"I am terrified too," Hassan responded. "How do you think I feel?"

"Let me at least check why they threw the shirt into the room, OK?"

"My concern is how the hell they know where we are. . .is anyone else in the building other than you and the cleric?" Hassan raised his voice angrily. The Imam watched his cleric as he shook his head and said "Just us and the children, we are all in the room. Besides there is a helicopter in the distance probably watching us, that's how they knew where we are."

Another helicopter flew close by and dropped a combat team fully geared for a battle. Ambulances and firetrucks took position and a dozen police cars and emergency vehicles responded with special team vehicles.

A group of parents assembled outside praying for the safety of their children.

"Turn the window shade down," commanded Hassan. Then a megaphone called decisively, "Hassan, pick up the phone. We want to talk."

"The phone in the shirt," the Imam said and pleaded with Hassan to pick it up.

The megaphone continued, "Have the children lie on the floor. We don't want anyone hurt. Pick up the phone, please."

Hassan ignored the call and let the Imam pick up the ringing phone and answered bluntly, "Hello."

"This is the chief of police. Hassan, is that you?"

"No, let me transfer you to him," said the Imam.

"I don't want to talk to anyone!" shouted Hassan angrily.

"Who are you then?"

"The Imam."

"Keep Hassan calm, that's very important, and if he doesn't want to talk to us directly it's OK, we will communicate through you."

"OK," the Imam answered.

"Tell him to get the fucking helicopters away," Hasan yelled nervously.

The chief heard the scream and answered, "Tell him it's OK, we are not doing anything to arm anyone, are the children on the floor?" he asked.

"Yeah," the Imam answered.

"What the fuck are you talking to him about?" Hassan continued holding the loaded gun in one hand and grabbed the phone from the Imam.

"Listen, I didn't do anything, it was self-defense and I was manipulated into all this shit!" yelled Hassan into the speaker.

"We are not judging you, Hassan. We would like to talk to you for your benefit." The chief was calm and relaxed.

"Oh, yeah, the minute I lay down my gun, you will shoot me in the head," Hassan's tone was sarcastic.

"Absolutely not, you have information we want and that is very valuable data that can help you with your plea."

"Plea? What plea? I am not getting out of here alive!" he screamed.

"You would be able to go back to school where you registered for engineering." The chief showed knowledge of Hassan's plans prior to the assassination attempt.

"No way will you ever send me to school after all the shit I went through."

"At least let the children go?" asked the chief.

Outside, the unfolding drama attracted many bystanders whom the police moved away for safety and for fast exit in case of emergency. The two helicopters disappeared and landed in a safe area for fast response.

They kept Hassan occupied on the phone. The squad was on the roof and got into the building through the open bulkhead door. They descended two floors from the emergency stairs into the main floor, even though they weren't sure where the classroom was.

Their rubber shoes made no sounds as they inserted a tiny camera under each closed door, one by one. It was the third and last classroom.

"I clearly see the people in the room," whispered the squad leader.

"Do you have a clear vision of Hassan?"

"Yes, a young guy holding a gun and two adults next to him."

"Are the children on the floor?"

"Yes, all of them, but they're very restless," the squad leader replied.

"OK, let's keep him busy and focus on me when you are getting ready to act."

"The door is locked, and we will need to break it."

"Not a battering ram, because that will give him enough time to shoot and kill someone or commit suicide by the time the door falls."

"Stand by, we will use an explosive door breaching procedure—the fastest method."

"Be careful. . . there are children."

"They are at a safe distance, chief."

The explosives expert inserted the plastic explosive into the latch area.

Outside, the chief occupied Hassan with promises to help him be released on minor charges, and to get him back to school in exchange for the information. Hassan was speechless and petrified by the situation and was listening to gain time to think how to get out of this situation with minimum threat to his life. He really had no clue on how to proceed.

The explosive was ready.

"Oh, wait," whispered the police officer monitoring the windows with binoculars.

"What?" asked the chief, keeping his volume down as well, even though the officers were wearing air pods.

"He is moving the kids to the windows," he said, concerned.

"Of course: human shields."

"I'll leave this up to you. We are ready at your call," added the chief and wished them good luck.

The plastic charge exploded loudly.

The door opened, slamming against the wall and the latch blew off and flew across the classroom. It hit the cleric who instantly fell on the floor, ricocheted, and landed on the opposite wall.

Hassan and the Imam turned around, horrified. Once each of the policeman immediately took positions with their backs to the wall on each side of the room, they aimed their guns. The team commander aimed at Hassan and shot him in the leg. The Imam fell to the floor uninjured. The children screamed in panic on the floor with no one to protect them.

Hassan fell bleeding on the floor and dropped the handgun. The policeman kicked it away, and the rest jumped on the injured fugitive, tackling him on the vinyl floor.

"All secured," said the head of the squad. "Get in the response team. Cchildren are in trauma. We have one dead, and Hassan has a heavily bleeding leg."

"Good job there. Thank you, chief."

A minute later, the children were evacuated, and two ambulances rushed the dead cleric and the injured Hassan to the nearest hospital in Alexandria, Virginia.

The Imam was treated for trauma and was taken in for questioning at the FBI headquarters.

A couple of hours later, Hassan was operated on to save his life and his leg was amputated.

He had a secured private room in the medical facility under heavy guard, 24/7.

Hassan's capture was kept confidential. Only a few top figures knew.

"Tell us everything Hassan!" demanded the investigator when Hassan opened his eyes for the first time.

"You don't waste time, do you?" he slurred.

"We don't have time to lose either, it was easy to eliminate you, so be respectful if you don't want to lose your hands, too."

"You won't believe my story," he said and raised his eyes to meet the investigator's eyes. . .but I really do love America!"

"We all do, Hassan!"

Chapter 30

The American Airlines Dreamliner Boeing 787 landed in Bogota, Columbia in the late afternoon and Patrick went straight to his hotel room to prepare for a meeting with Julio Esperanda, "The Little Jackal."

Patrick's cover story was that he was a horse-breeder investor looking for a good deal on racehorse for his aging inventory. What brought Patrick to Bogota to meet the drug- and arms dealer turned sober, was that he now invested his fortune on his love for horse breeding.

The question Patrick really wanted to ask Julio could wait for the right moment and would have to be done using his talents. *There would always be someone who would agree to talk for a good amount of money,* he thought.

He situated himself in the JW Marriott as a successful investor would do to spoil himself. The first visitor in his hotel room was a messenger from his own embassy who brought a diplomatic bag and planned for his short stay.

"Patrick Stevenson?" he asked, even though he recognized the photo his boss prepared for him in advance.

"Chico?" asked Patrick.

"That's me!" answered the tiny man.

"Glad to meet you." Patrick was polite and looked at the man and hoped that his mission would get the results he wanted. After all, Chico was his local contact agent who was supposed to rescue Patrick if the shit hit the fan.

"Wait, don't go," said Patrick as Chico made himself comfortable on the sofa.

Two handguns, a Glock 500 series with the fire power of a bazooka, scoffed Patrick. *Also, a silencer and a hefty round of ammunition which was tacked into a wooden box, heavy as hell.* Someone probably thought he was about to start a war with the South American drug cartel. He smiled.

He checked the guns and the barrels as an expert would, and loaded them in case he might need to use them.

Patrick reviewed Esperanda's thick background file.

Although it looked like a simple task for any secret agent to handle, it was not meant for an amateur. Any mistake could be his last one. The drug cartels killed anyone that could have been a threat, sometimes killed for pesos–life had the same value as a paper bag.

As a CIA agent in the lion's den, Patrick's life was worth even less than a peso. He took this upon himself in order to keep the circle of people involved closed and confidential.

"What do you know about Esperanda?" he asked Chico.

"Be straight with him, tell him what your meeting is about," Chico advised and Patrick chuckled.

"Are you kidding? It's suicide to come and ask if he dealt with Israelis on an arms deal? Don't you think, Chico?"

Chico went silent. "Perhaps, Patrick, you don't understand the South American mentality that a powerful man respects another powerful man. This is how it goes!" he said softly.

"The cartel despised the CIA due to their counter drug smuggling activities." Patrick opened the rest of the packages he got from the embassy and took off his tie and jacket and put them into the closet.

"That's my advice, come and ask just what you came for, he will ask you a favor in exchange, all the horse interest is bullshit, excuse my French, and he'll know in two seconds if you are bluffing," he said with a sly smile.

"OK, you've convinced me, now you have to convince me that your rescue operation will work," Patrick scoffed, and Chico looked humiliated.

"The last I know is that The Little Jackal, is living in a mansion on the outskirts of Cartagena, a booming town with many new skyscrapers. It's about 17 hours' drive from here. Due to your armament there was no other way to travel by plane with guns in this country. So we need to rent cars and drive." Chico waited for Patrick's reaction.

"Chico, you convinced me; what can I offer Esperanda in exchange? He has money, women, he lacks nothing."

"Patrick, offer not to disturb his operation for six months, and he will love you!"

"I love this idea," chuckled Patrick as he saw Chico's happy face.

The next day, Chico rented a Chevrolet Impala equipped with Car Play and drove south on Route 45. A short distance behind them, his shadow agent used a SIM card on their phones so they could communicate.

"This sucker made me drive 17 hours, I could fly while Chico could drive with the armament, shit," murmured Patrick. "Not thinking!" he scolded himself. As always, agents used to say that the worst enemy of any agent was agency planners.

Julio Esperanda seldom left his compound, but when he did, he informed the local police who granted him an escort. He was allowed to perform legal business and Julio chose to breed thoroughbred horses for the racing industry. The 250 acres had everything he needed to live in a luxury lifestyle: a tennis court, two pools, a twenty-room main compound, and a staff to serve him and his three wives.

Julio's twelve children were home studying and teachers came in and out all day through the armed security booth and its 16 feet high steel gates that read "Esperanda Farms." The deal with the Colombian government was simple: pay to play and don't interfere with the election process. When needed, also provide protection to its political partners from political assassination.

The only catch was that Julio was not allowed to do business with the United States. He auctioned the horses to countries other than Australia, England and the United States, which had the best breeding industries for a special type of racehorse. However, the price in those countries was exorbitant and Julio could offer a better value to a race professional. Patrick studied everything he could about Julio's passion, to the point that he could have been a horse breeder himself. The lucrative export to the U.S. of the popular thoroughbred breed would appeal to Julio.

Patrick contacted Julio's office and pretended to be Evan Stevenson. He kept his last name but changed his first. His shadow agent followed, and about half a mile from the long driveway, he pulled off the road and removed a few bags from the car. A 10-foot drone was assembled within 15 minutes, fully equipped with a camera and fake plastic rockets. He selected a perfect spot overlooking the racetrack that Julio used to train his horses.

Patrick pulled into the dirt driveway toward the security booth behind a food truck. The security guard stopped the truck and frisked the driver and checked the truck thoroughly.

"Shit," Patrick murmured and put the guns in the glove compartment, an easy place to find them. The best strategy was to be upfront and when the truck driver was allowed to cross the gate, the security guard signaled Patrick forward.

The shadow agent watched the event with his binoculars from the distance and just before Patrick stopped next to the booth he managed to say on the phone, "You have three hours."

"Ten-four, but start 15 minutes after you see me walking in."

"Granted."

The security guard took his job very seriously.

"Good morning. Nice weather today," Patrick said, cheerfully.

"Good morning, *señor*. Do you have an appointment?"

"Sure, *Señor* Esperanda is expecting me," he smiled.

"Your name?"

"Evan, Evan Stevenson, *señor*!" he said confidently.

The security guard looked into the guest book and marked the time Patrick got into the compound.

"Very good, *señor*. Step out of the car, please!" he ordered.

Patrick stepped out and used the straight approach. "I have my personal handguns in the glove compartment. I was told to disclose this when I stopped in the security post."

"Thank you for telling me!" he exclaimed and frisked Patrick thoroughly and used a Magnetometer all over his body. *He would be a good candidate for a TSA job,* Patrick thought to himself. Then he searched the car, found the weapons and shoved them into his belt.

"*Señor*, we do not allow visitors with any weapons in the farm, Mr. Esperanda is expecting you in the greenhouse on the left side of the main entrance."

Patrick, just before getting back into his car, took a long glance at the approximate location of his partner agent, then slowly drove the rest of the driveway to a guest parking lot close to a circular stone planter with full grown tropical vegetation. Parrots, llamas, and horses roamed freely and gave the site an exotic feel.

"It's a fucking Jurassic Park," Patrick mumbled to himself and chuckled. He felt good and searched for the greenhouse entry. The door was open, and a few ducks came out quacking their way to the open fields. A servant stood at the door and greeted Patrick with *"Buenos dias, señor."*

"Buenos dias," repeated Patrick, who was escorted to a glass topped table with six chairs around it. He put aside his bag and waited with anticipation to meet the man who spent 16 years behind bars as a plea bargain with the government.

"Oh, Mr. Stevenson."

A short man in his early 50s approached with a fast step with his hand stretched forward. He was dressed in white army uniform clothing, like a navy admiral. He wore cowboy boots and a large explorer white hat, ready to explore the jungles around him. His round face, mustache and a week-old beard made him look like Che' Guevara, the mystical Argentine Marxist who died in a Bolivian rain forest.

"Hello, *Señor* Esperanda, I was looking forward to meeting you."

Patrick sounded as cheery as possible but he could not stop the wheels in his mind from turning to find a way to get the information he needed about how the sniper rifle might be connected to the assassination attempt on the U.S. President.

They sat down and Julio asked Patrick, "What would you like to drink?"

"Too early for an alcoholic drink, but I'll have a cranberry juice with lime."

He ordered the drink in Spanish from his servant that looked like he was in the middle of a wedding dinner preparations. He came back a few minutes later with a tray full of tropical fruits and a few types of juices.

"So, you are an expert of thoroughbred horses," he said confidently and gazed into Patrick's eyes.

"Oh, yeah, I love horses, I lost my breeding farm and I turned to international horse brokering," Patrick shot back and hoped he sounded enthusiastic enough. "It's my passion!"

"Gambling, Mr. Stevenson?"

Patrick was not surprised. He figured this out when preparing a fake profile page on Facebook, Twitter, and Instagram. Computer science interns loaded his profile with horse's photos and fake auctions around the world. *Now it's show time*, he said to himself.

"Oh, yeah, I lost it to gambling."

"Where in Vermont was your breeding farm?"

"Close to the Appalachian Gap. Are you familiar with the area?"

Patrick didn't like anyone digging into his profile, but it looked as if Julio did his homework as thoroughly as Patrick did his.

"No, I never put my foot on U.S. soil, I was just wondering. So tell me, how can I compete with the American breeders? As you know I am banned from doing business in the western world due to sanctions by your fucking agriculture department."

"Fifty-fifty," Patrick shot back and scratched an imaginary point in his skull.

"Fair enough!" he exclaimed and emptied the mango juice from his glass. "Do you want to see my horses?"

"I was waiting for an invitation like this," he said and they both chuckled politely.

The cranking sound of two-cylinder model engines sliced through the air. The men got up and walked toward the horses. Patrick noticed that the servant followed them closely and realized that he had another job and was probably armed for it. *Something to watch,* Patrick thought.

The drone pierced the farm airspace and vanished behind the hills. The horse's acute senses were heightened by the unnatural sounds but relaxed when Julio appeared. His host showed a real compassion seeing the interaction between them.

"This is Sila, a two-year old champion," he caressed the horse and watched Patrick do the same then asked, "Do you want to ride?"

"Oh no, I am not dressed for it."

"I insist. I'll loan you a riding uniform."

A short while later they were both on horses when Julio ordered his shadow servant to stay away while they are on the racing track.

Patrick rode Sila and Julio chose a three-year-old mare he kept for breeding.

"Heehaw," he roared, and the mare shot forward like a Porsche on a race track. Patrick had a little trouble controlling the young stallion, but a gentle kick convinced it to shoot fast after the mare.

Patrick never rode a racing horse and struggled to stay on its back. Suddenly, the horses stopped, and Patrick flew forward and landed on the grass, rolling a few times before he came to a stop.

Julio rode back as quickly as he could and helped Patrick get to his feet.

"Are you OK?" he asked with fake concern.

Patrick wondered if "The Little Jackal" wanted to get rid of him in a horse accident by giving him an untrained horse. He wiped the grass from his chest and look straight at Julio's eyes.

"It almost killed me."

The drone came back from another direction and this time flew much lower, zooming right above their heads.

"Mr. Stevenson, you made one mistake that showed me that you have no clue about the breed I raise," Julio's voice became more aggressive.

The horses went free and they walked back on foot.

"What mistake?" Patrick played naïve.

"I know who you are, but I don't know what you are looking for."

Patrick found it silly to play dumb, but asked to satisfy his curiosity anyway.

"Tell me, what was my mistake? Educate me, Julio!"

"Well, the thoroughbred horses started in the seventeenth century, more than 200 years ago in England, not in Austria, and not last century. In addition, your web designer might be a good one, but your web page is terrible. One of my horse's photos was copied and pasted to your website resumé."

"Did I say that?"

"You see, the drone is yours, I could shut it down, but I didn't," he scoffed. "CIA, right? Who sent you? Marcus?"

"That's very nice of you, so maybe now we can get down to real business." Patrick got serious and added, "We have nothing to lose, right?"

"There were some other mistakes, but I won't go into it, you chose a very difficult subject to learn about in a very short time." He walked slowly and confidently, while his bodyguards watched in the distance, ready to take action if needed. Julio signaled to them that it was all right.

"Well, I do like horses!" Patrick chuckled, and Julio laughed out loud, he called his bluff.

"Yes, you like horses, who doesn't? I had visitors from the CIA before you. . . helping them with information about my ex-competitors and they chose the direct approach, Mr. Stevenson!"

"I'm learning. By the way, call me Evan!"

"Why not Patrick." Julio chuckled, and Patrick put on a cold smile and kept an ice face.

"You knew I was coming, didn't you? But. . .how?"

"Yes, I was told to eliminate you, since you are a double agent trying to frame me and tie me to the assassination attempt against President Barker due to the sanctions. I didn't try to kill you. It was an honest horse accident," he added with a confident smile on his face. Then, he got serious. "I just want a deal with the Gringos, *entendido*?" he emphasized the last word—Spanish for 'it is understood'?

They got back into the greenhouse and the table was full of food prepared by Julio's personal chef.

"Holy cow!" Patrick called loudly when he noticed the anaconda snake curling in the corner of the room. Julio was amused seeing Patrick's expression.

"Oh, that's Pichu."

"It's a snake!" Patrick was loud and petrified. He hated snakes.

"A 24-foot anaconda," explained Julio, amused at the horror on Patrick's face.

"What do you feed this thing?"

"People like you!" Julio laughed hard, but Patrick was not amused. "Every once in a while, I miss an employee, you know?" Julio teased Patrick and continued laughing at his own jokes.

"Seriously, get him away from me!"

"I feed Pichu mainly deer, it's enough for one year. Anyway, I was thinking, if I can help you, would you help me?" asked Julio, changing the subject as he pushed the snake away from coiling his leg.

"It depends on what you are looking for?"

"Lift the sanctions, it's been too long already. I helped the CIA in the past many times without profit, and everyone said OK, we will help you. But nothing is being done," he said, sounding frustrated.

"I am looking for information regarding a special sniper rifle," Patrick said.

"So, it's true that I was tied to the assassination, then!"

"Not you, but the rifle, yes!"

"How did you tie the rifle to me?" asked Julio, surprised.

"The Israeli intelligence agency, the Mossad." He checked Julio's facial expression and added, "They sold you a bunch of AK-47s and a few sniper rifles some 20 years ago."

"Oh yeah, that crazy time," he said and laughed. "When I was young and had my army!"

"One of those rifles found its way to the United States, perhaps by a broker or another arms dealer. Do you remember who?" he pressed the issue.

Julio wrinkled his forehead, trying to draw the information from the back of his mind.

"No, I didn't sell any guns to anyone. I am on probation for the rest of my life and do legal business. Why risk it?"

"Perhaps, it was stolen from you?"

"Perhaps, I didn't check the inventory for a long time," he added sincerely.

Patrick hit a brick wall but continued.

"I'll help you with the sanctions, Julio. Just help me find out who brokered the gun? Tell me who contacted you about my arrival? There must be a connection."

"It was an unidentified man, he asked for me and simply said that he was a friend and to expect a double agent to visit in a week. He also added the purpose was to frame me to the assassination attempt and then to kill me. It must be some very powerful man in your agency!"

"All options are open, Julio; it could be anyone, including me, as a suspect."

Patrick's thoughts gave him a splitting headache. Who knew about his trip to Columbia? A handful of people in the agency and in the White House involved with his investigation. . .those who knew from the first circle of confidentiality could spread the news or even worse, someone was digging for the news. *But who?* Patrick asked himself. *Señor.*

The servant who stood close enough to listen intervened. "The government confiscated all of our weapons. Perhaps the government sold the guns?"

"I'll check that with the police chief!" Julio said and then looked at Patrick. "Let me get to the bottom of this, I'll help you."

"I'll will not forget this, Julio."

The drone buzzed lower over the mansion and Julio followed it with his eyes and murmured, "Get this damn toy away from my property, please."

A few minutes later, the drone landed on the grass next to the greenhouse. Julio was amused to see the plastic rockets under its wings. He laughed.

"Look, Patrick, let me know where you are staying, I will check the inventory and let you know ASAP. Worse comes to worse, I'll call you at your office."

"Deal."

Patrick changed back to his clothes and departed the compound. On the way back towards the booth, he saw his ghost agent giving the drone controls to the security guard as he requested, a gift from the CIA.

Chapter 31

The US Embassy, Moscow

T he embassy gate closed behind Katarina and Evan. The guards blocked police entry into the embassy grounds, and aimed their machine guns at the car tires to shoot, if necessary.

Katarina rejoiced with a scream of victory as she got into the car. She drove it into the parking lot behind the 12-foot steel gate, while Evan hung onto the door handle to steady himself in the seat. Katarina had a habit of flooring the gas pedal and the brake, and Evan already sustained a few head bruises from banging his head on the windshield. Now, he knew better.

The car came to a screeching stop in front of the taller embassy building and the two rushed out of the vehicle, watching the two police officers in cars next to the gate talking on the radio in Russian. *This is a far as they could go, at least for now,* Katarina thought.

"That was close," stated Evan and held her hand to pull her into the building without irritating the Russian officers still watching as if to say, *Wait. . .you still need to come out!*

Suddenly, it was a different Katarina, not the shy, polite, minding-her-own-business woman, but one who could carry herself.

264 • WILLIE HIRSH

"Why does the CIA want to eliminate you?" Evan asked. Katarina just squared her shoulders.

"I know something they think I know!"

"To be honest, looks like you saved both of us."

"The equations must be solved, so perhaps then I will know why someone wants to eliminate me and why!"

"Well, that won't happen on my watch," Evan promised.

"*Spasibo!* Thank you. I will remember this promise!" she said sarcastically.

She let all her buried emotions burst like a volcanic eruption as she watched the police officers vanish back down the dark Moscow street.

"What do you know about the terror attack in Washington?" Evan asked.

"Huh?" she replied.

"Look, you're cool, smart, and you know your way around. You were not worried at all. Was this all just a show?" On second thought, Evan asked, "Are they really police or imposters?"

She blinked, her face frozen.

"We'll talk inside," she replied and then lowered her voice. "Russian sensors are all around the embassy. They can hear everything we say out here." She smiled like she shared a small secret with a friend.

She pulled him into the building when he said, "You know that you are a prisoner in the embassy now?"

"So are you Mr. CIA agent, but not for long, Dima is waiting for us!" She smiled.

Evan could not wait for the moment when he could trap her into a closed room, hold her sexy neck to the wall and force out everything she knew. Sure, she was pretty; beautiful, even, but he really just wanted to get into her head.

Evan and Katarina knew it would not easy to escape the embassy, which was always under surveillance. But it seemed not to be a concern. They always had a backup plan for that reason.

"They will redirect a dedicated satellite into new orbits to catch every move or activity on the embassy grounds," she said when she thought it was safe to talk.

"The agents who attacked us, who are they?" Evan asked.

"I am not sure; they could have been hired by a third party, or they were imposters. The fact that there is a police car in front of the embassy means there is some collaboration with Russian intelligence."

"I am sure we will hear back from them."

"No doubt, but let me tell you something," she whispered in his ear. "I am on a mission and there are only two men in America who know about it." She stared at his face, checking his reaction.

"What mission?" Evan asked.

Katarina said, "You interfered with my investigation, Evan. My next step after leaving my apartment was to go elsewhere and from there, escort Dima to a hideout apartment and force him to reveal all that he knows about The Chameleon to complete my investigation."

"What are you talking about?" He glowered. "You were on your way out to escape; I noticed your suitcase. You were ready to disappear!" he snapped. "My mission was to find out what you know, and I was not aware of your assignment!"

"True, I was on my way to a new hideout apartment as I told you, yours or our, agency rented using a third party until I finished my investigation so I could bring all my evidence to Patr-" She was calm and very serious.

"What do you know about the men? What were you working on?" Evan asked anxiously.

He sat down and looked at Katarina.

"Dima disappeared; he did not show up for our usual meeting. I'm concerned that he was kidnapped or eliminated by the same agents. I wanted to find him first. Hopefully he was still in his apartment. . . time is of the essence," she said.

"Was Dima an FSB agent? If so, he might know a few things about the operation."

The empty office was dark and they kept it like that. There was no stationary or office equipment available, perhaps the person who used it was one of the agents Russia demanded to expel.

"Yes, he was," Katarina replied, "But he was also a double agent, perhaps even a triple agent, selling information on the side for a fee."

"A double agent, huh? He paid you for the info you transferred to him?"

"In rubles." She chuckled. "You see, Evan? Dima was hired by a group to gather information about the President's schedules, and he hired me."

"We know that. How many people knew that you were hired by the two men in America?" Evan tried to keep his mind clear and focused.

Katrina stared at him, hesitating to answer the question and simply said, "I can't tell you, not now."

"That means that you are working on an investigation by someone who works within the investigation but as a separate entity?"

"Exactly!" she said.

"It also means that probably someone who knows that you are a double agent wants to shut you down. . .to kill you!" Evan suggested.

"Exactly. And it's not either of the two men!" she repeated. "They want his identity, understood?"

"And the 'someone who wants to kill you' is in the United States?" he asked.

"That's what they think!"

"The two men?"

"Yes!"

"And Dima might know as well, right? But they sent me to kill you, without knowing that I knew your mission!"

"Evan, Patrick and Marcus are smart men. They figured out you would discover my true identity. Think about it: if they told you I worked for them, then your actions might have been different and that man, The Chameleon, that we're looking for would know that he is cornered and try to escape," Katarina explained.

"I am just shocked that I was supposed to be the executioner!" Evan shrugged. "What if I had not seen that and killed you?" Evan was troubled.

"Yes, in order to let 'someone' believe that they cooperated and agreed to be sent, you had to eliminate me. They suspect that this 'someone' has some connections to a group that calls itself The Chameleons. Until I come up with evidence, there is nothing they can do."

"You disclosed the people who sent you, Katarina. I can't imagine it's not Marcus and Patrick running a small private investigation. They connected the dots. 'Someone' hired you to spy on our President's schedules and he didn't know you work for us!"

"Yes," Katarina answered.

"That means the man is not a CIA employee and doesn't have any access to our files. This 'someone' has an interest to murder our President," Evan continued.

"Once we know who he is, we can find out his motive. Right now we don't believe he is a top government official because if he was, he would have access to the information that I collected and transferred to Dima."

"True, that's exactly what I thought," said Evan. He put his gun on the table and then asked, "So why The Chameleons? What is their connection to all this?"

"I asked Dima that in one of our meetings. I told him we intercepted a cable with the word *Zikit,* a Hebrew word for a Chameleon, and I asked him to clarify."

"How did you intercept the cable?" Evan asked.

"A copy of that cable was sent to us from the Mossad, its 8200 communication interception unit," Katarina replied.

"What did it say?" Evan continued.

"*Zikit,* ready," Katarina said.

"When was that?" he pressed.

"January 19th, a day before the assassination attempt. What else can it mean?" she asked.

"To whom was it originally sent?" Evan asked.

"IH, the Hungarian civilian intelligence service. They are involved with non-military intelligence and collecting information ab-" Katarina started.

"I know!" Evan cut her off. "I checked this out," he said.

"Let's connect the dots, Hungary, Hebrew, a low ranking American government official, ready on January 19th." Evan winced, concentrating through his exhaustion.

"We can't wait, I know you are very tired but we must mobilize, especially now that I know where Dima stays!" she insisted and nudged Evan to wake him up. "I'll make coffee!"

"Perhaps, it is a trap. This whole thing doesn't make any sense. I don't understand how this is connected to the assassination yet," he continued.

"It's all about sabotage, Evan. It's worth exploring," she said.

Evan put on a tired smiled. "Then please explain!"

"Dima might not be involved at all. He was just a messenger spreading information and disinformation, and getting the Russian FSB agency involved. This way, the CIA would think that there was a Russian connection to the assassination, while the one person who was responsible was able to act freely to achieve his mission."

"Go on, Katarina. I am tired but I'm listening!"

"That's what I think, Evan, the agents firing on my apartment started to eliminate the trail of evidence. Do you understand?"

"So, whoever wanted to kill you, also planned to kill Dima and me, and silence the whole case?"

"That's what Marcus and Patrick thought, and they trusted you since they said you are one of the best they had!"

"I am the last one to know what's in their heads. They can twist things up but, in the end, they trust their agents to untangle the knots," Evan explained.

"In exchange, it was confidentially agreed upon to help me escape and to grant me United States citizenship and a job at the agency," Katarina said with a note of happiness in her voice, as if there was still hope in all of this chaos.

"Perhaps Dima didn't work for them of his own free will? Was he extorted? Did you think of that?" Evan asked.

"It doesn't matter what the reasons were. Dima is a dead man walking; this is why we need to find him tonight, any other day we will find a corpse," she said with all the seriousness she could muster.

"I'm not sure the agents who fired at your apartment are not from FSB," Evan assumed aloud.

"I'm not sure the Russian intelligence agency would get involved with the President's assassination attempt," she said with confidence.

The information sank in as a man approached them from the end of the corridor and entered the room without knocking.

"Robert Murphy, our head of security," Katarina introduced the two men.

"We met when I came here," Evan said.

The security officer led them both into his office in the lower building. It faced the street.

Robert Murphy was a thin person of medium height, far from resembling the stereotypical Hollywood spy that he really was. He wore a dark charcoal suit, white shirt and red tie, and radiated power and confidence. He was a very articulate and analytical person; he was the right agent in the right place at the right time.

"What the hell happened?" he growled out loud once the door was closed behind them.

Katarina and Evan sat on the leather chairs in front of his desk and both started talking at the same time.

"Katarina, you go first!" Robert exclaimed before he noticed Evan frown.

Evan wondered if they were keeping anything from him. The most important questions were, *who initiated it, why send him to kill Katarina, and how was all this tied to the terror attack?*

"Are you part of the coup with Katarina and her private investigation?" Evan asked.

"Katarina works for us!" exclaimed Robert. His face was as serious as a judge sentencing someone to death row. "We needed to burn her identity to see what would happen," he said calmly without explanation.

"What am I missing, Bob? Who reports to whom?" Evan was furious. "You are not telling me the truth. Are we on the same side here, or are we not?"

Bob relaxed in his chair and gazed at Evan. He pulled a Cuban cigar from the mahogany box on his desk and offered one to Evan, who refused politely.

"Cuban cigar?" chuckled Bob.

"Does the President know?" Evan asked, ignoring Bob's sarcastic sense of humor.

"The President?" Bob was surprised. "He is on his way to Saudi Arabia. He doesn't know anything!"

"We got warnings from a couple of foreign intelligence agencies of an apparent Air Force One sabotage. Hope all goes well, otherwise we have another dot to connect somewhere in the puzzle."

"True!" added Katarina.

"No one knows what really is going on, Evan, including me. . .this is a spy game. All I can tell you is that Katarina is working for us an-"

"We were shot at, we were almost both killed and that is all you can say?" Evan raised his tone and stood up.

The intimidating posture didn't help. Then Evan stretched his arms out and hammered the table with both palms as he yelled, "Who is responsible for all this, Bob? Tell me!"

"It's for you and Katarina to find out!" Bob exclaimed.

He kept his cool, but Katarina tried to put her two cents in to diffuse the tensions.

"We are working directly for Patrick Stevenson. . . it's confidential. He and Marcus are pulling the strings. No one else knows that, not even the VP!"

"I figured that much already. Who else knows about it here?" asked Evan.

"Just us!" Bob was determined to share with Evan, after all, he was the President's bodyguard and a close aide to Patrick himself. "Patrick suspects that we have a mole in the government!"

"No shit! How is that?" asked Evan. "We had so many meetings putting all our minds into all this looking for the wrong guy!"

"True, Hassan Abu Shikri won't know much, these were international professional killers. We think The Chameleons hired him and set him up as a main suspect!"

"After they approached Katarina to work for them, Patrick and I had a conversation and Katarina became a double agent. We are not sure if any of the information Dima received could have been used to plan the terror attack in D.C. since it was insignificant. Schedules can change. However, we think that Dima was used to sabotage the trail to the real people behind this attack," Bob explained.

Evan absorbed every word and his mind raced. "This was going on for the last few months, when this all started?"

"Three months or four, before the ceremony," answered Bob.

"That brings us to before the election, when the President was still a candidate."

"True," jumped in Katarina, "but he was the front-runner!"

"So that alone gives a motive to someone who predicted that Rufus would win and plan his attack," Bob clarified.

"That's what Marcus and Patrick believe, right?"

"Yes!" both answered in tandem.

"So why didn't they tell me?" asked Evan, surprised.

"They figured that you would find out. Plus they wanted to keep it as confidential as possible as long you were on American soil," Bob sounded confident.

"What we thought was that they might find out some of the information to Dima was fake and they would try to kill me. That's why I was ready to move. Understand?" Katarina added.

"If the idea was to blame the Russians, how come the intelligence community was not acting to counter it?" Evan asked, puzzled.

"They were after The Chameleons themselves!" Bob said calmly.

"They saw it as rival gang war," added Katarina.

"Gang war," scoffed Evan.

"We need to act fast Evan, Katarina is burned-"

"I am the only one who can finish that, Bob," she insisted in defiance. "Spread the news that I was killed in action, someone in the United States will be happy," she advised.

"I prefer to send Yuliya with Evan. They will track all of your moves, but they do not suspect Yuliya!" insisted Bob and straightened his tie.

"They are not stupid, Bob; we can leave in three cars and they would not know which one to follow," Katarina suggested.

"Where to?" asked Evan.

"Dima's new address before it's too late!" Katarina repeated, concerned.

"Who is Yuliya?" asked Evan.

"One of us, it's her code name. She is an American who speaks Russian, very competent," said Bob and then cheered up as he added, "OK, let's do it, make sure all of your equipment works and get ready to depart in 10 minutes. Yuliya will join you as well."

Evan realized that he was being used as bait in what Bob called the spy game. Someone used his passion to act as a covert CIA agent and he fell into the trap by agreeing to the mission. *So, this man knows me,* he thought. Someone used everyone in Moscow from both sides. They were just marionettes being controlled by someone in the United States.

Later that night, about 2:00 a.m., the three cars left the embassy grounds headed in three different directions as they outflanked the black Lada SUV that monitored the embassy activity 24/7.

The first and third car were driven with no passengers. All the embassy car windows had tinted glass, so the Russians would not know who to follow. Evan, Katarina, and Yuliya rode in the second car.

It was a strange act in the middle of the night, and the Lada decided to track the last car and chase them around in Moscow until they made their way back to the embassy.

"Where does Dima live?" asked Evan as the driver assumed a normal driving pattern to prevent suspicion.

"Not far from where you found me," Katrina answered.

After they were sure that no one followed them, Katarina directed the driver to Syoromyatnicheskiy Street, behind the Russian Academy of Lawyers. It was a quiet street.

The driver slowed down as he entered the side street behind the row of three-story garden apartments, and they spotted a car parked just next to the number that Katarina mentioned.

"This is suspicious. Pass him and go around," commanded Katarina.

They passed the Lada. Dim light came from the building's exterior fixtures. They saw two people in the back seat and a driver in the front, busy, with his engine on.

Once they drove around the building, they came back to discover that the Lada disappeared.

They parked at a distance and Katarina and Evan approached the building carefully. Yuliya stayed behind as a cover with the driver, who was ready to floor the gas pedal if needed.

A distant gunshot made them freeze where they stood.

"It's from the park behind us!" Katarina exclaimed in distress.

They ran back a block, signaling Yuliya to flank them from the other side. Neither agent knew what to expect. They crossed the Russian Academy of Lawyers easement to Malyy Poluyaoslavasky Street along the forested park.

The street was empty, and the shot didn't alarm anyone enough to call the authorities. Perhaps here, everyone fended for themselves and stayed out of other peoples' business. "That's life here," mumbled Katarina as she watched Yuliya crossing the street on the left.

"The SUV!" exclaimed Katarina. "It's the same car parked on Dima's street!"

"Be careful!" Evan warned her.

She didn't listen and took off to reach the car. Evan was a footstep behind her as two figures emerged from the trees and approached the SUV.

The men saw Katarina and Evan approaching fast with guns drawn, and they opened fire immediately. Without staying to check for casualties, they tried to get into the car and escape.

They shot back at Evan and Katarina through the car windows while the driver tried to zoom away.

Yuliya was just on the other side of the escape route and with one shot, she hit and killed the driver. The uncontrolled car flipped three times and hit a large tree before exploding in a big ball of fire.

Yuliya tried to get closer to identify the men but the flames quickly consumed them.

"Dima!" shouted Katarina.

"Yuliya, stay here and we will search the park," Evan yelled.

The park spanned a few city blocks with natural landscapes. They entered the dark park trying to find something they were not sure of.

"The gun shot we heard must be Dima," stated Katarina. "It's my gut feeling!"

"Stop!" Evan said. "Listen."

They heard the soft moan of someone in severe pain and walked toward the noise carefully.

The body on the ground was Dima, according to Katarina. At first glance, Evan decided he was shot once in his chest and his life expectancy was a few minutes, at best.

"Dima, it's Katarina," she whispered.

Dima opened his eyes and managed a weak smile as he gasped for air.

"Dima, who did this to you?"

"Bastards . . .I. . .I. . . trusted them," he whispered and he spat blood from his mouth. He closed his eyes again and laid motionless.

"Who were they?"

"Chamel. . .eons."

"Who is The Chameleon, the one who calls himself *Zikit*? Dima?"

"They hired me. . .hired you. . . information, delivered to me," he said slowly choking and coughing.

"Does your boss in the FSB know?"

"No!" he whispered and let out a painful grunt, "Hurt!"

"Go on!" encouraged Evan. "Who do they work for?"

Dima, bleeding heavily, struggled to talk with his last breaths. Katarina tried to stop the bleeding, but it was too late. She felt mercy for the old man and turned his torso around to breathe easier. She made a signal to Evan as he didn't have much time to live.

"They are with. . .with. . .connected gang. . . in America, leader's name is Z . .Z . .*Zikit*."

"Who is that man? Any info will help!" Katarina said in Russian.

Dima's breath sounded like a whistle, as it was difficult for him to talk. He opened his eyes to look at Katarina and what he said was barely heard.

"*Zikit,* Israel. . . trained there with other Arm dea—"

Dima went quiet.

"He stopped breathing." Katarina checked his heartbeat and shook her head.

Yuliya appeared and urged them to leave, since some neighbors evidently called the police.

Police and an ambulance approached the area fast and they all decided to leave the park. They called the driver to pick them up on the other side, away from the authorities' commotion.

"Do you know what the fuck he was talking about?" Evan asked Katarina as they drove back to the embassy.

"Somewhat," she replied.

"What did he say?" Evan insisted.

"Something like Arm."

"Arm? Hand you mean?"

"No, in Russian it means Armament, Armament Chameleon, and the last word was unrecognizable."

It was past 4:00 a.m. when they arrived back at the embassy.

Evan was surprised to see the expensive selection of vodka bottles on the shelf in Bob's office: "Beluga," "Jewel of Russia" and one unopened "Trump Premium" vodka in a golden bottle and the letter 'T' inscribed on the glass. It cost almost $2,000 a bottle.

Without permission he opened the expensive bottle as Bob nervously examined his movements. "Are you celebrating anything, Mr. Harris?"

"You bet. You bet, man," Evan murmured, chuckling to himself. He poured four glasses, but not before he looked through the window to look down at the empty street. He raised his hand and toasted, "To The Chameleon!"

"To The Chameleon," toasted Katarina. *L'zarovia.*

L'zarovia! Evan repeated. "Hail to our President!"

"Yes, I like his vodka!" joked Yuliya and downed the drink in one shot, something Evan needed to learn about Russian women.

"What are we celebrating?" asked Bob, confused.

CHAPTER 32

There is a plan to rescue you and Katarina and escape from the embassy," said Bob after they all had a short rest.

"I want Yuliya with us!" Katarina insisted.

"Not sure, but we-"

"You know, she is in danger here. . .will not survive, she-"

"I know, I know, but it's not up to me," replied Bob.

"We'll take her with us," said Evan. "What's the plan?"

The British ambassador is visiting our embassy in an hour, and you all three have to squeeze into the limousine trunk when he leaves for the airport. He is scheduled to fly back to London on a British military plane."

"London?" cried Katarina.

"It's better to get stuck there than here," Evan pointed out.

"I am sure half of the Russian intelligence force is now looking for all three of you!" Bob wasn't joking.

"How will we board the plane?" asked Evan, curious.

"I don't know, Evan; someone is handling it, and has assured your safety." Bob could not give any additional information. "I was told by headquarters. It's clear."

"The British foreign minister came for a meeting with his Russian counterpart to discuss the situation in Syria and the coordination with the coalition."

"It's a summit!" added Katarina.

"Yes, the Israeli foreign minister, German, and the French are all here."

"People will see us leaving the trunk to board the plane," Evan was concerned.

"They used the Globemaster, C-17 for this trip. The limo will drive straight through up the airplane loading ramp."

"Who the hell thought of that?" Evan and Katarina asked at the same time.

"It's a diplomatic car, so no one will search it," Bob said with a smile. He prayed the plan would work, otherwise, the three agents would be dead.

They had little time to prepare. Katarina and Yuliya would travel only with the clothes they wore, no papers, passports, no identification cards, just like the refugees who entered Europe.

Two hours later, a little after noon, the limo stopped and anchored into the Globemaster deck and the loading hatch closed. There were no hurdles in the plan and the simplistic idea worked.

The trunk was opened, and three agents came out groaning and moaning barely standing and Evan recognized the man who helped them out.

"Dan!" he screamed. "What the fuck are you doing here?"

"Helping a friend as an unregistered tourist!" he said, and they shared a hug. Evan introduced him to Katarina and Yuliya.

"Patrick!" Evan screamed again when he saw him emerge from behind the car. He genuinely hugged him and repeated the introduction of the two ladies.

"Is this a British plane?" asked Evan, confused.

"British paid in full," Patrick chuckled.

"We are ready to depart, gentleman. Let me direct you to your assigned seats." A military serviceman in an aviator jumpsuit led them to the passenger's quarters.

"We have a lot to talk about, and I prefer to do it over the ocean," said Patrick when they were all seated. "It was all Dan's idea to smuggle and rescue you from the embassy after the commotion struck an emergency code."

"That's unbelievable, but for both of you to leave the country to be here means that there is something brewing in D.C."

"Yes, yes." Patrick looked for the right words, but they didn't come out.

"The foreign minister just boarded, and we are ready to taxi," said the captain over the PA.

"Wasn't he in the limo?" Evan asked.

"Yes, he was delayed by his Russian police escort who wanted to ask him few questions, personally."

"Shit!" said Katarina and Yuliya hugged her and smiled nervously.

An hour later, the plane embarked into the Russian Federation air space and headed to London at its cruising altitude, 34,000 feet.

"Let me grab a few words with the minister," said Patrick and asked permission to enter his private chamber.

"Hey, Patrick, hope your colleagues are in good shape," he said.

"Thank you, minister. Out of curiosity, I know you will brief our government about your meeting, but what exactly did the police ask you before you boarded the plane?"

"Oh, they told me that they are looking for American agents who killed one of their own and if I knew anything." He smiled and poured two full glasses of Johnny Walker Black label and offered one to Patrick.

"Were they convinced?"

"We are toasting, aren't we?" he chuckled. "I told them, of course, if I hear anything, they will be the first to know."

"I am sure you will!" Patrick exclaimed and laughed out loud. "It will be a heart-pumping situation, sir!"

The minister rolled a cigar and ignored the 'no smoking' signs. It was his office and he felt in control and then said as he lit the cigar, "Sorry for your country's turmoil these days."

Patrick shared the gloomy face and nodded "Yep, we will find them, sir."

"I am sure you will!"

"Thank you, sir. I'll join my colleagues."

After they calmed down, Patrick briefed them on the President's situation and the crash of Air Force One in Sinai. *It was shocking news and terrible timing* they thought.

"There were a lot of crazy events in D.C. since the assassination," said Patrick. "We stitched in a computer model of the events from the day the President was shot at and his wife killed, to the President's crash landing. We came to one conclusion, that someone. . ."

"Wants to kill Rufus Barker," Evan responded emotionally.

"Yes!" said Patrick and continued, "Then to kill you, Evan. It was to get you out of the game as the President's bodyguard, therefore your car exploded and you almost died!"

"You forgot Frank Dabush's car explosion, too," said Evan.

"I'll get to that," Patrick replied as he took a sip from his glass, "You see? The President's plane was monitored by adversaries and someone was expecting him at the right place at the right time. All this data was transferred to the people who pulled the trigger and shot those deadly missiles that almost killed him and his entourage."

"Which country is behind it?" asked Evan.

Dan intervened, "Wait, we are sure it's not a country!"

Evan and the rest paid utmost attention and Patrick continued, "It takes a great effort–with money, logistics, arms, and people–to plan and perform like a country if you are not a country!" said Patrick.

"If not a country, it must be a rich fucking gang. . .a Mafia?" added Katarina.

"You are getting close." Patrick smiled. "And we are looking for the top member, who must be rich, influential, and power- ful." Patrick scrutinized their faces for their reactions.

"And motive?" asked Evan.

"Many fit this political category, starting with the vice presi- dent who will take the President's post, speaker of the house who is the next runner up, any political figure adversary, really. The President has enemies, you know," exclaimed Patrick.

"Something doesn't fit the model, though," Evan said. "I un- derstand the vice president will be President and the speaker of the house might then kill the VP to be next in line for the Presidency, but it's a crazy scenario! It doesn't feel plausible." Evan sounded excited. "Tom Phillips is the most pleasant man to work with. This is why Rufus chose him carefully to be his running mate."

"Yes, it's a crazy scenario," Dan said, adding "the motive is essential to the puzzle."

"I went to Marcus and he gave me a green light to have a confidential independent probe into those people we just mentioned," Patrick said. "Then, we branched out to the second circle of people after the President's inner circle– their lives, beliefs, likes, lifestyles, health–all confidential. If the media knew that we would be lynched," Patrick said with a serious expression. "We all would pay the price."

"Well, we might have some information after my excursion with Katarina," Evan put his thoughts in the mix.

"Evan, after the unsuccessful attempt to kill you, the same someone wanted you out of the state–not to interfere with his affairs—so you were marked to be assassinated by Katarina, and not the other way around as you thought."

Evan and Katarina exchanged surprised glances.

"So, you knew I would come," Evan directed his response at Katarina.

"True, and I told you that," she said, "but the command I got through Dima was to kill you, and it was given by the head of The Chameleons. And as you see, I was a double agent trying to expose the head of The Chameleons gang. I was very close to finding out until you came along."

"So, they knew I was in your place and decided to kill us both!" stated Evan.

"Precisely," said Patrick.

"So our suspect is a man who has connections with the Russian Mafia, Armament, Sinai insurgents, military explosives, Presidential schedules and trip data information. Who the hell is this man? What position does he hold? It's not the VP or the speaker, then who is it?" asked Evan.

"Might be someone who has access to all this information, someone with connections to the White House?" said Patrick as Katarina nodded in agreement. Yuliya was stunned by the information.

"Who it can be? I know everyone and see no connections whatsoever," Katarina said.

"After gathering the information about our White House staff, from top to bottom, we found that the vice president started new cancer treatments," Patrick said sadly.

"He recovered and also shared this openly to the public when they questioned his health to lead in case of an emergency," Evan said.

"True," replied Patrick. "It seems that it came back deadlier and was kept a secret before the election. Once the President established his cabinet, Tom Phillips would resign and probably Frank Dabush would take his place."

"What? That doesn't make any sense, the President hates Frank."

"Tom might have a few more months or weeks to live according to his physician," added Patrick, "I found that out after I visited his clinic."

"So Frank is out and Tom Phillips is out," said Evan.

"I never said they were out," claimed Patrick.

"I am not sure who is screwing around with us," Evan said. "This fucker can't hide for too long."

Yuliya was silent, listening to the unfolding events as Patrick peeled them back, layer by layer. He was trying to get them all to solve the case by putting all the information gathered in one mixing pot.

"So what was my excursion here then?" Evan asked. "A game?"

"It was all sabotage, we knew you would prevail. The man we were looking for was connected with The Chameleons gang, not only because he knew them, he wanted to get the Russian intelligence involved so the assassination could be blamed on the Russians."

"Yes, the Russians had nothing to do with this case," confirmed Katarina. "This is why I was recruited by The Chameleons. Dima was recruited by them as well to smear the Russians into all this." She was confident.

"The sabotage trail is very simple," Dan said. "There is no terror group called Soldiers of Allah. It was created for sabotage only. It simply doesn't exist." He inhaled deeply. "It was created to blame the Muslim world and create confusion with the investigation and more chaos, The Chameleon gang connection was to blame the Russians. They almost took the bait, and created more confusion. But now the question is what sticks to the wall?"

Patrick concurred, "Interesting but true! We flew Aslam Abu Mansour in our white plane to Guantanamo for interrogation. The guy has no fucking clue who hired him to create the fake Soldiers of Allah video," Patrick chuckled.

"He was paid?" Katarina asked.

"Probably not!" chuckled Patrick and they all laughed.

"He is on his way back to Israel now," added Dan.

"Yes, meanwhile I am now burned!" exclaimed Evan, changing the subject.

"We all have to pay a personal price, and don't forget in your case, the entire world saw you protecting the President during the assassination. . .every intelligence agency knows who you are. Sending you to Russia was a calculated risk," he explained.

"It was a decision made by Frank Dabush," Evan said.

"It was his idea, but we agreed, it was our decision. Again, a calculated risk," Patrick said, annoyed.

Katarina intervened and jumped from her seat. "Now we are all in on this!" she said, excited but not sure about her future assignments with the CIA.

Patrick refrained from lighting a cigarette and instead put it in his mouth and chewed the tobacco and offered one to all, who declined.

"The interesting thing is that SVR RF, the Russian intelligence agency, stayed away from this case like the plague," added Katarina enthusiastically.

Evan glanced at Patrick, looking for him to clarify this issue. "What else can you tell me? Did the agency find out who the three people were who were shot by Hassan Abu Shikri in

Washington?" he asked and looked at Evan with a funny face and lolled his head slightly.

"Yes, one of them was identified by Julio Esperanda as the one who bought and smuggled the sniper's gun into the United States via its southern border."

"Really?" All were surprised.

"Yes, he was aided by refugee smugglers," Patrick explained as he saw Yuliya's face tighten.

"Why was it so important to get an Israeli gun to shoot the President?" Yuliya finally asked.

"It's to blame Israel, adding to the confusion, another trick to sabotage the investigation," Patrick commented.

Patrick pulled some photos from his briefcase and put them on the table.

He looked at the photos and raised his eyes. "Are these Russian agents?"

They examined the dead bodies and the photos marked with red pen showing scratches, tattoos, bruises, surgeries, anything that could identify them.

"These are The Chameleons!" exclaimed Patrick and pointed at the photos.

"And Langley knows that?" asked Evan.

"Since last night everything, names, emails, cell phone numbers, agencies." They waited to hear the rest of the story. "We have two attempts to sabotage the real people behind the assassination and there is only one man we had to investigate and check his motive." Patrick completed his last drop of the superb whisky that the British Minister gave him and he smiled with satisfaction.

"I think I know the man we are looking for!" he exclaimed.

CHAPTER 33

A week later, after analyzing all the information compiled in the CIA and FBI databases, Patrick concluded his investigation and asked to meet his boss.

The President was brought back from Israel onboard Air Force One and was recovering quickly from his ordeal. The defense secretary took command to secure the country once he landed, since he was in better health than the President. He immediately met with Tom Phillips, who was still the acting President, to patch up issues until Dr. Rintler cleared the President to return to his post. The President was briefed on the CIA meeting plans and Dr. Rintler could not stop him from participating in this Oval Office meeting. The physician made sure he had the medical inhaler and an oxygen tank was with him at all times.

It was the first week of May and a beautiful spring day. The cherry blossoms painted the Tidal Basin in pink and the sweet fragrance perfumed the air and smelled like freedom.

Patrick deliberately drove through slowly to capture the beauty of nature in the garden where millions of visitors came every year to witness the cherry blossoms blooming.

Many tourists congregated in front of the White House south lawn hoping to catch a glimpse of the recovering President. Patrick entered the government executive's gate to the

White House grounds to brief the President and pursue his plans.

One by one, they entered the Oval Office, where the President sat at his desk. Evan was already situated next to him. The main switch was on, lighting the oval office with a bright light, and the curtains were closed shut.

Unprecedented security measures were taken and it was normal to think that the President was over-protected after what the country went through. Also, it was the first time the President was back in the Oval Office since his departure to Saudi Arabia. It was a historical day.

Patrick invited Dan to attend the briefing. Dan was let in before everyone else and asked to stand next to Patrick.

The vice president sat opposite the President. The defense secretary, National Security adviser, the CIA and the FBI directors also came with their top brass and crowded into the office.

"I want to hear it from you, Evan," the President wheezed. He was vigilant.

"Mr. President, we suspect one man behind the conspiracy. We've connected all the dots."

"Go on," he directed his bodyguard. Marcus, Dan, and Patrick tensed.

"How do you feel, Mr. Vice President?" Evan asked Tom Phillips, who looked surprised at the question. His face hurt and he squeezed his lips tightly as if he was holding a big secret ready to erupt in the open. He had nothing to lose.

"OK. It came back," he said sadly and sniffed.

"What came back, the cancer?" asked the President, concerned.

"Yes, and now it's spreading into other organs like the pancreas," he added.

"Oh, my goodness, you were sick all this time handling the shit I went through and keeping the county safe?"

"I did my best, Mr. President." His voice was so low now, it was almost a whisper.

"One of the motives we investigated was someone who wanted to take the presidency if you were gone, and of course the vice president came up as a suspect and ruled out immediately, only no one knew his cancer came back," said Marcus.

"Nonsense," cried the President, angry and coughed. "Even if you ruled it out!"

"Sorry, Mr. President, it's the process. We agree, Mr. President, without finding a motive it's hard to move forward in any investigation, many options came up and—"

"What about the Russians? The Soldiers of Allah? Revolutionary Guards? All the intimidating news you all briefed me on before my doomed trip?" He coughed and used the inhaler to take a deep breath. Dr. Rintler sat behind the President and grabbed his arm to assist him and calm him down.

Evan waited a couple of seconds for the President to regain his focus and catch his breath. Once they made eye contact, Evan continued.

"It's all fake, sir, but that's not our fault," he answered, and the President was comfortable in hearing it from his trusted bodyguard.

"All avenues of the investigation we took got us nowhere, until the idea 'thinking out of the box'–like a different motive. This idea actually came from the Mossad. By the way, here with us is agent Dan Eyal. He can explain." He looked at Eyal and nodded.

Dan, encouraged by the gesture, cleared his throat nervously, as he'd never before spoken to the President. He stood close to Evan as he watched him put a book on the President's desk.

"I want to present to you this book called *The Greatest Spies in History*. Pay attention, especially to the second spy after Mata Hari."

The room chattered with curiosity and it started to get stuffy.

The President looked through the pages and landed on the No. 2 spy in the book, Eli Cohen, a Mossad agent captured in Syria in the mid-1960s just before he was to be appointed as the next Syrian Defense Minister.

"Why are you showing this to me?" Rufus asked, surprised.

"Mr. President, a spy defense minister. . .Eli Cohen was spying for Israel for years. He mingled with Syria's top brass as a businessman who donated to top politicians and bribed top brass in their ambition to be promoted. He partied all the way up the social ladder. He bought them all with charm, a lot of booze and a lot of money."

"How is this related to our case?" asked Rufus again.

"That's the motive!" Patrick and Dan stated at the same time.

"No one was trying to assassinate you, Mr. President to take your post, the motive was not political," Evan added.

"Is this a spy motive? If yes, which country is involved?" the President asked.

"Someone who could not be the President, since he was not born in the United States, or vice president, but could go as up as far as he could. Just like the Mossad spy, Eli Cohen, to copy his success without being captured. It's an obsession!" Marcus said without pointing fingers yet.

"Kissinger was not born in the United States and became a successful Secretary of State," chuckled the President and coughed hard.

"Kissinger was not a spy. That's the difference," said Patrick.

"Don't they all go through the FBI security clearance, and background checks? What are you saying? Can you get to the bottom of this?"

"We fucked up!" said Marcus, taking responsibility on behalf of all the state law enforcement agencies including the FBI and his own agency the CIA. "We only hope we are right about the man!"

"Why don't you arrest him for questioning?" asked Rufus.

Tom Phillips moved uncomfortably in his chair as he listening to the tense conversation. "Am I a suspect?" he asked dead serious.

"Absolutely not!" exclaimed Marcus. "But we know who he is."

"Then, the President is in control now, and I shall resign from the vice presidency effective immediately. I want to deal with my health issues and spend my remaining time with my family," he stated with a sad, weak voice.

"Tom, you have been a very brave man to take the responsibility to run the country in my absence. I can imagine how difficult this is for you to show strength when the devil is eating you from the inside out. Your courage to make decisions to bring me safely back home and run the evacuation of the remaining Americans will cast you an honored place in history." Rufus took a break to inhale his prescription medicine. "The country salutes you," Rufus grew emotional. "I accept your resignation but do not give up your friendship, sir!"

"I suggest escorting the vice president home to his family," said Marcus.

Tom stood up, shaky and on his own and slowly walked out of the Oval Office escorted by two Marines. "Can I have Frank, my Chief of Staff, help me?" Tom asked just before the Marines open the door.

"No," said Marcus. "We will call him to the room with the rest of the cabinet members waiting outside for briefing." Marcus glanced at the President, who looked puzzled.

Marcus followed Tom a couple of steps out and called the rest of the cabinet members waiting outside to get into the Oval Office. Frank approached them and asked to help but Marcus denied politely and said "We need you for a briefing with the President."

When they moved out a little further away from curious ears Marcus asked Tom, "Can I ask you a question, sir?"

"Sure," he replied and his dark brown eyes caught Marcus' gaze.

"Did you promise to nominate Frank Dabush to be your defense secretary if you would be elected President after Rufus?"

Tom was puzzled and lightly scoffed "Oh, Frank, yeah, he asked me that and started to believe he would."

"But you didn't promise, did you?" Marcus insisted.

"Not a promise, just a discussion, when you repeat a lie many times, you start to believe it, remember?"

Marcus signaled the two marines to take over and call for the vice president's limousine.

The cabinet members and Frank Dabush entered the Oval Office. Frank stood between Evan and Dan. Additional fully geared, armed, riot-ready Marines entered and took positions around the room.

The White House compound looked like a combat zone and it was attributed to President Rufus Barker's return to power. Evan checked his handgun to ensure it was still tacked under his shoulder and situated himself closer to Frank Dabush and a Marine standing still like a statue behind him. Dan stood on the other side of Frank.

On the other side of the room next to the fireplace, two Secret Service agents watched in silence.

"You have enough force to start a war!" Dan whispered in Marcus's ear.

He nodded slightly and whispered back, "We don't want to take any chances."

Everyone was surprised to see the President, who came back confidentially. They greeted him and wished him a fast recovery and took seats on the couches and a few chairs as Evan asked—a tactic all planned in advance.

Frank Dabush, the VP Chief of Staff whispered in Evan's ear, "When did you come back? I was not informed."

Evan ignored the question at first and then whispered back "With Air Force One from Israel," he lied. "By the way, I am glad you survived your car explosion. I am sure it's the same people who wanted to hurt us both, right?!"

Frank's face was like ice. His hazel eyes blinked when he asked, "You came back with the POTUS?"

Evan nodded his head slightly and watched Marcus grow tense beside Dan.

Donovan, the special investigator on the assassination attempt was in the room as well, and submitted his intermediate progress report shortly after the President landed. That report occupied the office of the Chief Supreme Court Justice who walked into the room and sat on the couch across from the President's desk next to Donovan and both took a quick glance spotting Frank next to Evan.

The White House Chief of Staff walked in and instructed four more police officers equipped with machine guns to take positions around strategic points outside the Oval Office. Alex, "The Little Big Man," White House Chief of Staff, signaled the President with a short nod and locked the doors.

Everyone glanced at the President with anticipation.

It was 9:30 a.m. just a short time after the 7:30 a.m. Sunday mass at the churches. Some came straight from church and others from their breakfast at home.

Did the President lose his mind? Some participants thought as much, looking at the FBI director as he stood next to Marcus on the other side of the President's desk. The whole secretive procedure was orchestrated to 'pull the mole out from the skin' on his own, as Patrick said. The rest of the attendees just guessed that the President wanted to make a welcome statement and start taking over government control. More importantly was if the mole had any partners in crime.

The President was not briefed on the entire plan, his physician knew, since he advised Marcus and Patrick to plan it this way so he could attend and watch the President as to not overload him with excitement. Rufus Barker, only four months in office, cleared his throat and began.

"The vice president just asked to be relieved from his duties and commence with his private life. We thank him for his patriotism and love for this country."

The people murmured. Frank, his Chief of Staff, was caught by surprise. Frank didn't know that Tom's cancer had come back.

"On January 20th, I was targeted by an assassin. Two innocent people died; my beloved wife was one of them. The bullets were directed at me and missed. . .I don't know if it was a miracle or a curse!" he exclaimed, elevating his tone of voice with much effort. He scrutinized the tense faces in the room.

He nodded at Marcus to take over. Marcus took his time, looked over the attendees, and his glance landed on Evan. "The weapon was discovered; and its bloody history was traced from the first day it was manufactured in Israel, to the bloody day in history that shook the world. Checked by our labs, we followed its journey from Israel to Bogota and to the United States. The assassin who pulled the trigger was discovered as well, a limping gang member known as 'The Chameleon.' "

A dramatic starting statement indeed, thought Dan. The book near the President sat on the desk, opened on the Israeli Mossad agent's page.

Marcus continued, "The assassin was trained to shoot a sniper rifle right here in the United States." He stopped when he saw the President sitting uncomfortably and Dr. Rintler helping him with his oxygen tank.

Marcus took a long pause and then continued, "You were all in one way or another, part-time or full-time, investigating the events, but no one could come up with what really happened. Was the crash of Air Force One in Sinai a coincidence?" he asked and examined the people especially making sure the police and guards were in full attention before the revelation.

"No!" he answered his own question. "It was another assassination attempt on the President!" he declared. "The assassin who pulled the trigger apparently was not an expert and that saved the President's life but killed his wife instead," he paused again.

"Under the Constitution, if the President dies who is next to take his position?"

The people just looked at Marcus and the President with full skepticism and suspicion. *The vice president's gone for God's sake,* some thought.

No one answered Marcus's question, so he said, "You all know the answer, it's in our Constitution."

The Supreme Court Justice nodded.

"If the President would not recover then Tom Phillips would be the President!"

Dead silence settled in the room, and they all realized that the President was partially in on the planned meeting and the show was for them to watch.

"The motive in this case was covered up with layers of sabotage, bizarre developments brought us to believe it was a simple espionage exercise that the intelligence community's imagination could only dream of."

Evan watched Frank tense. He breathed heavily, blinking his eyes quickly and suddenly was as uncomfortable as the rest of the people in the room. They understood that the mole was in the Oval Office. How dangerous could that be? Is that why all the heavy security? Would this not be considered putting the President in danger? They looked around nervously to find who in the room might fit a glamorous spy persona like Eli Cohen?

Patrick gave Evan a signal and Evan shoved his hand into his shoulder pouch holding the cold handgun ready in case of any development.

No one smiled.

"The spy is in this room, an ex-arms dealer and mafia director, who hired insurgents and equipped them with weapons just to kill our President so he could claim his top post in the government. He successfully thwarted our investigation with sabotage around the world. The man is. . ."

Dead silence fell in the room, only the humming of the air conditioning system could be heard. That was the moment Frank thought the rope was actually put on his neck. He jumped forcefully behind Evan, put his arm around him and hit Evan on the head to soften his reaction. Frank grabbed Evan's handgun from his pouch before Evan or Dan could react. All the armed security personnel got into combat position.

"*Zikit!*" yelled Marcus and jumped to protect the President, shielding him from the other side of the desk.

"Are you blaming me?" shouted Frank in a vicious voice as he struggled with Evan before aiming the gun at the President's head.

"You just turned yourself in," said Marcus and the room went into a panic. The police and the Marines were ready to fire, and a few joined Marcus to shield the President.

"This is the man, a gang member, who sold surplus arms to third-world countries, a man who had enough money to buy the most corrupt people in our industry, an ex-member of the NRA," yelled Marcus and pointed his gun at Frank.

Frank used Evan as a human shield but hit him on the head again to daze him. He held the cocked gun with a tight grip and aimed it directly at the President's chest now covered by a human shield.

"It was Hassan Abu Shikri!" Frank yelled with all his might and his eyes crazed.

The rope was given to the man who was responsible for hanging himself. I hope he will grab it, thought Marcus.

"He was your hostage, Frank!" replied Patrick calmly. "Frank, it's over, you are *Zikit*, the head of The Chameleons. You formed the group years ago in Russia, and you planned all of this for many years, joining the NRA first, a very strong political lobby, and step-by-step you bought junior politicians and grew up with them into the White House."

"Shut the fuck up, Patrick!" Frank yelled and shot Patrick, hitting him on the hip.

"You have no proof!" he shouted at Marcus as he looked at the Supreme Court Justice for moral support.

"Attacking Evan and shooting Patrick is enough to put you behind bars for the rest of your life. . .this is proof!" said Marcus.

"Don't forget that someone tried to kill me, too. My car exploded!"

"That was sabotage, just to get us off your back. You bought a bomb expert from the mafia to kill Evan and exploded your car, it's a 'one-o'-one' trick, Frank!"

The President ordered the Marines and officers to lower their guns and stay calm. They could shoot and kill Frank after his first move but that would leave a few dead people behind.

"This is the third time you tried to kill me Frank, and the game is over!" announced Rufus calmly, the room watching the shocking drama unfold before their eyes.

"No one move, or your President is dead!" stated Frank with a strange smile. Patrick regained consciousness and could not wait to act. He was bleeding and looked for signals from Marcus or Evan. He sought the attention of the Marine next to the door. Even with a splitting headache, Evan saw the signal from Patrick and got the idea to turn off the main light switch.

The Marine finally saw Patrick and Evan staring at him both lifting their eyes up and down from the lights to the switch and so did Alex Mann next to him.

Frank, with a slur in his voice, cleared his throat said, "I want the President as hostage. I want a plane full of fuel to fly me out of here."

Alex Mann, the White House Chief of Staff, got the message that Patrick and Evan were trying to signal the Marine, helplessly.

"No negotiations, Frank, just drop your weapon. You can't get out of here alive. I offer to fly you to any third world destination you want. I promise!" said Marcus.

"I also want Alvin Nelson, the defense secretary, too, as hostage."

Rufus raised his hands and asked his Chief of Staff to get on with Frank's request and then he said, "It's OK, I'll go!" he was decisive and added, "No more killing!"

"I need to arrange this from my office," said the Chief of Staff.

"No way, no one leaves the room!" shouted Frank decisively.

Marcus and the secret agents thought that the POTUS forgot that he was a public domain. His life did not belong to him anymore, but to the American people. However, he saw the signals of the two injured men and thought that there was no other choice. He volunteered.

"Take me as a hostage!" snapped Marcus.

Alex was thinking of a solution when he said, "The phone on the President's desk is dead during sessions. It was disconnected when Tom took the oath to be the active President," Alex convincingly lied.

"I want Hassan Abu Shikri with me on the plane!" requested Frank.

"OK," said Marcus. "We can arrange that!"

"Don't play games with me!" yelled Frank at Marcus who stretched his hand to his sides as if to say, *What did I do?*

"Why Hassan?" asked Marcus and the Chief of Staff asked again to leave the room. "Hassan is in Guantanamo, to release him, I need my office phone."

"Go now, you have three minutes, if you don't come back, Evan gets the first bullet, then Patrick!" he yelled as "The Little Big Man" nodded.

"I want to throw Hassan from the plane," Frank said, and he laughed a short crazy laugh.

"I wonder, are you the man who trained the sniper? I know you are an expert sniper trained in Israel."

"Shut up, Marcus, you have talked enough!" Frank shot back loud enough to rattle the walls.

Dan stood a breath away from Patrick and helped him to stand up and stop his bleeding. He was calm but his head was running scenarios very fast. *It must end now,* he thought.

Alex opened the door to leave for his office, greeted the Marine, and in a blink of an eye pulled the main light switch off and the Oval Office became pitch black, like deep space. Now the closed curtains made sense.

Frank, surprised, felt a hand twisting on his arm which was holding the gun and he pulled the trigger. A shot was fired in the dark. Evan was released from Frank's grip despite his pain and twisted Frank's right hand tightly behind his back, pushing it all the way up to his shoulder blade. Frank screamed. Dan, ready for action, grabbed Frank's other hand and twisted his palm in a *Jujitsu* martial arts trick and the handgun fell on the floor. It dispensed another bullet on impact.

"Turn on the light," screamed Evan. The light was turned on.

The plan was not perfect, and did not go according to its original idea to expose Frank in a heroic publicity stunt. The FBI and the CIA desperately needed the public approval rating to be raised. The President agreed to whatever was disclosed to him. *Not everything and probably the Secret Service would object to it, but it's done,* thought Marcus.

It was the second time that a Supreme Court Justice was hit by a bullet in four months. A pool of blood stained the carpet and the sofa from the shoulder wound where the Supreme Court Justice was hit.

The second shot originated from the floor, shot the ceiling and broke the light fixture.

Frank was finally restrained and handcuffed as half a dozen Marines and police officers laid on top of him and the rest shielded the President.

Everyone took a deep breath and sighed as the worst was over. *Was it really the end?* some wondered.

One by one, the officers and Marines stood up and Frank was detained.

"Frank," Marcus called out. Frank looked at him with one eye as the other was swollen and closed. "We also know who you were in contact with, and who might have benefited from selling your position as future defense secretary–the post you were seeking. But what I don't understand is your stupidity in thinking that this position would pass the House and the Senate, only because Tom Phillips may or not have promised you that position once he became the President, or perhaps you bought them, too?"

"Go to hell!" spat Frank.

"You are already halfway there, Frank, you will join the three bodies of your Chameleon members soon. By the way, Evan, can you remove the leather wrist band on his left hand?"

"Sure, my pleasure, it's the third time he tried to kill me. The explosion once, with Katarina in her apartment the second time, and now. You found out that she was a double agent, hired by your Chameleon mafia, and convinced Marcus to send me to kill her. Smart shit, Frank!" he said and removed the leather band very cruelly, hurting Frank on purpose.

"Oh, what a surprise, a small tattoo of a chameleon and there is some word in a foreign language," Marcus continued sarcastically.

"*Zikit* is Hebrew–my second language," said the Chief of Staff, victoriously examining the tattoo.

"This case, Frank, is like the fool who threw a diamond into the river and thousands of scientists could not find it," claimed Alex, seeing the President alive and well in his chair.

"A fool with money is a dangerous thing," scoffed the President. He blessed God for the outcome, despite the few painful casualties. *It always could be worse,* he thought.

"Just to show you how money can buy your government!" cried Frank and in return was brutally pushed out of the room.

The door was shut behind the law enforcement officers who dragged Frank Dabush screaming all the way to the police car that awaited him. The rest in the Oval Office were escorted to another room for questioning. Paramedics entered to treat Patrick, Evan, and the wounded Supreme Court Justice as well as others affected by the trauma. Dr. Rintler immediately checked on the President's condition and signaled a thumb's up sign.

The President nodded in sadness and said, "So many dead just to win a spy game fantasy inspired by a real spy story. Remember friends who are friends that only money can buy, are not friends. In the end, history is written by the winners!"

"Marcus, you still didn't tell me how you managed to convince the Secret Service and the President to have this meeting in the Oval Office?" asked Patrick as they exited the White House compound in Marcus's car.

"I asked and gave them my reasons," he said, shifting his voice to sound satisfied.

"I am happy it's over. We have a lot of work ahead to clean this up," Patrick said, thinking of his new future tasks, "but still Marcus, you know, to me, it looks like it was a great publicity stunt to make us and the FBI look good!"

"True, in this case, *our* reputation *is* important as well," he put on a mysterious smile and asked, "and you Patrick, how did you know it was Frank Dabush?"

"I didn't!" explained Patrick and returned the same mysterious smile, "I guess he thought that he was amongst and above all!"

Revelations

A congressional inquiry by Gordon Donovan, could not determine if Frank Dabush was supported by a foreign entity or not. No connection was found. He was brought up in a Communist environment, his family immigrated to the United States and probably acted alone using his wealth and connections worldwide to become a spy for hire.

Perhaps the adversary intelligence agencies were waiting to see how successful Frank would be before they tied the knots.

Hassan Abu Shikri was sentenced to 15 years in jail. He was released after three years from Guantanamo and was sent back to Iran in exchange for American Sailors kidnapped in the strait of Hormoz, international waters.

Frank Dabush was sentenced to death. Kept 10 years on death row, his Supreme Court appeal was eventually rejected. He was electrocuted in Kentucky and his body was incinerated. His ashes were scattered over a secret location in the middle of the Atlantic Ocean.

The landlord died from frustration in a witness protection program's secret location. He never got his apartment back, which was kept as evidence for a few years after his death. It was auctioned later.

Katarina and Yuliya accepted offers to work in defense agencies. Katarina was shot three years later by an assassin in broad daylight in Mexico City on a secret mission chasing human trafficking lords. Yuliya disappeared with no trace a year later and her body was never found. Apparently, a foreign agency's retaliation.

Jamila and Farouk were granted asylum and moved to Cincinnati to live within a big Muslim community where they felt comfortable. They raised their son Jamil, who later joined the FBI terror counterintelligence in New York City.

Imam Afshin Shiraz was sentenced to jail due to his lack of reporting to the FBI and assisting with hiding information of a fugitive. He was deported to Iran rather than serving jail time right after the judge's sentence, for respect of the Shiite community in town.

Major Jeffrey Ahmad was awarded the Distinguished Service Medal by the President for his handling of the rescue operation that saved so many American lives. He was promoted to major general.

Patrick recovered from his injury, resigned from the CIA, grew a long, wild beard and started a very successful career as an abstract oil painter, signing his art with "*Zikit.*" He moved to Florida, the sunshine state.

Aslam Abu Mansour continued to produce porno videos but moved his business to Berlin, the porn capitol of the world. He had to learn how to speak German.

Mossad agent Dan Eyal, went back to Israel to another mission awaiting. There was never a dull moment in the Mossad headquarters.

Alex Mann moved on to become United State Ambassador to Israel, since he spoke Hebrew. He understood the Middle East cooking pot culture and loved hummus and falafel.

Alvin Nelson retired as secretary of defense and moved to Florida not far from Patrick and became his best customer.

Marcus Barbour, the CIA director, moved up to take over the NSA. He still didn't like the Mossad and lost valuable information that they could share with him to keep America safer.

Evan Harris recovered from his injury and suffered a slight concussion. He married Katarina (who remained a closeted lesbian). After her death, he remarried, resigned from the CIA as a condition from his new wife and ran a small security company in Las Vegas.

Vice President Tom Phillips passed away four months later. His partnership with Frank Dabush was scrutinized by the Congress long after his death with no conclusion, as always.

President Rufus Barker dismissed any member in his administration who had any contact with Frank Dabush or received a campaign contribution from him in the past. He never married again, but always checked out the interns in the White House.

Poopoo, Katarina's doggie, was rescued by the police who were dispatched due to the gunshots fired in her building and was adopted on-the-spot by the upstair's neighbors. They lived happily ever after.

~The End~

ABOUT THE AUTHOR

W illie Hirsh recently published two novels: *Regicide, The Shadow King* (2018), and *Constellation: The Second Race to Space has Begun* (2018), which was an American Book Fest Finalist in 2018.

Willie currently spends his spare time traveling, photographing nature, and painting landscapes in oil. He loves writing spy and political suspense books. He pursued his career in engineering and currently is working full time managing a construction firm.

willie@williehirsh.com
twitter-@WillieHirsh
Instagram
Facebook-The Odyssey of Art by Willie Hirsh

CPSIA information can be obtained
at www.ICGtesting.com
Printed in the USA
LVHW110742120120
643055LV00003B/3/P